ASCENSION
RAZOR'S PASS

A LESBIAN ACTION ADVENTURE

L. FERGUS

ARTICLE94

Contents

Ascension: Razor's Pass Second Edition Hardback ISBN 978-1-949789-45-4

Ascension: Razor's Pass Second Edition Paperback ISBN 978-1-949789-46-1

Ascension: Razor's Pass Second Edition eBook ISBN 978-1-949789-47-8

Cover Art by Mrinmoy Kar

Scene Break provided by Freepik designed by upklyak / Freepik

Return of the Fallen Angel wings designed by pch.vector / Freepik

Game of the Gods katana and Children of the Fallen Angel skulls designed by Freepik

Irruption circuit board designed by Harryarts / Freepik

PLAYLIST

MANY HOURS GO INTO writing and publishing a book which means I accumulate lots of hours listening to music—usually one song on repeat (I believe Blue Monday has almost 5000 plays). Many songs inspire scenes or conversations and can help set the mood. I've included a playlist of the songs that helped inspire me as I write. You can find the playlist HERE

- Chapter 1: The Moment—Professor Elemental & Mister Frisbee—The Good Dad Club

- Chapter 2: Death Wish—Royale Lynn & Danny Worsnop—Death Wish

- Chapter 3: Disturbia—Rihanna—Good Girl Gone Bad: Reloaded

- Chapter 4: She Drives me Crazy—Fine Young Cannibals—The Raw & The Cooked

- Chapter 5: Brave—Sara Bareilles—The Blessed Unrest

- Chapter 6: Fallen Angel—Three Days Grace—Human

- Chapter 7: Sign of the Cross—Iron Maiden—The X

ONE

THE MOMENT
PROFESSOR ELEMENTAL AND
MISTER FRISBEE
THE GOOD DAD CLUB

"**W**E'D BE THERE ALREADY if you walked in a straight line," Cowboy chided as Kita and Sarge jumped, dashed, and rolled in the snow.

"This is the first time Sarge has seen snow," admitted Kita.

"We've got a four-day hike, so you might want to conserve your energy. Even you can run out. And Zidin probably doesn't want to carry you."

Kita was about to give in when Sarge tackled her from behind. The pair wrestled, kicking up snow. With a slinky maneuver, Sarge sat on Kita's chest.

Kita relented. "Alright, you win."

Kita and Sarge joined the line up the pass. The lower valley was open and filled with pine trees. As they went up, there were fewer.

"We're at the timberline if you're curious," said Zidin.

"What is that?"

"The altitude at which trees will no longer grow. Notice we have short scrub pines. Those are the last trees we'll see for a while."

"Why does altitude matter?" Kita asked.

"Various factors," answered Cowboy. "Most conditions aren't right: insufficient nutrients, water, and wind. You'll be surprised at how robust life is and how fragile."

Sarge stopped and growled.

Four war cats hopped down a rock face and greeted Sarge. They seemed to have a conversation.

Sarge looked at Kita and motioned with his head forward. Then he left with the other war cats.

"Sarge! Come back!" Kita wailed.

"I think he wants you to follow him," said Zidin.

"We don't have time to look for a lost cat," huffed Cowboy. "Don't forget what the mayor said. The war cats have attacked their herds and even taken people."

"Well, I'm going. Don't worry, I'll catch up."

"Kita, you'll never..."

Kita placed a hand on a rock and pulled. She stuck fast.

"There's not a place he can go that I can't. Now, the longer I waste talking, the further they get."

K ITA SLOGGED UP THE trail after the war cats.

They wouldn't have left a trail if they didn't want me to follow.

Kita traversed cliffs, avalanche chutes, and rocky outcroppings to catch the cats. As she jumped to a clearing, she found twenty war cats and Sarge looking at a tall, faded red wooden structure built into the mountainside.

Under it, carts delivered coal and took out something in war cat-patterned bags.

Why would they pattern it after the war cats?

The cart drivers each received a coin bag on the way out.

What are you making? And where is it going? I should get the others, but they'd never traverse the deep chasm separating them from the cart trail. I guess I'll do it myself.

At the head of the chasm was a frozen waterfall formation.

Kita put on her toe spikes as insurance against slipping. She trusted her nanites, but it was best to be prepared. She took her first hesitant step onto the ice column and stuck, letting out a sigh of relief as the formation held her weight.

It's a long way down.

Climbing across the ice, Kita kept her caps' spikes firmly in the ice. She maneuvered around three frozen columns and stopped when she reached a void a dozen feet across that went deep into the mountainside.

What do I do now?

There was no way to climb around. Her only option was to jump. Hanging onto the ice, she leaned back and swung herself until she had enough momentum. Releasing her toe spikes, Kita pushed off, leaping across the chasm with a loud yell.

As she neared the frozen formation, she reached out and slapped her hand against the ice. She swung, trying to get her other hand on the column. She dragged her toe cap spikes against the ice to arrest her motion. Her spike caught, and she slapped her other hand against the formation. Digging her caps in, she rested her cheek against the ice, taking deep breaths to counter her adrenaline.

A vibration was followed by a *crack*. The piece of ice that Kita's cap was anchored to gave way. Kita's legs swung out over the chasm. Thankfully, her cheek and hands held. The chunk of ice was caught on Kita's cap. She shook her leg, trying to dislodge the dead weight.

Then her right hand slipped.

Jerking her hand away, she slapped a different section of the ice. Her hand held, but her other hand and cheek slipped.

What's wrong? Why am I slipping? Am I not thinking sticky enough?

No...ah, the sticky nanites don't work on a liquid surface. Too much movement of the molecules. Your body heat is melting the ice, causing you to slip. I suggest keeping your hands moving and only holding onto dry ice.

Bloody moons! Kita screamed in her head as she slipped again. I've got to get this weight off.

Twisting and turning the chunk of ice, Kita tried to dislodge her cap. She lifted the ice and kicked with her free leg. The ice gave some as Kita slipped further. Her hands had reached the edge.

I've got to hurry.

Another swift kick, and the ice gave way partially, leaving Kita dangling, twisting, and swinging wildly. She slammed into the side of the ice column, shattering the chunk of ice. Kita watched it disappear into the fog of the chasm.

When the blood stopped pounding in her ears, Kita followed the formation until she came to a flat spot with several war cats and Sarge waiting, overlooking a large wooden building.

"Let me guess, you knew an easier route?"

Sarge wrapped his tail around Kita.

"Hu-huh."

It must be a factory—a big one, said Omega from the computer inside Kita's head.

Yorq had few factories, and they were small, unlike the large steam-driven ones found in Champignon.

"So, let's see what we can see. Coal is going in, and something in war cat-patterned bags is coming out. I guess I need a closer look."

Kita turned invisible, and the cats waited as Kita slid down the slope to the edge of the factory. She inspected the conveyor that took the coal inside and the chute that brought the sacks outside.

Kita hopped on a waiting cart full of sacks. Using a throwing blade, Kita sliced open a bag and gagged at the smell. It was rotting meat, bone…it's like they threw the whole animal in the grinder. Kita had a funny vision of the butcher making hamburger.

The cart moved forward, and Kita hopped off. The line of wagons moved at a steady rate, loading and unloading.

Yuck. I've seen enough. Let's see why the cats are upset.

Kita climbed back up to Sarge and the other war cats. He bumped Kita's leg when she appeared.

"Let me guess, whatever has your friends' tails twisted is in there."

Several cats bowed their heads.

"Don't worry. I'll free them. I don't know what they're doing, but I'll stop it."

After scratching Sarge's ears, Kita turned invisible and returned to the loading area. Without direction, she climbed on the coal conveyor to get inside.

It climbed several floors before dumping the coal in a large pile where sixteen pigmen shoveled it into four boiler fireboxes. The steam was pumped into some kind of contraption.

It's a generator. The steam turns the shaft, generating electricity.

The steam engines were massive, two stories high, but produced a sweltering heat, making it hard to breathe.

Kita skirted the coal pile and dodged the pigmen, spotting a door with a wheel latch.

How am I going to move that unseen?

Kita inspected the wheel, and not only would it require a lot of force, but she also bet it would be noisy if the room weren't already a cacophony. Unable to leave, Kita settled in and watched the pigmen's routines. Once they were on the far side of the room, she took her chance and opened the door. She gently shut it behind her after Sarge darted in.

"Where have you been hiding?"

Sarge licked his nose.

"Treats. Come on. Let's see what this place is up to."

A maze of rusty pipes leaking water went in every direction.

Kita touched one.

Oh, that's hot.

You have to learn the hard way, don't you?

"Where does this all go?" Kita said in wonder.

I don't know, but we should figure out what it's doing and fast. Your best bet is to follow the big pipes.

Kita jumped and stuck to a large pipe. She needed to keep moving to avoid burning herself.

The pipe turned ninety degrees, and Kita landed on the top, thankful her boots could take the heat.

Following the large pipe, Kita jumped a series of smaller pipes to a platform with a door. Turning invisible, she stuck her head in as Sarge arrived, upset over his paws.

Her recon didn't reveal anything other than a stack of crates.

"Wait. I'll be back," Kita told the war cat.

She vanished and slipped through the door. The noise reminded Kita of pieces of wood rubbing. She climbed to the top of the crates to get the best vantage point. Large wooden gears and leather belt driven machines did bloody moons what.

In the corner is an electrical generator. I'm going to guess it runs this freakshow.

Omega wasn't kidding. Limp war cats came down a chute where a pigman with a spiked hammer smashed the cat's skull. Next, the cat's head, legs, and tail were removed. The carcass was hung on a meat hook and gutted. The bodies were skinned, and what was left was mixed with a powder and put through a grinder that fell into a room below.

Kita sat down hard and covered her mouth.

How can they do that to the war cats? I have to figure this out. There's no way I'm going to let this happen.

Peering over the crates, Kita spotted a human directing the pigmen working at each station.

Kita let him go for now. She wanted to know more about where these war cats came from.

Climbing the stairs next to the chute, a team of pigmen were throwing war cats from a cart down to be killed.

Having had enough, Kita drew her swords and appeared balanced on the cart's front edge.

"Why are you doing this to the war cats?" she demanded.

The pigmen looked confused.

"Fine. Have it your way."

Kita spun to a knee, removing the five workers' heads.

Picking up a war cat in the cart, Kita wanted to cry. This was a war cat in name only. It was so deformed, mangled, and sickly that it should have died.

Heartbroken, Kita laid out the seven cats and stabbed each through the heart.

You've suffered enough.

Kita pushed through hanging plastic sheeting into a world of unimaginable suffering.

Female war cats were chained to the ground with feeding tubes forced down their throats. They were forcibly inseminated, and by Kita's guess, gestation lasted a week and then a few more to let the cats grow.

A group of ravagers pushing a cart reached into cages, pulling out cats.

Enraged, Kita performed a handspring, landed balancing on the cart's walls, and with a flurry, she stabbed each pigman in a place where they would take days to die.

Kita wondered about the giant facility, looking at the cats until she found a room with United Earth Empire livery.

These are the computers that control the hormones, food, and waste of the creatures.

What do I do?

Ask your advisors. That's what they're there for.

They're not here. I'll destroy the place if I have to.

We should look more before we do that.

Kita searched the gestation area and found a barred door. She undid the wooden crossbeam and opened it.

Her heart sank. Hundreds of real war cats were kept in cages. What made the situation worse was that the feeding crew gave them the ground-up mush.

Furious, Kita drew four throwing knives and threw them between the ravagers' eyes.

Kita drew her swords and attacked the locks, cutting open the cages. The cat's hopped out, but none left.

What is it?

"Do you know where to look?"

A cat lashed his tail, and Kita followed back to the meat factory.

"You guys want your revenge?"

Sarge led the charge, jumping down the chute to the processing plant. A live, angry war cat wasn't what the worker was expecting. The cats came down the shoot and ran down their prey.

"Leave him!" Kita pointed to the human.

Kita let the slaughter unfold around her. She didn't have much to do until the cats finished.

"You really shouldn't piss off a war cat. I know. I have one. So, we're going to play a game. I ask a question. We'll move you to the next station if you fail to answer. First question, who's paying for this?"

The man shook his head.

"I'm not answering stars for you. Whoever you are. The Master will have your head."

Kita grabbed one of the kill hammers and slammed the spike into the man's shoulder.

"I can't kill you too quickly. What are you making, and for whom?"

The man pressed his lips together.

Kita grabbed two large cleavers and stuck them in the fire.

"I guess you don't need all this extra stuff."

She slammed him down on the table and with swift strokes, Kita removed his feet and hands. Using the flat of the red-hot cleavers, she cauterized the wounds.

"You're going to need your head."

"Answers?"

The man's screams died to a whimper.

"Believe me, whatever they're going to do to you, I'll be way worse."

"Kill me. I'll never tell. But take care of the boy. He's in the barracks area."

"Don't worry. I'll make sure he's well taken care of."

Kita grabbed the man by his waist and slammed his shoulders through a pair of meat hooks.

"The last step is skinning," Kita giggled. "Something I'm good at."

She made a slice across his forehead and around his face. Taking her nail, she dug under the skin, then yanked the man's skin free as he howled.

"I can take more."

Kita grabbed the body and climbed the grinder platform.

She extended her barb.

"This will keep you alive for days and make sure you don't pass out."

Kita dropped the screaming man into the grinder. When he was halfway, she hit the disengage lever.

Kita injected him with her barb.

"I'll leave you here to think about your life choices and see if you want to answer me."

"This is cruel. It's torture!"

"Then what do you call what you did to the war cats?"

Kita retraced her steps out of the room, looking for the barracks. She crossed one of the covered passages inside the mountain and found mostly empty rooms with straw.

She opened a door, which was nicer than the others. Inside were comfortable beds, bathrooms, a lounge with games and entertainment, and even food. A giant circular metal door stood embedded in the back rock wall. A smaller door was on the right.

What's behind door number one?

Three women, one older and supervising two younger girls, were sitting around a table talking about how bad the ravagers were at sewing.

Sarge sniffed the air and put his nose to the ground. He tracked someone to the smaller door. Opening the door for the war cat led to an office. Kita smirked as she came around the desk.

"Don't eat me!" a boy screamed at Sarge.

"He's not going to eat you," assured Kita as she pushed the cat out of the way.

"What...how'd a thief get here?" asked the boy.

"I'm investigating for the Legion and the Shadow Guild. Neither like what's happening. Who are you?"

"I'm Eazor. My Pa runs the factory."

Not for long.

"You should see the cat queen," exclaimed Eazor. "If you're with the Legion. You can put an end to her reign of terror."

Kita raised an eyebrow.

"Cat queen? Reign of terror?"

"It's their queen, I guess. They captured her and locked her behind the door. Before the factory, the war cats hunted the livestock and game."

Kita stroked her hair.

"Do you know how to get in?"

"I have the token."

He took it from around his neck and gave her the jewelry.

"Just push it into the center."

"Why do you have it?"

"My da gave it to me for safekeeping."

Oh...hmmm...

"I'm going to go check out the door. Why don't you and Sarge stay here and play? Just don't pull on his tail, fur, or ears."

"Oh, really? I get to play with a war cat?"

I wonder if he knows what this place does.

"Yep. Have fun."

Kita flipped the token as she left the room.

She turned invisible, went to the metal door, and pushed the token into the hole. It swung open to the grinding of gears and the whine of an electric motor. A blast of heat radiated from the opening of a lava tube.

The women jumped to their feet and ran out the room.

We may have visitors when I return.

Kita drew her swords and followed the tube, staying in the shadows. She, and several war cats, exited onto a semi-hardened lava pool.

In the pool's center was a large floating cone with a war cat—she looked like something between a human and a war cat. Around the large cone floated three smaller ones.

This shouldn't be too hard a jump. I just need to get the timing right.

While watching the small cone pads, Kita went as close to the pool's edge as she dared. Each pad moved at different speeds and directions.

I can't do this without help. Omega?

Sure, this is what adventuring is all about. Just don't miss.

A red halo appeared in Kita's vision.

When the cones aligned, she jumped. The pad tilted when she landed, sapping Kita's momentum and nearly dumping her into the lava pool. Only dropping to her stomach and redistributing her weight saved her.

Ah, what happened?

It seems this is an elaborate booby trap. But they're set by wireless controls. Give me a second, and I'll make them stable.

Kita wasn't sure what that meant, but her red aura faded as tears trickled down her face.

Great.

The pads stopped their orbit and lined up.

There you go.

Kita bounded between the pads and landed gracefully on the large platform.

Momentarily.

Her weight tipped the platform, causing Kita and the queen to slide toward the lava.

Kita threw herself down next to the queen and spread her arms, righting the platform.

You missed one.

Oops, it's on a separate area of the network. I'm going to teach you something. These things have a wireless connection. They connect through the air. I can connect to them and control them. I'll show you.

A picture of lines and bars appeared in Kita's mind.

These bars move up and down the lines, controlling the platform's stability. There. I've made it so you can stand.

How is this possible?

You've got much to learn, youngling.

Kita rolled the queen over, and she gasped.

She's beautiful.

The queen had war cat features that fit a human face. She was covered in white and gray fur with black rosettes and walked erect, except her legs looked like a war cat's from her knees down. Her front was covered in fine, soft, silky fur, while longer hair covered her backside.

The queen's eyes focused on Kita.

"Food?" she asked.

"Yeah. Let me get you off this first."

Kita picked up the queen. She jumped back to the waiting war cats using the platform's superior height. Kita fumbled the landing, and the queen rolled into her subjects. The cats licked and nuzzled her.

"Ok, ok," she said, pushing off an aggressive licker.

Kita offered the queen her ration pack.

"Here, it's all I have."

The queen tore it open and took a bite, ignoring Kita.

Kita frowned. Shrugging, she walked back toward the door.

Rats.

Kita punched the wall, spraying rocks across the passage. It tore the skin from her oddly colored bones.

It should hurt more.

"Do you always leave without asking the name of the person you saved?" said a voice from behind.

"Huh? Sorry, you looked busy."

"Don't mind the cats. They're excited to have me back."

"And you are?"

"The locals call me Cat Queen. I live among the cats, tending, studying, and protecting them. The cats call me Snowy."

"Kita. I think your cats sent me to save you. They took my cat and left."

"You have a war cat?" the queen said darkly.

"He's been with me since I was six. He's busy guarding a child of the person who ran this place."

"When I catch up to him, he will suffer."

"Not a problem anymore...They're dead. Speaking of dead, maybe you can help me with a problem."

"I don't know if there's much I can do."

"Help me make a decision."

Kita led Snowy out of the large circular door to the office, where Eazor and Sarge played.

Eazor came out, stopped, and screamed, "It's the Cat Queen! She'll eat us all!"

"Not until you've had a bath," muttered Snowy.

"It's alright! She's with me!" cried Kita, jumping between the pair.

"You made friends with the Cat Queen?"

Kita looked at Snowy.

"I think so."

Snowy laughed and then scowled at the boy.

"I know his father. He runs this place."

"Not for long. Eazor, I need you to get in a cart and tell the driver to take you to The Forges. Your father will join you later."

"What's going to happen?"

"Not now, go. We'll find you. Tell Leader Murdock that Commander Kita says he's to take care of you."

"But my da."

"We'll get him, I promise. But I'm a Legion commander, and you must do as I say. Now, go."

Eazor nodded and ran out the door.

Kita explained what was happening as she escorted Snowy to the processing room.

"This is ghastly!" she exclaimed when they entered and she saw what was being done.

"You might know him."

Kita motioned to the man stuck in the grinder.

Snowy leaped to the platform.

I guess I'm not the only one with superpowers.

Kita followed and landed as Snowy scolded the man.

"You're a disgusting, vile waste of life," Snowy snarled as she grabbed a piece of the man's intestine and shoved it in his mouth. "See how your own filth tastes, pig."

"I think he's a human."

Snowy laughed.

"Not for long."

She extended a bony claw and scratched out the man's eyes.

"Now you know how I felt waiting alone in the dark to die."

Snowy faced Kita.

"I'm sorry, but—"

"Don't worry on my account. I've been killing workers all day."

Snowy looked at Kita's bloody knuckles.

"Are you always so hard on yourself?"

Only when I don't get what I want.

"Just frustration."

"Who are you to be here?"

"I'm the Legion Commander of Yorq and Rose of Arcone."

"Your royalty?"

"Not really. I tell them what to do, but I'm not treated special or anything."

Snowy looked star-struck.

"I can help you get back to your people."

"Right now, I need to get rid of this factory."

There were boilers below. Overload those, and this place will explode.

"We can blow the boilers," said Kita.

"Oh, good idea," said Snowy. "I should be able to."

Her nose turned red.

"I'm a scientist and know a bit of engineering."

"Great. Let me show you the big problem."

Kita led Snowy into the gestation room.

Snowy gasped, and her whiskers twitched.

"These are not war cats but meat vegetables."

"Can we do anything for them?"

"No. Death would be a release."

"How do we kill them?"

"There must be a feeding tank."

They split up. Even Kita's hardened stomach was upset by the brood mothers and the lifeless babies.

"I found it," called Snowy.

Kita hurried over.

"How do we poison so much?" lamented Snowy.

"I can."

Kita jumped atop the tank, opened the lid, and extended both needle-like barbs from the heels of her hands. She released a stream of a nerve agent known to kill in seconds.

"I hope that's enough," said Kita as she resealed the hatch. Her hands were numb.

It should be. Sarin nerve gas is potent stuff.

"If not, they'll go when we blow the place," said Snowy.

She has a callous side. Not that I mind.

Kita led Snowy into the cage room.

"They kept hundreds of war cats here. I cut them free. That's why there are so many around."

"We'll have to get them out."

Snowy called over a cat and had a conversation of meows, growls, and chuffs. He passed the orders to the others. As a group, they left.

"Thanks for the help," said Kita. "I was going to bring my advisors here, but you know just as much."

Snowy giggled.

"I enjoyed spending time with you. Come. Let's blow this place."

T HE DOOR TO THE boiler room burst open. Kita performed a sideways layout, cutting a pigman into pieces. She corkscrewed through two more workers. Launching off the side of the conveyor, Kita cut three pigmen in half. She charged forward, stabbed a worker, twirled, and slashed another. After splitting a hog man's skull open, she flipped her grip and stabbed another worker through the eye. Spinning, Kita cut through two more. As she came around, the last pigman jumped down the coal chute.

Ok, let me have a look at these boilers.

Kita looked at the piping and valves scattered along the large cylindrical boiling tanks.

There! Tighten down those large valves. Those are the emergency shut-offs. After that, we need to stock the fire and get the boilers overheated.

"Snowy! We need to shut these valves."

Kita pointed.

"Then we need to feed coal into the fireboxes."

"You want me to get covered in coal dust?"

"Or I can do it."

"It's fine. You can help me clean my fur later."

That sounds like fun to me.

Once the valves were shut, Kita hurried around the room, throwing in as much coal as the tinderboxes would hold.

"I don't see why you need me," scoffed Snowy at Kita's progress.

"It's better with friends."

Snowy carried an armload of coal over and threw it in a box. She turned up her nose at the dark streaks on her fur.

"It'll come off," Kita promised.

Once the boilers are full, shut the doors and set the pressure to maximum.

"Shut the fire doors," ordered Kita, "and set the pressure to max."

Kita and Snowy hurried around the room, setting the boilers.

"Now what?" Snowy asked when they finished.

Run.

"We need to get out of here. Come on, we'll take the food chute."

"That's gross!"

"It's the only way. Come on."

Kita grabbed Snowy's hand and pulled her down the chute.

On a table next to the chute were bags of coins. Kita scooped up a bunch and jumped.

It was a slow ride to the bottom, and they landed in a cart full of meat sacks.

"Yuck!" exclaimed Snowy.

"It washes off," protested Kita.

"I bet it tastes awful."

Kita didn't doubt that. She jumped down from the cart to find Eazor running to them.

"Commander! What happened?"

"We have to go. Tell the drivers to get out of here. Here, give them the money for the shipment."

Kita passed some of the money to Snowy, and they gave instructions and payment to each driver.

Kita, Sarge, Snowy, and Eazor jumped onto the last cart.

Kita moved up the empty cart and put Dawn on the driver's back.

"Where are you supposed to take the food?"

"To—to an army in the mountains."

"You're to take the boy to The Forges and never return by order of the Legion. Your job here is done. Eazor, come sit up front."

The boy went to the front, and Kita lifted him into the seat next to the driver.

"We'll get off when we reach the main trail."

A WAR CAT JUMPED into the cart and gave Snowy a message.

"This is good," Snowy ordered the driver.

"Why are we stopping?" asked Kita.

"The cats found the army that the factory was producing for. I thought you'd like to come and help get revenge."

"Sure. Just a second."

Kita leaned into Eazor. "Take this message to the mayor of The Forges. I've solved the war cat problem. They should be left alone."

"My cats will bring fresh kills for a year to make up for what they've taken," offered Snowy.

Kita pulled her marker, a wooden coin with a S and G burnt into one side and a raven on the other, from her belt.

"This is my marker. Show it to a legionnaire or thief, and they'll take you to see my dad, and he'll help you."

Eazor didn't look sure.

"Here," Snowy called over a cat. "This is Norway. He's big and strong and will protect you. Ok?"

"He'll be my pet?"

"He'll be your friend," corrected Kita.

"Yes, Commander."

Kita and Snowy jumped off the wagon and were joined by a group of war cats.

"They say it's toward the rising sun," said Snowy.

K ITA CROUCHED WITH SNOWY and Sarge, waiting for the
noonday sun.

Below them was a camp holding a large force of ravagers.
The camp was laid out like a wheel, a large tent with flapping
banners in the center.

*That's Earl John of Montfort's banner. What's a
Champignon noble doing here?*

When the sun peaked, thousands of war cats descended on
the camp. Stalking became charging the surprised ravagers.

In the beginning, the cats had speed and surprise on their
side. Most of the ravagers couldn't organize, and only those
around the main tent showed any discipline, forming a series
of battle lines to protect their headquarters.

Kita let the cats take their revenge, only making opportunistic kills.

The ravagers weren't the only ones with casualties. Kita
knelt beside an injured war cat and injected it with a nanite
solution to heal it. Soon, the cat was on his feet, returning to
the hunt.

Not far away, a pigman squealed, calling for Kita. She went
and knelt over him.

"What do you want?"

The pigman shoved his wrist into his arm.

"You want me to heal you like I did the war cat?"

The pigman squealed.

"Why?"

The pigman pointed to his arm and then Kita's black bracer.

"You think because I wear black, we're the same?"

Kita stood.

"I know if I heal you, you'll return to attack us again. Better to let you die now."

She walked away.

A commotion at the main tent drew Kita's attention. When she arrived, she found that the war cats had a man wearing plate armor. He was bleeding from multiple puncture wounds to his armor and claw marks on the face.

"*Strange finding a Champignon noble out here,*" Kita said in French.

"Please, you must help me. Stop them! I have done nothing wrong."

"Have your ravagers seen where their food comes from?" asked Kita. "And what's an army doing way up here?"

"We destroyed the King's forces, and these mangy felines helped," John said proudly. "The Yorqians ran like the dogs they are."

"I believe the cats only helped because you had their queen. And my legionnaires?"

"Cowardly mice running around with their tails chopped off."

Kita glared at John as she picked up his helmet.

Intricate metalwork made the helmet look like a dog.

"Who are you?" asked John.

"Commander Kita of the Legion of Yorq. It was my men you called mice. Now, we'll see how well you do."

John nodded to the helmet.

"Keep it. It's been in my family for generations. A real warrior should have it."

Kita scoffed, then crushed the helmet.

"You really shouldn't get attached to things," Kita told the gaping man.

She motioned to the cats.

"He's yours."

The group of war cats fell on John.

"I have to get to Razor's Pass to see what's left," Kita told Snowy.

"We know a shortcut."

"I have to catch up to my companions first."

"Then I will send the cats to find them."

P^{*IFF!*}

The snowball struck Cowboy in the back.

"Hey, did you miss me?" Kita called as she, Sarge, and Snowy came down from a ledge.

"I wondered where the hell you'd been."

"Gathering information. We need to get to Razor's Pass. According to our enemy, they wiped out the King's and Legion Armies."

"How do you know this? And who is this?"

"You're such an ass," huffed Snowy.

"Darla?"

"I'm not some fat, dumpy, four-eyed loser now," Snowy snarled.

Cowboy raised his hands defensively.

"I called you fat to motivate you. I never said the rest."

"Bastard."

"I take it you know each other?" said Zidin.

"We have a history," chuckled Cowboy.

Snowy put her nose in the air.

"Sounds like a long, spiteful history. Right now, we don't have time to get into it. We need to get up the pass."

"You're right," said Cowboy. "Darla will just have to deal."

"I'm not dealing with you. I have a new girlfriend. And Kita's amazing."

Girlfriend? Me! She wants to be my girlfriend! She's so pretty and smart. And she'll give me someone else besides the boys to talk to. I can't believe I have a girlfriend! Squee!

Cowboy laughed.

"See how long that lasts."

"Ass."

"So, are you behind the booms?" Cowboy asked Kita.

"Yep. I found a factory making food for an army. So, we blew it up, and Snowy and her war cats wiped out the enemy."

"You don't say?" said Cowboy, rubbing his chin, which was hidden by his bandana.

"I'll tell you all about it. I almost brought you, but Snowy solved the problem."

"Next time, let me have a look. We may need what you blew up. So, what did you girls get up to?"

TWO

DEATH WISH
ROYALE LYNN AND
DANNY WORSNOP
DEATH WISH

"THEY DIDN'T LEAVE MUCH," commented Zidin.

"No, they didn't," said Kita, looking at the frozen field of bodies.

The bodies froze before decay set in. It was like walking through a freak show of death.

Kita wanted to find her Legion, her brother's banner, to prove he was dead, and Arbol's banner to prove it no longer existed.

The macabre killing field being frozen helped Kita's stomach. There was no smell and just the wind to speak for the dead.

"What are you looking for?" asked Snowy.

"Ah, my family and brother's banner and anyone in a blue Legion uniform."

"Your family was here?" gasped Snowy.

"My brother. He led my father's army. I was supposed to join the Legion as a junior commander. Now, as commander, I've lost everyone."

"Their deaths are not your fault," said Cowboy, stepping around the bodies. "You weren't even in the Legion when this happened. I bet the force you destroyed got the drop on them."

"Doesn't help me know."

"You don't know that," said Cowboy. "Wiping that army out probably saved us an attack on The Forges."

"It wasn't me who destroyed the ravager army. It was the war cats."

"You're the catalyst—the spark—that set it off. That's a rare talent. But like a good leader, you get recognition for your soldiers, not just yourself."

"I'm not my brother."

"I haven't had the pleasure of meeting him."

"His body's around her somewhere."

"I'm so sorry," said Snowy.

"It's not your fault," whispered Kita softly. "But thanks."

Kita was glad her hood, mask, and scarf hid her blush.

"You know what's interesting?" said Zidin.

"How *this* was allowed to happen?" muttered Cowboy.

"That rock is oddly human shaped."

The group gathered around.

"It has a heartbeat," said Snowy.

Cowboy knocked on the rock.

"Hey! Anyone in there?"

The rock swirled and twisted like taffy. It receded into the ground, revealing a man in an elegant robe, gold belt, and fur collar.

Kita was instantly jealous of his hair. Not a strand out of place. It was long and luscious and framed his perfect face. It looked like he went to a Champignon hair salon daily.

The man saw Cowboy and Zidin and yelled, "About time! Where have you been?" with his back to Kita. "Where's the army?"

"One girl army," chuckled Zidin, pointing behind the shaper.

He turned, and Kita's heart skipped a beat. His piercing gray eyes made her want to melt. His pleasant, deep, and rich baritone voice was the kind she'd do anything to hear more of.

So, this is the mythical man you could switch horses for.
Kita gulped.

"K-K-Kita L-Logine."

"Kita Logine? Well, you're a rose among the brambles. I would have never guessed to find someone so—what in the ten thousand blazing suns is that?" he said as Snowy walked up to Kita.

Snowy's face, whiskers, and tail drooped.

The man's spell broke.

"Hey, be nice. She's with me. Who are you?"

He gave Kita an amazing smile.

"My apologies. I did not think I would see something as exotic as your cat."

"This is Snowy," Kita said defensively. "She is the queen of the war cats. I'm grateful to have her as a traveling companion."

The man's face contorted in disgust and anger.

"Did you know your traveling companion set her cats upon us? They attacked with the ravagers. She should be killed for what she did. Those cats chased us down like mice and dragged the bodies away to be eaten."

"That's not true!" cried Snowy. "The cats were forced to attack you. They didn't want to. They took the bodies to a slope facing the sun, trying to give the soldiers a proper burial."

"You knew your cats were involved and didn't say anything?" Cowboy demanded.

Kita stepped between the three parties.

"I knew of their involvement. I went with them as they took revenge and earned their redemption. They're innocent players forced to do something ghastly to protect Snowy."

"There is no redemption for these vile creatures," said the man. "We should hunt them to extinction. Starting with that one."

He pointed at Snowy.

Kita's anger exploded.

"Listen, whoever you are!"

Zidin and Cowboy stepped back.

Snowy took the cue and did the same.

"I was with them as they destroyed the army that attacked you. The field was littered with dead and dying war cats. They have earned our forgiveness and trust. You try to hurt her, and you'll have to come through me."

The man laughed.

Kita's feet went rigid, encased in rock. She scowled.

"Let me go. First and only chance."

Kita folded her arms.

The rock receded.

"I don't want to hurt that pretty face. It would be a shame," the man said with a dazzling smile. "I thought you should know who you're dealing with."

Kita returned a sinister smile.

"You would have to be able to hit this pretty face first. Do you have a name?"

"Bartholomew Jackson Van der Hoost the Sixteenth, rock and fire shaper in the service of his Majesty, the King of Yorq."

He bowed low to the group.

"Why are you here? Instead of reporting the defeat to New London?"

"Why, awaiting rescue, of course. I'm no soldier, and these mountains are dangerous."

Bart looked at Snowy.

"It's not my job to report a defeat. I'm not a member of the army. I'm a specialist in the service of the king."

Kita scoffed.

"While you waited for rescue, which may or may not have come, our enemies now have a head start. All you had to do was walk down the mountain."

"My dear lady, I do as I am paid to—to use my shaping powers to help the army as needed. I'm not paid to be a messenger. These are not my enemies."

"Not what you said about the war cats. These enemies don't care. They'll tear you apart because they can. Come on, everyone, let's go. Keep looking for food, water, and the Legion. We'll leave this fool to his fate."

Kita motioned for Snowy to follow, but the cat queen looked distraught.

Kita leaned in and whispered, "Don't worry about him. I think you're beautiful, and that's all that matters."

Snowy's tail twitched as her ears perked up.

Kita searched the area, looking for her banners. She found her family banner broken and lying in the snow. She picked it up and brushed it off.

"What's that?" said Snowy.

"It's my father's banner."

"Your father was here?"

"No. This is the estate banner, but I don't see my brother's banner. Maybe he survived. He wouldn't go anywhere without it."

"Maybe he escaped or was out on patrol? He could be waiting for help—like that idiot Bart."

Snowy growled and chuffed. Six war cats came down the steep slope and talked with her.

"They say they've seen several bands of human soldiers roaming the mountains. I will tell them to keep looking. If any humans are found, they'll let us know."

Snowy gave the orders, and the cats returned to the mountains.

"Thanks. You didn't have to send them. I figured Jeffrey was dead when I heard the army was gone."

Snowy looked at Kita quizzically.

"He's your brother. Don't you want to know if he's alive?"

Kita shrugged.

"I...I'm not sure. We're not close. My family life is a mess. It's a long story, but thank you for looking."

Snowy hugged Kita.

"Don't worry, that's what friends are for."

Kita hugged her back.

"Thanks."

"WHAT DID WE FIND?" asked Kita when everyone gathered.

"This camp was a mess before the ravagers arrived," muttered Zidin. "There was at least one other army. I found elf, hoof, paw, and *other* tracks."

Kita agreed. She'd seen the same.

"We should get down to Outpost Twenty-four and report to LCOM," suggested Cowboy.

Kita shook her head. "We're going to call LCOM from whatever environmental station is running amok."

"We'll die if we go into the Unfinished Wastes," exclaimed Bart.

He's an idiot. We have enough supplies and water to get to the station. It's only a three-day walk from the base of the pass.

"We'll be fine."

She looked at Cowboy and Zidin for confirmation.

"If we don't have to go far," said Cowboy.

"Three days."

"We can manage that. But *Why?*"

"Because I have an—inkling—our ravager armies are coming from there. I want to destroy their rear. They've already passed us by. But if we destroy the source, we just have to eliminate the armies."

Cowboy and Zidin exchanged a look.

"She's right," muttered Zidin.

"All those lessons on strategy," Kita said with pride.

"You're learning faster than I expected," said Cowboy. "But that's not a bad thing. Is this inkling sure?"

"Have I been wrong yet?"

"You haven't had many chances to be right."

"Touché."

"We should send those furballs after the attackers," suggested Bart. "Let them continue their redemption."

Kita sucked in a deep breath as she fought to control her temper. A battle she was losing.

"The war cats are not an army and are in no condition to fight. We don't have an army, but we need information—how big? How many? Who's in charge? What's their objective? And who the bloody moons asked you?"

"I thought my insights on being present during the battle would be helpful to you, my Lady."

Kita frowned.

"I'm not *my Lady*. You'll address me as commander."

"As you wish, Commander Kita Logine," Bart said with a suave smile.

Snowy frowned at Bart, and Kita sighed.

I feel dirty.

"Let's get going," said Kita. "There's nothing here for us."

"Commander, uhm, what about myself?" said Bart.

"Sorry, I don't have money to pay you. You'll have to fend for yourself."

Kita shrugged and walked off.

Bart followed.

"Maybe we can make a deal. I can work for you for the promise of protection...and maybe some company on the cold nights?" His eyes twinkled with a promising grin.

Kita slapped him to the ground.

Zidin pursed his lips, Cowboy's eyes widened, and Snowy covered her face while she laughed.

"I'm not for sale, trade, or anything. I won't offer protection because these people have better things to do in a fight. I don't have enough food for you and won't ask them to sacrifice for you. What I do offer is a chance to make it back to somewhere safe when I decide it's time. How's that for a deal?"

Bart grinned.

"Fiery. I like that in a woman. It's a deal. As long as I can enjoy the view."

Enraged, Kita walked off.

Now I really feel dirty.

K ITA ONLY STOPPED TO rest for Bart. He didn't have the energy nanites the others had.

Snowy returned with a large stag dangling from the jaws of a war cat. She removed a leg and gave it to the cat. It bound up the slope, clutching its prize. Zidin helped Snowy clean and cut the meat.

"You're throwing away the best parts," said Snowy.

"This?" said Zidin, holding up a kidney.

Snowy took a bite out of it, and Zidin turned green.

Kita laughed.

"Shaper, come get a fire going so we can roast the meat," Kita yelled at Bart.

"Now you need me, eh? First, it's for the fire I'll light here. Later, it'll be for the fire I'll light elsewhere," Bart said as he went by.

I'm seriously reconsidering my stance on usefulness over personality.

Kita picked at her dinner, still full from eating days before, but she ate what she could—she wasn't sure when she'd eat again.

Each person ate differently.

Zidin ate with his hands, ripping the meat off in big chunks.

Cowboy used a knife to cut, and then he stabbed the meat to get it to his mouth, though he didn't remove the bandana.

Bart somehow produced a fork, knife, and plate and created a rock table with a stool.

Snowy refused to let her share be cooked. Instead, she happily tore away the flesh, making a bloody mess. Kita giggled at her when she stopped.

"What?" Snowy asked shyly.

"You've got a red mustache."

Snowy licked at it with her tongue, then licked her hand and cleaned her face. "Better?"

Kita laughed.

"Now, it looks like you've got lip makeup on."

Snowy's ears and whiskers drooped.

"It looks good on you."

"Anything is an improvement," Bart chided.

"Ignore him. I think you're beautiful."

"I know you do," Snowy said.

Kita blushed.

"You're cute when you blush."

Kita's blush deepened as Snowy winked at her.

K ITA WAS ANNOYED AT the slow pace. Bart needed to rest every few hours, even going downhill.

At the base of the pass, Kita didn't hesitate to step onto the *deadly* sand. She climbed the first dune and marveled at the sandy sea with tall rock spires reaching for the sun.

Everyone else, except Bart, joined Kita. Only Bart refused.

"The sand is cursed," said Bart. "I don't carry a ward of protection."

"Neither do I," said Kita.

She picked up a handful of sand and let it fall between her fingers.

"It's just sand. There's nothing cursed about it. Come on. We're losing daylight."

The others each gave Bart an amused look as they walked away.

Even Sarge snickered.

"How do I know you're not in league with evil spirits?" yelled Bart.

"Let me ask you a question," said Kita.

"Ask me a question now, and soon you'll ask for other things."

Ugh, why am I putting up with this?

"Do you want to take a chance with a curse or take a chance with me? Because you only get one shot with me."

Bart's ears perked up.

That's it. Hear what you want to hear.

Snowy looked worried.

I promise it's not what you think.

"Come on," Kita told her group as she led them down the dune.

"Don't I get some motivation to get me out on the sands?" called Bart.

Kita turned without stopping.

"Yes, either come or go. I care not which."

Bart hurried to catch up.

"I love a girl who plays hard to get."

Kita scowled.

"**A**RE WE GOING TO make camp?" Bart asked as dusk fell.

"No. We'll push on through the night and rest during the day. I don't want that perfect skin of yours to sunburn."

Bart touched his face and smiled. "Been looking, have you? My skin is perfect—everywhere."

Gag.

"We can rest in the shade of the spires," Cowboy motioned to the large, hundred-foot-tall rock formations that dotted the landscape.

"How are we going to see?"

"Besides by the light of the moon? Some of us can see in the dark."

"I believe the creature can, but you're not whatever she is."

"She's superhuman," said Zidin. "As are the rest of us. You're the only plain human here."

"I'm anything but plain," huffed Bart as he lit a flame in his hand.

There was a *woosh* and an eerie laugh. Cowboy stood as a flaming skeleton.

"Son, you know nothing of what can be done!"

"Stars above! What kind of demon are you?"

"A cursed cowboy chasing the devil's herd."

"The what?"

"Never mind. You're not the only one with nanites—what creates your flame and rock shaping. Everyone here has some. You're the only one without the constitution, energy, and endurance. We'd be there in a few days if it were just us. Instead, we have to wait for your sorry ass to sleep, eat, and rest. If you're not careful, I'll bury you up to your neck and let the insects have you."

"What's a nanite?"

"What makes your *magic*," grumped Zidin.

"I am a magical being. MY magic is—"

"Science," said Cowboy, turning back. "Which you don't understand, and I won't teach you. I already have one apt pupil, and she's learning fast."

"Let's go," ordered Kita. "You can teach me something cool as we go."

They walked through the darkness, and Cowboy, with help from Zidin, gave Kita a lecture on surviving the desert.

"You'll find the Unfinished Wastes have some unique critters. Most are harmless, but there are a few. Sand sharks, for one."

"Sand shark? What is that?" asked Kita.

"A shark that swims through the sand like water. There are also seals, a food source for the sharks."

"Nothing like that exists," scoffed Bart.

"If I see one, I'll feed you to it," said Zidin. His marking turned his bald head blue with a large shark-like smile.

"You need me."

"For what?" asked Snowy.

"Creatures don't talk."

"Hey," said Kita as she grabbed Bart. "She is a she, not a creature. Just because she looks like a war cat doesn't mean she's bad. She's helped us and will continue. So far, all you've done is complain and whine. Start being helpful, or you won't be at all."

"Whatever it takes to get your attention. I know you like what you see."

"Yes, but can you back up that pretty face?"

Kita swallowed some bile.

I think I'd rather rip my eyes out.

Snowy's whiskers and lips quivered.

The group traveled until the early morning rays turned the sky lead-gray. They made camp in the shadow of a spire.

Curious about their surroundings, Kita climbed the spire to see the desert. The sand was empty except for the rock columns.

Kita cycled through the lenses in her eyes to look closer. Odd-looking creatures basked in the early morning light at the base of a distant spire. Zooming in, they were black with a dog's head and a fish's body. One dove into the sand like water. The other creatures joined it.

"What are you doing up here?" said Snowy.

Kita jumped, startled.

"I came up to check our position. We're going in the right direction and should reach our destination in two more nights. I scanned the horizon and found we're not alone. There are some odd dogfish creatures at that spire over there."

Kita pointed to where she'd seen them.

Snowy smirked.

"Dogfish? You mean a seal?"

Kita shrugged.

"I guess, sure. All I know is that it dove off the rocks and plunged into the sand like water."

"We'll have to be careful. Where there are seals, there are sharks."

A long, awkward silence hung between them.

"It's ok if you're more interested in him than me," Snowy blurted through tears. "I know he's gorgeous, and I understand. I'm still willing to come with you to make up for what we've done. Just tell me now."

"What! Never," Kita said firmly. "The last thing I want is to touch that slimy bastard. On the other hand, you're what I'm most definitely interested in."

"But you flirt with him and give him these looks."

Kita laughed.

"I'm stringing the bastard along. He'll be willing to do anything if he thinks he has the slimmest of chances. I'm sorry. I'm doing it without realizing it. It's a skill I mastered as a teenager to get what I wanted from the guards."

Snowy wiped away her tears.

"I was never able to do that. When I was human, I was frumpy, overweight, and happy when Gerald looked at me, and I was ecstatic when he talked to me. Even when we were married, I always felt insecure, afraid he'd leave at any moment. I must sound foolish."

"You're not foolish, and I'm sorry. I should have mentioned my intentions with Bart to you earlier. I didn't mean to hurt you."

Kita bit her lip and then said hesitantly, "You're happy a girl's looking at you, right?"

Snowy giggled.

"I have no problem swinging—being with a man or woman. My parents always taught me to fall in love with the person."

She let out a long sigh, and her eyes darted away. She returned her attention to Kita with a shy smile.

"You really do like me and the way I look?"

Kita smiled wolfishly.

"I think you're the most beautiful thing I've ever seen. You want to watch the sunrise?"

She took Snowy's hand and invited her to sit.

The sun peeked over the horizon.

Kita found she wasn't concentrating on the sunrise, but on other things.

What do I do? It feels like my heart is beating out of my chest. What if she can hear it? I'm so going to screw this up. But if I do nothing, will she think I'm rejecting her? Gah! Kita quit being foolish. Just put your arm around her. DO IT!

Kita faked a yawn and stretched her arms.

Oh, I feel ridiculous.

Slowly and carefully, she placed her arm on Snowy's shoulders.

Oh, please, oh please, don't reject me.

Without a word, Snowy leaned in and placed her head on Kita's shoulder.

YES! She does like me.

Kita swallowed to keep her racing emotions and heartbeat in check. She then settled back, trying to relax and bring her anxiety under control.

"I SAW A GROUP of seals diving into the sand north of here," Kita said when she and Snowy returned to the desert floor.

Cowboy looked up from his notebook. Everyone else was asleep.

"Seals mean sharks, so be prepared."

Kita, not tired, let everyone sleep and stood guard. Just before dusk, she roused the group.

Leading the group on a path from spire to spire, Kita led them into the night.

As dawn approached, Kita stopped at a random spire.

"I'm going to the top to see where we are," she told the others.

"I'll come with you," said Snowy.

Together, they climbed the side of the formation. Snowy used her claws while Kita stuck to the rock.

"The dawn is pretty," Snowy said after they reached the top.

"I like the stars. They always bring me peace. You want to sit and watch the sun rise?"

"Sure."

When the sunrise was over, Snowy was fast asleep. Kita decided a nap sounded like a good idea.

ZIDIN SAT ON A rock cleaning Great White when Kita and Snowy reached the spire's base. The Arconian didn't look happy.

Kita touched Snowy's arm.

"Get some sleep. I'll deal with this."

Snowy smiled, showing a fang.

"I hope we get to see the sunrise again sometime."

Kita was glad her roses hid her blush.

"M-me, too."

"You're late," said Zidin when Kita went to relieve him.

"Sorry," Kita said, trying to be apologetic. "I'll take your shift tomorrow."

"We wouldn't need shifts if we didn't have Bart. So, what's between the three of you? You're not leading her on, are you?"

"No! I am Bart. I think his shaping might be useful. If I have to flirt to get him to bend to my whim, I will. I wish you'd said something earlier about leading Snowy on. She got the impression I was interested in Bart."

"You girls want some alone time? Tell me. I'll shoo the others away."

"That's why we've been going up the spire. But thanks for offering, someday..."

"If you want, I'll gladly break Bart in half."

Kita chuckled.

"I like the idea. We'll see if it comes to that. Get some rest. Or you can stay up and teach me something."

Zidin laughed.

"Let's talk about hydraulics."

"What are those?"

"Remember what we saw in the room with the cone? It's lifted by hydraulics."

"Ok, now you have to tell me."

Zidin laughed.

"It is nice to have a Rose who thirsts for knowledge. Your mother wanted nothing to do with anything unless it was wanting a family."

"The more I know, the better. Family, yuck. So, hydraulics?"

THE MOON HUNG IN the sky when Kita froze.

"What's wrong?" asked Snowy, coming over with the others.

"When I freeze, you should all freeze," scolded Kita. "There's something in the sand. I can feel the vibration."

"We know creatures live in this," said Zidin.

"Everyone, spread out, then don't move. I'm going to see if I can draw it out."

"You be careful," said Zidin, backing away but not far.

Kita yelled, stomped, jumped, and kicked the sand.

"This is a redfish," said Bart.

A large, black fish with jaws full of teeth exploded from the sand, tossing Kita in the air. It lunged, grabbed Kita by the arm, and tried to pull her under. When it couldn't, it dragged her along the top.

The wild tumbling kept Kita from drawing her sword. The creature rolled, shredding her arm.

As Kita banged against the fish, she was slickened with an oily substance.

I bet you burn.

She removed a thermite charge from her belt and slapped it beside the shark's eye.

The thermite set the fish afire. It released Kita and dove into the sand.

Recovering from her discombobulation, Kita found she'd been dragged far from the others. Careful of her arm, she pushed herself to her feet and went to help.

As she drew near, she could see the others fighting more of the sharks.

"They're covered in oil!" Cowboy yelled. "They burn."

Cowboy stood his ground. The demon was facing down a shark with a shotgun. He drew two brass cylinders from his belt, broke open his shotgun, and inserted the shells. Snapping the weapon closed, he fired, and the front of the fish exploded.

Snowy was on the back of another, attacking with her claws while Zidin faced the charging creature, sidestepped, and sliced the fish longways.

Bart blew flame in all directions, trying to keep the creatures away from him.

"Are you ok?" said Cowboy, rushing over when he saw Kita.

"My arm hurts."

"Ah, no shit. It's shredded. We have some foam left, but you'll have to let your nanites heal you."

Kita nodded.

"I know some first aid," said Bart. "I work with healers to sterilize and cauterize."

"Don't touch me," huffed Kita. "I'll be fine, let's go."

"**I**NTERESTING CREATURES," COMMENTED COWBOY. "They must use the oil to glide through the sand. I—Kita?"

She'd been leaning against Zidin listening, but was listing as she walked and couldn't focus.

"I'm alright. It just—"

Kita collapsed in Zidin's arms.

KITA AWOKE WITH A pounding headache. Water droplets hit her face, and her arm hurt.

"I'm awake..." she said weakly.

Zidin pulled the waterbag away.

"When was the last time you ate?" asked Cowboy.

Kita shrugged.

"The stag."

"Healing uses energy reserves at a rapid rate. You need to keep eating."

"Here," said Snowy.

She cradled Kita's head in her lap.

"Gerald, give me some of that jerky."

Cowboy handed over a strip.

Snowy tore it into little chunks and fed it to Kita.

"What does a cat know about first aid, anyway?" mocked Bart.

"She knows a helluva lot more than you," retorted Cowboy. "Zidin, once she's strong enough to move, can you carry her to the next spire? We'll rest there."

Kita nibbled on the meat, annoyed she should know better, even though she had no idea.

"How much further do we have to go?" whined Bart.

"We're not far," said Cowboy. "So quit yapping and be on the lookout for more of those things."

As Kita ate, Snowy stroked her hair, making her sleepy.

"Kitten, you must eat before you sleep," said Snowy.

"But you're comfy," sighed Kita.

Snowy giggled.

Kita ate four slices before she could stand. Even then, Zidin carried her while Cowboy taught her genetics.

"**T**HERE IT IS."

Kita pointed in the distance.

A structure sat atop a spire.

"Finally, we can rest properly," huffed Bart.

There is no ground-level entrance to the Razor Reef Conservation Center. You have to go through the Visi-

tors Center. A neighboring spire has a walkway we can take.

"We're going up there," Kita pointed to the spire Omega gave her.

"I do not fly," said Bart sarcastically.

"Then make stairs. Be useful or not at all."

"What my Lady requires, I will do."

"You better be careful. She'll take you up on it," said Zidin.

"I'm looking forward to it."

Kita ignored the banter. She was annoyed at herself for wasting a day healing and eating the group's food. She didn't want to be a burden. It caused the anxiety in her chest to build.

When Snowy took her hand, Kita forgot her troubles, and her heart soared.

During the night, Snowy lectured Kita on nanites and genetics. Unlike Cowboy and Zidin, who were thoughtful and took time to explain when Kita had a question or made a mistake, Snowy became upset when Kita didn't understand or gave an incorrect answer. Kita wasn't sure she wanted any more teachings from Snowy.

Nobody's perfect. It'll create an interesting spark between us.

"Start shaping," Kita ordered Bart when they reached the spire's base.

She and Snowy climbed as the boys approached the top one stair at a time.

That funny rock formation near the edge of the spire will extend a walkway to the Razor's Reef Visitors Center.

Kita went to the formation, and following Omega's instructions, she found the switch to extend the walkway.

"Wow!"

Kita ran and jumped on the clear plastic floor. She hung over the rail, looking down until Zidin grabbed her.

"Kitten!" scolded Snowy. "You must be more careful. It's a long fall, and even you can die."

Kita sighed.

"I just want to look."

"That's why it's clear, so you don't have to hang over the side to see," scolded Zidin.

Snowy took Kita's hand.

"You can't die on me."

Kita laughed.

"I, ah, wasn't planning on it."

"Poshé," said Bart. "We're all going to die. Even the mangy furball."

Kita spun, grabbed Bart by the neck, and dangled him over the rail.

"Call her anything but Snowy again, and we'll see if you can fly."

Bart grabbed Kita's wrist.

"Put me back, or I'll burn your hand off."

"Wouldn't you fall anyway?" asked Snowy.

Kita squeezed.

"Before or after, I pop your eyes out."

Bart heated his hand.

Kita snarled against the pain and squeezed harder, pressing down on the arteries in Bart's neck. His head lolled to one side as he lost the contest of will. Kita tossed him back on the walkway.

Bart awoke, rubbing his neck and head.

Snowy stood over him.

"I'm over seven thousand cycles old. You will be nothing but a blink in time and gone like dust."

"Then so shall she," Bart said flippantly, looking at Kita.

"She has healing nanites like the rest of us," commented Cowboy. "The only one who doesn't is you."

"That means you must protect me."

"I'm willing to lose the weakest of the herd."

"I am not the weakest. I'm—"

"There's no rock out here," said Cowboy menacingly.

"I, ah, I'm in the service of his Majesty the King of Yorq, King James. Injuring or killing me would be a capital offense."

"He asks me where you went...if he remembers who you are...I'll tell him you went to Champignon to get your hair done."

"Remember, Bart," Kita cooed, "you're here by my grace. I warned you once: be helpful or not at all. Those who are helpful get rewarded."

Bart's smile looked like he practiced every day.

"My Lady, how can I be helpful if I keep getting attacked by this oaf and giant?"

"They're looking out for your well-being. If you can care for yourself, I'll tell them to leave you alone."

"I'm perfectly capable of caring for myself."

"You heard him, boys. He can take care of himself."

Kita took Snowy's hand, and they crossed the walkway, taking a moment to admire the view.

Snowy sighed.

"I can't imagine what this will look like when finished. So many fish and coral."

"I thought it was a desert?"

"That's because there's no water. Giant gates hold the water back so the creative landscaping crews could work. They built the spires, visitor's center, walkways, and underwater passages."

The group exited the walkway and went to the doors of the Visitors Center.

The domed Visitors Center was glass, built out over the edge of a spire so tourists could walk over the reef, letting them see in all directions. Inside, you couldn't see anything. Some kind of fog or haze filled the building.

"What's in there?" said Bart.

Kita shrugged.

"We'll have to go and see."

Cowboy looked closer through the glass.

"They look like spiderwebs."

"That's not hard. You and Bart can clear the way."

"At best, I can do a flame lance, and we'll be here for weeks."

"Then we better get started."

"I'll go with the shaper," announced Zidin.

Bart smiled.

"Don't worry, big guy, I'll keep you safe."

"It's your safety I'm after."

"I think I've proven I can take care of myself."

Great White flicked to Bart's nose.

Bart grew flames in his hands.

Zidin sucked a stream of water from him.

"Do you think you can torch me before your dust?"

"I vote for dust," said Snowy.

Kita drew a sword and put it between the two.

"I'll side with Zidin. If you don't want to help, leave. If you want to help, do what Zidin says."

"Son, I understand you're used to being the most powerful group member," said Cowboy, "but your shaping is based on the nanites we have. Ours are more powerful and can do more. So, shut up and do as Kita tells you. I like her saying: Be useful or not at all."

He drew a revolver and pointed it at Bart.

Bart laughed.

"What is a crossbow piece going to do?"

Cowboy fired, hitting Bart in the ear.

"Stars!" screamed Bart as he grabbed the side of his head.

"Kita, remember that lesson on Force?"

"Force equals Mass times Acceleration."

"This is a prime example. This bullet is tiny and light, but it's moving faster than the speed of sound. It can do a lot of damage. I should have blown his head off."

Kita snickered.

"Oh, let's see, you big baby."

Bart removed his hand, covered in a trickle of blood.

"He barely touched you. Next time, I'll run you through, and then you can have something to cry about."

"Are you going to bandage it?" said Bart, aghast.

"Why? It's already stopped bleeding."

Kita went to the visitor center door, but it wouldn't open.

"Let me," said Cowboy.

He tapped on the number pad and used the biometric scanner.

It's odd such a building would have such security.

The door opened, revealing sheets of cobwebs with thousands of tiny spiders.

Kita sliced through a web to find more.

"Let's go. This is going to take a bit."

THREE

DISTRUBIA
RIHANNA
GOOD GIRL GONE BAD RELOADED

"WE'LL SPLIT UP," ORDERED Kita. "Cowboy and Snowy will go right. Zidin and Bart go left, and I'll go down the center."

"What if this sticky stuff gets in my hair?" whined Bart.

"One, I expect you to burn it, and two, you can't possibly love your hair as much as I love mine. So, if my hair has to do this, so does yours."

Kita cut sheets of webs down as Cowboy turned into his demon. He walked through the cobwebs, burning them and taking time to remove them from the furniture, tables, and computers.

Bart used lances of flame to slowly burn a path wide enough for him. Zidin was left using his sword to cut through.

"She's going to make you come back and clean this. You should be doing what Cowboy's doing."

"Let the cat do it."

"I don't think that'll happen."

"What does she see in that furball? I'm better looking, smarter, far wealthier, and know how to please a woman. All the cat has is fur."

She's not you.

Kita ignored Bart's whining and remarks about Snowy. There would be a time and place to settle the score. Right now, she wanted the whiny shaper for the information she could extract later.

As Kita cut a web, it fell on her. She groaned and then, with a tug, smiled when she easily pulled it off.

Huh. I don't stick.

You're a quick learner.

That made the job go much faster. Kita slashed and cut her way through, shrugging off the webs as she went.

A gunshot echoed through the room.

"Kita!" yelled Cowboy, "We've got bigger ones."

"Anything you can't handle?"

"No. They land on me and pop."

As Kita cut her way deeper, the webs thickened. She sliced through a dense wall into the queen's nest. Thousands of little spiders climbed the walls, while larger ones tended to the queen. The queen was the size of a horse, with a large abdomen and fangs.

The larger spiders frenzied and attacked. Some came at her, and some climbed across the ceiling. Kita stabbed and slashed those on the ground, but had to retreat from those coming from above. She backed into the hole she cut and used the bottleneck to kill the spiders singly or in pairs.

The tiny spiders fell on Kita like rain, and she cried out when the first bit her.

Don't worry! Don't worry! The nanites will clear any poison.

It still hurts to get bitten.

Kita flourished her swords and stepped back into the nest to face the queen.

The queen raised her abdomen and fired a webbing rope, hitting Kita in the chest and knocking her to the ground.

"Ah, ah. I'm not lunch."

The queen charged, and Kita rolled to the side, taking two of the spider's legs.

The spider tumbled and struggled back to its feet.

It opened its mouth and fired a stream of venom.

Kita flipped over the stream and landed on the spider's head. She slashed Dusk through several of the queen's eyes and removed part of a fang with Dawn.

The spider bucked, throwing Kita over it. The queen pounced and bit her in the lower back.

Ok, that's a bit much.

The spider reared and tossed Kita across the nest.

She landed in a soft pile of webbing, but her back was on fire. Kita jumped to her feet and charged, flipping into a layout over the spider. As she went over, she slashed a hole in the abdomen and dropped in a thermite patch.

The spider thrashed around the nest until boiled spider and thermite fell out of the bottom of the bulbous body part.

Kita, with a smirk, slammed Dawn through the queen's head.

Her triumph was short-lived as her stomach became violently ill, and she dropped her swords and fell to her hands and knees.

"Kita!" yelled Zidin from somewhere to her left. "Bart's been bitten. I don't think he's going to make it."

Kita grabbed Dawn and leveraged herself to her feet. Using the katana as a crutch, she slashed her way through the webs with Dusk. She found Zidin treating the shaper.

"What happened?"

"He was bitten by one of those large spiders."

Kita grabbed a spider's body and jammed its fang into her arm.

What are you doing?

The more venom in my veins, the faster the nanites find an antivenom.

That would be me, and I can't make a cure if you're dead.

Work fast.

You're crazy.

Kita collapsed, dots before her eyes as her veins burned.

Oh, come on! You have to give me more time than that!

"Kita, what in the Emperor did you do?" exclaimed Zidin. "Cowboy! Snowy! I need your help!"

Kita's head lolled side to side as she entered a fever dream, making Zidin into a mouse and Bart into a giant leech.

"Kitten!" exclaimed Snowy as she landed on her knees next to Kita. "What happened?"

"She sucked down a bunch of spider venom to save Bart, I guess."

"Humph. It's better than he deserves."

"True," said Cowboy, "but Kita wants him for something badly if she's willing to do this."

"How do we save her?" Snowy said apprehensively.

"There's nothing we can do. She'll have to save herself."

Snowy pulled back Kita's hood and used the assassin's scarf to wipe away the sweat.

Cowboy pushed an emergency injector against Kita's arm. "That's all we got."

"See if her secret weapon works," muttered Zidin.

Oh, please. I'm almost done.

So am I.

Hang on. There! I sent it to your barb gland. You can inject yourself...

I can't move.

That is a problem.

Kita extended her barb.

"Inject me."

"What is it?" gasped Snowy.

"A barb," said Cowboy. "It works like a needle. Put it in her arm. I bet it has what she needs."

Snowy angled the barb on the heel of Kita's hand and pressed it against the assassin's other arm.

Kita screamed. Her back arched, and she convulsed. When she fell back to the ground, she rolled over and slammed her barb into Bart's neck, then collapsed.

"Kitten?"

"I'll be alright," Kita groaned. "I just need to clear the venom from my system. Keep clearing the room."

"I'll stay with her," offered Snowy.

"There are four spiders the size of horses in here some-where, so everyone be careful," instructed Cowboy.

How does he know there are only four?

"Kitten, how are you feeling?"

"Better. My veins don't feel like they're on fire."

"You shouldn't do such things," scolded Snowy. "We could have found another solution or let the fool die."

Kita chuckled.

"I need him."

"What could you possibly see in such an ass?"

A spy.

"He'll be useful when the time comes."

We have a problem.

Oh?

Someone shut off the wireless connection.

What does that mean?

It means I can't control the facility. Someone is here and knows how it works. We need to go to the server room to turn the wireless on.

What is this place?

The Visitors Center for Razor's Reef. People came here to rent bungalows around the reef and do whatever humans do in such places.

There's no sea here.

There will be if I open the gates. All those spires will become islands connected by walkways. The reef's beauty is watching it grow and come to life.

How do we open the gates?

Why would you do that? Do you want a reef?

To keep this place from producing more ravagers.

We'll have to find who's ever in charge and turn on the connection so I can.

I'm sure it'll be interesting.

"Run! Run!" yelled Bart as he ran toward the door.

Kita rolled her head to see Bart covered in cobwebs. He reached the door but didn't know how to open it.

The spider appeared from the webbing. Its eight eyes gleamed like oil drops. The giant fangs moved back and forth as the spider seemed confused by Kita and Snowy.

BAM! BAM!

The head of the spider vaporized in an explosion of goo.

Cowboy came around, his shotgun smoking.

"Always amusing what a twelve-gauge shell will do to a head," he chuckled in the eerie baritone of his demon form.

"Oh, so gross!" exclaimed Bart as he picked at the goo on his robe.

"Son, until you've had your arm up to your shoulder in a cow's rear end, you don't know gross."

"What kind of sick weirdo are you?"

"Inseminating cows with good DNA. The only way to get it there is to put it there. Now, hush. We've still got two more."

Cowboy pushed two brass cylinders into his shotgun and snapped it shut.

"How're you feeling?"

Kita rested her head on Snowy's thigh.

"Better. I'll be ready to go in a few minutes. That stuff you gave me helped."

"That's the only one I had, so we'll have to look for more below. I know this place has a medical facility. You can relax. I'll hunt them down. I'm immune to their venom."

"Then why didn't we get the antidote from you?"

"There's a difference between antivenom and immunity. They bite me, and nothing happens. They bite you, and we need to give you the antivenom before it kills you."

Can you make me immune?

If I had the right nanite.

"I..."

Out of the webbing lunged a giant spider at Cowboy. It plunged its fangs into his flaming neck, then released a hiss.

He must be too hot to handle.

Kita grabbed Dusk and threw it at the spider's head, hitting it between its eight eyes.

The spider sank to the floor.

Cowboy smashed its head with his boot.

"Damn things, anyway. I'll go hunt the last one."

"Are you going to be ok?" asked Snowy.

"Hurts like the dickens, but the holes will close. Helluva throw."

Kita shrugged with a smile.

"I'm feeling better. I can help you hunt the last one."

"Oh, no," said Snowy. "You're to stay here until we're sure that stuff is out of your system. Gerald and Zidin can hunt the last one."

"But—"

"I'm trying to take care of you. Hunting giant spiders while having venom in your veins sounds like an unnecessary risk."

On the other side, Bart moaned.

"Take him."

Snowy pointed at Bart.

Cowboy laughed.

"He's better used to keep the floor from floating away. Kita, you rest, I'll go. You can come with me, Darla."

Snowy frowned.

"I'm afraid my claws would be useless against a giant spider."

She extended the short claws on the back of her hands.

"I'm made to hunt game, not monsters."

"As you please. I'll be back."

He left, burning a hole in the webbing.

Snowy cradled Kita's head in her lap and stroked her hair.

"I miss my hair," Kita sighed.

"What happened to it?"

"My mother cut it off. It used to go past my butt."

"I love playing with hair. When I was human, I would put my hair in a different style every day."

"I can't imagine you as a human."

"I was, still partially am."

"Well, you're the prettiest partial human I've ever met."

Snowy's whiskers twitched as her nose turned red.

"Thanks. You're pretty cute, too."

Snowy bent down and kissed Kita's forehead.

Kita turned red.

"It's been a long time since someone kissed me. Years."

"For me, it's been thousands of years."

"Too busy howling for attention from those flea-ridden beasts," scoffed Bart as he sat up.

"I'd rather wait a thousand years for the right person than be like you and kiss slime mold," retorted Snowy.

Bart laughed.

"I can have any pick of women. They're all the same. You'll see. You won't be able to take your eyes off me in a few days."

"I'd gouge them out first."

"Good luck," muttered Kita. "I'm only watching you so you don't do anything stupid."

BAM! BAM!

"Die, you eight-legged freak," Cowboy yelled, laughing.

"Sounds like he got the last one," said Snowy.

"Yeah, but how'd he know there were only four?" Kita asked.

Snowy shrugged.

"Bart, it's clear. Go finish cleaning the room," ordered Kita.

"I promise you'll be taking me to your room soon."

Gag!

"I'll be there first," said Snowy. "You can wait in the hallway and listen."

Kita giggled.

"Women are *not* supposed to yell," Bart said condescendingly.

"If she's not screaming, you're not doing it right," said Kita. "I would love to have Snowy make me scream."

Snowy smiled, showing her fangs.

"Those are cute," Kita purred.

"Woman with another woman is unnatural," scolded Bart.

"How about you leave us and do what I told you to do?"

Bart turned and said, "Just wait," then walked away.

By the time the men cleared the room, Kita was on her feet, taking in the lobby of the Visitors Center. Sitting areas were arranged so people could look out over the reef. A long counter with computers and other equipment stood before a giant window showing the Unfinished Wastes.

"Here, I got something to show you," said Cowboy as he finished cleaning off a table.

"Does this have a holotable?" exclaimed Snowy.

"Sure does. Let me get it turned on and warmed up. We'll see what it was last playing."

"How exciting! I haven't seen a holoprojection in forever."

"What's a holo—whatever?" asked Kita.

"A holoprojector, in this case the table, projects a three-dimensional image."

"She's talking nonsense," said Bart.

"You don't even know what Three-D is," growled Cowboy. "There we go."

A dot of light appeared above the table. It expanded into a circle and spun.

"It's loading," Cowboy explained.

The dot expanded outward to show a model of the reef and a woman.

"Welcome to the Razor Reef's Vacation Destination, where you can see this wonder of the world first hand!" she said pleasantly with a tone that made you relax.

The woman narrated a flyover of the reef, a journey through the underwater tunnels, the private beaches and bungalows, and the many activities patrons could enjoy.

"The Unfinished Wastes are supposed to look like that?" said Kita.

"That was the idea," said Zidin. "The original colonists had over a hundred natural wonders planned. Part of the fun was watching them being constructed by the nanites. The Grand

Gorge, Savannah Plain, and the Amazonia Forest are the ones I know that were completed."

"See our representatives now to book your excursions and dining," said the woman.

"Would have been a nice place," said Cowboy, "but expensive at three vacation days a night."

"So where are the ravagers coming from?" asked Kita.

"My guess is below us. The reef is supported by an extra-large environmental station that monitors the reef and creates the wildlife. Morons."

"What's wrong?"

"Nothing that can be done. The UEE didn't send enough genetic diversity with the colony ship's human, plant, or animal DNA population. We have a serious problem with inbreeding. I was working on fixing it in humans before the war started."

"Isn't that why you started the war?" said Snowy. "Because most people wouldn't go along with your plan?"

Cowboy's eyes narrowed.

"They were fools who didn't want to believe the data I showed them."

"Yes, killing the vatborn was an ingenious solution," commented Zidin.

"I had a plan to repopulate. I'd been all for it if someone else came up with a better way. And you went along with it," Cowboy said to Snowy.

"And what was the black eye?"

"Trying to get through that thick head of yours."

"I'm not going to do this here or ever. I left. I'm with Kita now."

"You've never had a girlfriend," muttered Cowboy.

"I, ah, have. I—" Kita smiled and blushed.

"You would sleep with that thing?" exclaimed Bart.

Cowboy drew a revolver and stuck the barrel under Bart's nose.

"Darla is a brilliant mind. We had our differences, and she had the right to leave, but I'll be damned if I let some dandy give her a hard time. What she's done is incredible."

Bart snarled and blasted Cowboy with a lance of flame in the face.

Cowboy turned into the demon cowboy.

"Fireproof, remember? And there's no rock in here. You say another word about the girls, and I'll fill you full of lead. Understand?"

"Couldn't keep her satisfied?"

SMACK!

Bart spun like a top from Cowboy's punch. The shaper landed in a heap on the floor.

"I may be an ass, but what happened between us is none of your business."

"This doesn't change anything, does it?" Snowy asked Kita.

"No. Unless it does for you."

"No. As long as he doesn't hit me or is an ass."

"You touch her, and I'll skin you alive," Kita said to Cowboy.

To make her point, Kita flourished Dusk.

Cowboy held up his hands.

"I don't need an assassin working her trade on me. I want all the happiness for Darla."

Kita looked at Snowy.

"You're Darla, if I picked up on that?"

"My human name was Darla Chang."

"I like Snowy. Sounds soft and fluffy."

Snowy laughed.

"I am those."

"Alright. How do we get downstairs? I need to get the wireless working, and we need to stop this station from making more ravagers."

"I know the way," said Cowboy, leading the group to a door. "This is an elevator. It moves up and down. We'll take it down to the gestation room."

Kita followed Snowy's lead and stepped into the tiny room. Zidin pushed Bart in.

Cowboy tapped a circle on the wall, and the elevator moved, causing Kita to twitch.

She took Snowy's hand to reassure herself.

The elevator dinged, and the door opened onto a catwalk landing.

The dimly lit room was huge, with catwalks crisscrossing above hundreds of gestation pods—some small, others huge—full of ravagers. Some pods were empty, and the ravagers wandered through the room.

Kita led everyone out onto the catwalk. It amazed her that the holes in the grating could hold them.

"Shit," muttered Cowboy seeing the ravagers. "The control booth is over there."

He pointed to a room suspended among the catwalks. An elevator moved between the control booth and the gestation pod level.

"Darla and I can shut the system off and flush the ravagers."

We need to get to the server room. I can shut it all down from there.

"I can shut it down from the server room," Kita announced.

"If you can get in, that would make it easy," said Cowboy. "We'll stay and work while you get connected."

"I'll take the shaper and clean up the ravagers," announced Zidin.

Kita turned toward the main elevator, and her reflection caught her eye.

Uh-oh.

The ear-splitting roar made Kita fall to her knees.

The creature tossed its massive head against the catwalk, causing it to swing. It bit down on the walkway and shook, sending everyone tumbling to the floor below.

Kita landed in a heap between two giant gestation pods. One had a large creature in it.

"T-rex," said Zidin. "We've got to get out of here."

"Where's Snowy?"

Kita found her pinned under the wreckage and the T-rex sniffing her. It pushed aside a bent railing holding Snowy and picked her up in its jaws.

"Snowy!" yelled Kita as she drew her swords and charged.

I've got to save her!

The dinosaur heard her cries and swung its tail, smashing Kita into a plastic gestation pod.

The explosions of Cowboy's shotgun echoed in the room as he stood up to the beast.

Zidin attacked the underside, slashing and stabbing with Great White, but the dinosaur was more intent on its next meal. He kicked Zidin across the room into the walkway debris.

The ring of pain burned in Kita's chest, and at the same time, her red aura closed around her eyes. Kita bounced to her feet. With a loud war whoop, she attacked the creature's leg.

The T-rex spun, trying to stomp on Kita, but her speed and agility kept her ahead of the large, bird-like feet.

Kita slashed across the underside, leaving a bloody gash that caused the T-rex to stumble. Jumping on its back, Kita plunged Dawn into the creature's spine. She climbed toward the head and drove the blade through the top of the T-rex's skull.

The creature collapsed, and Kita jumped down to force the jaws open.

As Kita held the mouth open, Zidin and Cowboy removed the body.

"Is she dead?" Kita whispered through tears.

"Not if we get her to the autodoc on level five," said Cowboy.

Kita picked up Snowy.

"Then that's where I'm going. You take care of the ravagers."

Kita was in the elevator in a flash, repeatedly stabbing the button to level five.

We have a problem.

What's that?

I can't be in the autodoc while we take control of the server room.

We can't leave her!

I suggest letting the autodoc's onboard computer work on her until we gain control of the server room. Once I'm in, I can control the autodoc."

The door opened to level five. The waiting room had a large desk, and doors led to the back. Omega guided Kita to the autodoc. With tears in her eyes, Kita placed the cat on the table.

Here are the instructions for the machine.

Kita followed Omega's tutorial, and blue hoops moved over Snowy.

Now, all we can do is wait.

It'll be faster when I'm controlling the autodoc.

To the server room, then.

T HE SERVER ROOM WAS located on level two. Kita passed through an antechamber into a large room full of boxes with blinking lights.

These are the servers that control the environmental station.

There are so many.

You need a lot of computing power when you're controlling trillions of nanites to keep the environment stable.

Kita walked down a row, noticing how warm the room was. Ahead, she could see a giant screen filled with numbers and words she didn't understand.

A voice from a large screen on the wall said, "Well, you can tell The Master—"

Kita went invisible and crept to the end of the row.

"—The destruction of Army One wasn't my fault. Those damn war cats turned on us after the factory was blown up. We don't need Army One anymore. Armies Two and Three are in the tubes. They'll just have to make up for Army One."

The lump in Kita's throat was too big to swallow.

What do I do? They're going to slaughter my legionnaires.

I might be able to connect to your Central Hub and warn them.

I have to get back and lead them.

That's days away. The ravagers could wipe them out by the time you got back.

Yes, but they can hold out in the outposts.

Ah, these things can burrow through rock. The walls of the outposts are concrete. That won't stop them from coming in where they least expect.

Then we need to warn them and give them a chance.

Kita slipped from the server row through rows of computer workstations toward the man.

He was dressed like Cowboy, without the duster or hat. Kita saw them lying on a workstation.

"The Legion of Yorq must be destroyed. If you think you can do it with two armies, go ahead. Just remember, it's your hide."

"Have that fool Cunningham hire mercenaries to make the difference."

"That's a good idea. I'll pass on the recommendation to the council. The Master is out, so you're lucky."

"He won't care once the Legion of Yorq is destroyed. Is Cunningham ready?"

"Bah. He can't convince half the nobles he's king. We're going to have a civil war. We might have to deploy a battalion or two early to put down resistance."

"I'm almost done here. I'm corking as many ravagers as possible and will send them over the pass. That should give the dissenters something else to think about."

"Sounds good. I'll let you know what the council decides. For now, keep doing what you're doing."

The screen went dark.

That snake. Arbol was just the first step. I'll gut Cunningham.

I sense some hostility.

We have a history.

Kita crept toward the cowboy. Kita placed Dusk against his spine and Dawn across his throat as he huffed angrily.

"We need to have a chat," she said menacingly.

"I'm not telling you shit."

"I already heard the strategic plan. I want you to stop it."

"Bah, I couldn't if I wanted to. The ravagers are in the tubes and running wild. Cunningham isn't mine. I just made the ravager armies. You're too late to save Yorq."

Bang!

Kita's eyes widened as a painful, burning sensation radiated from her side. She stumbled back a few steps and put her hand to the wound.

You've been shot. Nothing I can't fix...as long as you don't take too many.

The cowboy turned and fired three times from the hip, hitting Kita in the thigh and stomach.

She sank to her knees from the pain and weakness in her leg.

He pointed the revolver at Kita's head.

"Whoever you are, The Master's going to be pissed some vatborn has messed with his operation. I have no idea where you came from, but I'm sending you to hell."

His thumb cocked the hammer.

Kita lunged, tackling the cowboy around the legs and knocking him to the ground. She severed his revolver hand with Dusk and stabbed Dawn under his chin, through his skull. Kita rolled off the body and lay on the ground, bleeding.

I could teach you first aid if you had some supplies.

I don't have anything like Cowboy, just strips of cloth and some salves. I wish I had Zidin's healing balm.

Normally your body will push the bullets out on its own but since we're in a hurry you're going to have to dig it out.

Kita followed Omega's instructions. She grit her teeth and dug the bullet out, then dressed her wounds using wadded-up bandages placed over the injuries, held in place with bandage strips.

Omega ordered her to rest, allowing the nanites to clot the blood on the bandages.

How do I turn on the wireless? Kita asked when her patience ran out.

It's that button on the screen in the corner with the three arcs. Press it.

I could have done that anytime.

Yes, but then you wouldn't wait to heal.

Kita tapped the button.

The background of the button changed from red to green.

Omega's red face appeared on screens around the room.

"By the Emperor, what a mess. This will take time to clean up."

"We don't have time to clean. Kill the ravagers. We have to get back to the tubes and save my legion. Oh, and call LCOM."

"Unfortunately, he was able to cork a hundred. He's gathered them outside."

"Then I'll kill those."

"Better idea. I can open the gates and flood the reef."

"Do it. I'll still kill those outside. I have to get back to the Legion."

"What about fuzzy and the others?"

"Can you heal Snowy?"

"Yes, now that I'm in direct control. She's got a lot of puncture wounds."

"I don't have time to wait. They can catch up."

"They won't like that."

"I—"

The elevator dinged, and Cowboy, Zidin, and Bart exited.

"Think we got them all," said Zidin. "Mostly elves."

"That's nice," said Kita. "I have to go."

Cowboy grimaced when he saw the other cowboy in a pool of blood. He took off his hat and placed it over his heart.

"Go where?" he asked, putting his hat back on.

That was unusual. Maybe it's a cowboy thing.

"More ravager armies are attacking my legion and invading the tubes. I have to go rescue them."

"There's nothing you can do," Cowboy protested.

"I need to do something. Now, get out of the way."

Kita pushed past the men to the elevator.

"Wait for us," said Zidin.

Kita pressed the DOOR CLOSE button.

"Where do I go?"

"There's a large hatch where the T-rex was. That'll take us outside. The compartment is meant to be flooded. There's already water in the sand."

The elevator dinged, and Kita hurried around the destroyed catwalk, passed the T-rex gestation pod, to the large door that rose with a grinding noise.

Outside, a group of ravagers were wandering around.

The red aura closed around Kita's eyes.

"Hello, boys. Time to die."

BLOODY MOONS, WHO DESIGNED this?" snarled Kita as she looked into the access panel of a telescoping walkway.

"I did. Components fail. We need a two-thousand-ohm resistor. We'll have to salvage one from another walkway control box."

"I don't have time for that!"

"It's fifty yards away. Calm down and relax. Getting upset doesn't help."

"About time we caught up to you," said Zidin, leading the others, including Snowy.

"I'd be there if this thing worked!" Kita yelled.

"I doubt that."

"Let me have a look," said Snowy.

She knelt in front of the control box and studied the circuitry.

"Gerald, give me a revolver casing."

Cowboy pulled an empty bullet casing from his belt and handed it over.

Snowy took it and placed it in the box. There was a loud *pop*, and the walkway extended.

"Got it!" she said excitedly.

Kita took two steps toward the walkway, but Zidin grabbed her.

"Why are you in such a hurry?"

"I have to go. They're going to die if I don't. You're all just slowing me down. I don't need you. Go away."

"Does that include me?" whispered Snowy.

"Wait a second," said Zidin.

He grabbed Kita's chin and looked into her eyes.

"She's still berserking from last night."

"Ah, what about the fact she killed over a hundred ravagers?" said Bart. "Does that not bother anyone else?"

"Kita has some special talents," replied Cowboy. "But I haven't seen a field like that in a long time."

Kita turned away. "I don't care. I have to—"

Rock crept up Kita's feet to her knees.

"Please understand, this is only for professional reasons and changes nothing between us," said Bart.

Kita snarled at the shaper.

"Let me go, or I will—"

"You're not going anywhere until you calm down," said Cowboy.

"But, but, they're all going to die, and it's my fault."

Tears tumbled down Kita's cheeks.

"I can get there faster than you. What did the man tell you?"

Kita told about the ravager armies going into the tubes to destroy her legion.

"I'll take this to Commandant La Forge and see what he wants to do."

"How are you getting there faster than us?" scoffed Bart.

Cowboy let out a shrill whistle.

A black flaming horse raced up the spire's side and landed before Cowboy.

He reached into his pocket and pulled out a lump of sugar.

"Even nightmares like sweets," he chuckled.

"Where—how—it's impossible," exclaimed Bart.

Cowboy chuckled.

"I got tired of walking and made myself a horse years ago. Kita, I'll ride ahead and warn the Legion. I will contact La Forge to see what he wants to do. I know he won't be happy having one of his legions attacked."

He mounted his horse and galloped off, leaving a trail of flaming hoofprints.

Kita gave Bart a nasty look. "Rock. Now."

The rock receded from Kita's feet and legs.

"Don't hold it against me. I was just doing what was best for the group."

"Can and will. Never touch me again, or there won't be enough of you to bury."

"You'll want me to touch you soon enough. I'm not worried."

"And do this?" asked Snowy as she leaned in and kissed Kita's cheek.

Bart's mouth fell open.

"You would let this thing touch you?"

Kita burst out laughing.

"You want me so bad, yet you can't stand the person who has my attention. Not a great way to court a girl."

"Sweets and flowers are hard to come by out here."

"I prefer things that are fuzzy, cozy, and warm."

"Just you wait," boasted Bart.

Kita looked at Zidin, exasperated.

The man does not give up.

Zidin shrugged.

"Let's go," ordered Kita. "We have a long few days' march."

"March? You mean walk?"

"Yes. How do you normally accompany the king's forces?"

"I ride in a coach."

Kita and Zidin snickered.

"No coaches out here," teased Kita. 'Walk or learn to fly. Maybe you can swim like those seals. Let's move. The longer we wait, the more the ravagers destroy."

"D O WE HAVE TO go so fast?" whined Bart for the count less time. "I need to rest."

"We can stop when we reach The Forges," growled Zidin.

"Come on, even you need to rest."

"Kita will give us time to recover when we get there."

He gave Kita a sharp look.

"I don't think anyone can keep up with Kita."

They crossed another walkway, and Bart sat down.

"I'm going no further until I relax, have a meal, and get some sleep."

"Leave him," suggested Zidin. "I'm not carrying him."

"I wouldn't ask you to," replied Kita. "I'd only ask you to carry me."

Zidin snorted. "Like you're heavy."

Kita gave Zidin and Snowy a wicked smile as she knelt before Bart.

"I thought you were supposed to be my hero, to protect and care for me. You do have fabulous hair. I'm jealous. And you are making me curious...."

"I knew you'd come around. Get rid of the fleabag, and you'll experience things you've never heard of."

"Maybe a taste to tide me over."

Zidin looked green, and Snowy looked horrified as Kita took Bart's face in her hands.

She leaned in to kiss him, then slammed her barbs into his neck, giving him a hypnotic drug.

"Stand up," Kita ordered.

Bart did.

"You will do anything, Zidin, Snowy, or I tell you. You are to keep up with Zidin. You won't get tired, nor will you slow the group."

"What did you do?" asked Snowy.

"I gave him a hypnotic drug. He'll do anything we say."

"Bart, act like a chicken," said Snowy playfully

Bart folded his arms and bent over, pecking at the ground.

Kita laughed. "He'll remember, so be careful."

The Bart problem solved, Kita led the others at a faster pace, hoping to reach the remnants of the king's camp in two days.

FOUR

SHE DRIVES ME CRAZY
FINE YOUNG CANNIBALS
THE RAW AND THE COOKED

"**I** DON'T SEE IT," sighed Kita after searching what was left of the Army of Arbol's camp for Jeffrey's banner.

"Maybe he's still alive," suggested Snowy, upbeat.

"Be better if he were dead," muttered Zidin.

"What gets me is, there are fewer dead soldiers in this camp than in the others."

"He could have been out on patrol," Zidin suggested.

"The cats have reported soldiers in the mountains," said Snowy.

"Just what I need," muttered Kita. "The past never stays dead."

"What's wrong with him?" asked Snowy curiously.

"What until you meet him," huffed Zidin. "Not much else salvageable from this mess."

"Yeah," agreed Kita. "Let's get down the mountain and to The Forges. At least we'll have good news to report to them."

She gave Snowy a loving look.

"Could it be under the snow?" asked Bart.

Since being hypnotized, Bart had no problem keeping up with Zidin during the climb, and he'd become polite and helpful.

"I doubt it," grunted Kita. "He was the kind that put it on a tall pole so everyone could see. He'd never go anywhere without it. Vanity is the least of his depravities. I expected to find it next to the Arbol Estate banner."

"Maybe they took it as a trophy."

"Eh, let them have it. We've wasted enough time. Let's go."

"**W**HAT IS GOING ON?" Kita asked as she stood on an overlook.

Neat rows of tents surrounded the village of The Forges.

"It looks military," said Zidin. "I see guards and patrols."

"Bloody moons. These could be Cunningham's forces."

"What is important out here?" asked Snowy.

"I know The Forges supply the kingdom with weapons and armor. I don't know how, but they do."

"How are we going to find out whose side they're on?" asked Zidin.

Kita vanished.

"Kita?" exclaimed Snowy.

"I'm here. I'll be back. Sarge, stay with Snowy."

"I guess I can babysit," huffed Snowy.

Kita ran down the trail. It became wider and flatter as she neared the base of the mountains, where fallow fields and empty livestock pens encircled The Forges village.

These fields should be nearing harvest.

Following a dirt track from the trail through the fields, Kita came to the first house in the village. She pressed herself against the wall, listening for anything unusual. She didn't hear children's laughter or vendors hawking their wares in the village square.

Turning the corner, Kita cautiously walked down the street toward the village's center. The empty market, an inn, a schoolhouse, and a council lodge ringed the square. A formation of legionnaires was waiting while a group talked on the inn's porch.

How did the Legion get here?

Cowboy was on the porch and ushered his group inside.

What is going on without me?

Kita skirted the group—young officers by their rank—to the inn. She climbed the stairs and slipped through the door. The men gathered around a table. Kita jumped and caught a rafter. Swinging herself up, she moved so she could hear.

"What kind of mess do we have, Commandant?" chuckled a general.

"It's twofold, but they're related. The first is armies of ravagers have invaded the Legion of Yorq's tubes. We're going to have to clear them and reestablish the Legion. The second is that Yorq has fallen into civil war."

"That's not our job," said another general.

"Commandant La Forge and I agree the attack at Razor's Pass and the Yorqian tubes were related, if not coordinated."

"So, we have to put down the civil war?"

"No, we're going to put a successor for King James on the throne. I don't know who that is, but we need to free the dissenting nobles to get a proper candidate.

"I requested each of you because of your experience. General Forrester will be my chief of staff and be in charge of day-to-day operations. That said, Commander Kita will arrive in the next few days. Let me deal with her and get her settled—"

Kita scowled. She'd spent most of her life being placated and forced out of situations. She sure as bloody moons wouldn't get pushed out of her legion. Taking two flashbangs from her belt, she dropped them on the table.

The deafening boom and flash stunned most of the senior legionnaires. Others ducked under the table.

Cowboy looked like he'd found a broken fence, and the cows were out.

Kita appeared on the table as the smoke cleared.

"I want to talk to Commandant La Forge now," she demanded.

"You're still commander," replied Cowboy. "You don't have enough experience to lead—"

"Eh-hem. Underboss in the Shadow Guild."

"—Military operations. I'm hoping your guild experience will translate to the Legion."

"I will not be pushed aside. You try to be like the duke, and you'll meet his fate."

"We're not taking your legion. The army you destroyed was supposed to attack from the south. I was able to rescue those from Outpost Twenty-two and a few others. I want you attached to my hip or Forrester's so you can learn how the military works."

"Fine. But I'm still in charge. My region. My legion. If people don't like me being in charge, they can go home."

"Let's talk to the Commandant and see what he thinks."

"I'll send him a letter," Kita said firmly.

"Why? When I can call him in a few minutes."

"This is technology you haven't explained to me."

"I'll tell you on the way."

T HEY WENT TO THE back of the inn and upstairs to a room taken over by electronic equipment. Two men sat and listened to a piece of equipment talking.

"This is a radio," said Cowboy, motioning to the equipment. "It lets us talk long distances. Some satellites in space bounce the signal anywhere on The Mass. This allows us to talk to the hubs and LCOM."

Kita didn't know what a satellite or space was, but would ask later.

"Patch me into LCOM," Cowboy ordered the legionnaires working the radios.

He picked up a hand mic, and Cowboy spoke when the legionnaire waved his hand.

"This Commandant Hennessey, I need to speak to Commandant La Forge."

There was a pause.

"Gerald, are the legionnaires arriving?"

"Yes, sir. We were getting set up when Commander Kita caught up to us. She's not happy with the arrangement."

"Is she there?"

Cowboy motioned for Kita to speak.

"I'm here, sir."

"And what is the problem with the legionnaires I sent?"

I'm not in charge.

"I understand they have more experience than I, and I'm trying to learn from them, but it's still my region and legion."

"And what makes you qualified to run a legion? Cowboy was already mentoring you on the basics."

"Sir, I have destroyed an enemy army and flipped the allegiance of the war cats. I entered the Unfinished Wastes and destroyed the enemy's command center, main supply, and replenishment depot. I've killed their commander. I've solved The Forges' food shortage. I may not know legion doctrine, but I am qualified to lead."

"Impressive. Angus was right about you. Still, that doesn't mean you know how to lead an army. Commandant Hennessey will remain in charge. I expect you to learn all you can. Gerald, see that she does."

"Yes, sir."

Kita snarled and stormed from the room. They were treating her just like the duke. No matter what she did, it wasn't good enough.

To the bloody moons with them. I'm leaving.

Kita burst from the inn and headed into the mountains surrounding The Forges on three sides. She didn't miss the fuzzy tails following her.

KITA SLAMMED HER FIST against the rocky cliff face. With every blow, more rock flew, and so did the damage to her fists.

At least something could put up with the punishment.

A growl from Sarge alerted Kita as she tried to punch the mountain into dust.

"I hate them, I hate them, I hate them," Kita snarled, ignoring her cat's warning.

Sarge snarled as soldiers turned the corner with swords drawn, getting Kita's attention.

Sarge stood his ground as the soldiers brandished their swords.

"Who are you?" demanded Kita.

"Same for you. What's a woman doing in the mountains?"

Finding something to take my frustration out on.

"I'm the Commander of the Legion of Yorq. I'm looking for refugees from the king's camp."

"We were out on patrol when it happened. You should talk to Captain Logine."

Kita burst out laughing.

"He'll be lucky I don't hang him. Take me to him."

"CAPTAIN LOGINE, SIR, WE found a woman claiming to be the Commander of the Yorqian Legion."

Kita bared her teeth. With a flourish, she drew Dawn and cut off the man's head, surprising everyone, including Snowy, who'd joined the group after visiting the war cats to get Kita's location.

"I *am* the Commander of the Legion of Yorq. I'll kill anyone who argues."

"Including me?" Jeffrey laughed while sitting on a rock.

"Especially you. Gather your men. I have a camp in The Forges that you can join. If you start marching now, you'll be there by sunup."

"And what of the ravagers? The mountains are crawling with them."

"I got rid of them. The route to The Forges is safe. If you hurry, you can march with me, and I will get you settled."

"I'm not going to play pretend with you. If you can lead us out of the mountains, we'll go to Leadings and report to the garrison."

"I doubt Leedings is on the side of the Crown. I'm sure Cunningham has taken it."

"Why would Cunningham take it? He doesn't have the troops."

"Earl Maybrow has probably sided with him. Let me bring you up to speed. The King is dead, and we don't have a replacement. Cunningham is taking the throne by force unless we stop him."

"I know the king is dead. I saw the battlefield and the body. Well, even if this is one of your games, you can get us out of the mountains. We'll go."

Kita and the others followed Jeffrey to his camp. He had twenty-five uninjured soldiers.

As she waited, Kita put an arm around Snowy and her head on the big cat's shoulder.

"Who is he?" asked Snowy. "You seem to know and dislike one another."

"He's my brother and the bane of my existence. To him, I'm a girl playing pretend, waving around a stick. No matter what I did, I was never good enough for the duke or him. Our differences go beyond that. He's like his father, thinking the serfs are slaves. I did all I could for them, trying to improve their lives."

Jeffrey came up to them. He looked at Snowy.

"I do admit, my sister finds delectable creatures. Captain Jeffrey Logine, miss?"

"Snowy. I lead the war cats."

Jeffrey took Snowy's hand and kissed the back.

"Ok, enough," grumbled Kita. "She's my girlfriend."

"Oh, really?" chuckled Jeffrey. "The boys were right. You do only like girls."

"At least I don't have any kids."

Jeffrey laughed.

"You're such a donkey ass. The least you could do would be to support the mothers."

"That's why I have you."

Kita pressed her lips together and reached for Dusk.

"You're worse than the duke."

Kita vanished.

"Where'd she go?" demanded Jeffrey.

"I don't know," said Snowy.

"But I'd watch your back. She has quite a temper. Good looks won't save you."

"I've handled my sister before."

That's because you always had the duke standing behind you.

Kita whispered into Snowy's ear.

"Let's go. He'll just piss me off."

"Nice to meet you, Jeffrey. I should go calm Kita."

The big cat turned and walked away.

"She'll settle. Her bark has no bite."

"HE SEEMS NICE ENOUGH," said Snowy as they followed the trail.

"He's charming like a snake. He'll worm his way into your bed, leaving you with a little one. I helped the girls take care of the children he sired."

"That's not unusual, and he has good manners."

"Oh, yeah. See if I kill him once we get to camp."

"Why would you do that?"

"Principle? He'll betray me as soon as he can."

"We'll keep an eye on him and watch your back."

A roar came from down the mountainside.

Kita drew her swords as a giant white bear stood in their path.

It's not trying to eat me, so what does it want?

From down a cliff face came three war cats.

"Wait!" said Snowy.

She talked with her cats.

"They report finding another factory, this time using bears. They freed them, destroyed the factory, and came to help."

"Can you talk to them?"

"Some. They don't make that many sounds. The giant white bear is Frostbane."

"Hello, Frostbane," said Kita pleasantly. "Tell him we're going to the village, and he and some of his bears can come. I need all the help I can get."

THE MOON WAS UP, and only the night watch was out...until Frostbane roared, waking the village square and bringing people running.

Kita held up a hand.

"He's with me. They're all with me. Back off."

The few guards formed a circle around the new arrivals.

Kita let them, knowing they wouldn't be a threat.

"What in Sam Hill is going on?" yelled Forester—his Confederate draw punctuated his words—as he came out of the inn partially dressed.

Kita patted Frostbane's head.

"Our allies, the war cats, freed the bears, and now they want to help. I also found some lost soldiers commanded by Captain Logine. We need to find a place to put them."

"Where the hell have you been?" yelled Cowboy from the inn's porch.

"Proving I'm better than just following you around," she screamed. "I've brought two more groups of allies. What did you do tonight?"

Snowy smirked.

Cowboy's eyes narrowed as he weathered Kita's fury.

"Get the logistics set up and a training regime made. If you come in, I'll show you. General Forrester can find Captain Logine and his men a place to sleep."

Cowboy had a twinkle in his eye.

"What are we doing with the bears?" said Kita.

"How are you talking to the bears?"

"Snowy and her cats."

"We'll talk and see what they need later."

"Now," ordered Kita. "I want all our allies assimilated into our forces and then have a short leader's meeting so each group knows what's expected in the next few days."

"Come talk to me," said Cowboy, waving Kita to follow him.

They walked down a dirt street to a quiet spot.

"I know you feel you should be in charge and have the experience leading...just not military. There's more than just logistics. You can run small missions, but you've never commanded a battlefield. You've got to learn that to be an effective commander. I'm willing to make you a deal. You can lead the greater campaign. You let Forrester and me handle the military. I expect you to pay attention and learn. I'll pull you aside and tell you when you're making a mistake. Zidin, too. I know you have as much to learn about the Arconians. But you can't throw a tantrum whenever you don't get your way...even if you prove you're right."

"Then how do I prove I'm right?"

"I'll give you the benefit of the doubt, but if I feel you need help. I'll step in."

"I'll agree to that."

"Good. Let's go get your new arrivals settled in."

"**C**OMMANDER! CAT QUEEN! YOU'RE back!" yelled Eazor, running up with Norway in armor.

"How are you?" Kita asked.

"Good. My new Pa is teaching me to be a smith. He made Norway's armor."

"Can I look at it?" Snowy asked.

"Sure!"

Snowy knelt beside the war cat and chatted with Norway as she checked the fit and movement.

"He says it's comfortable, like he's not wearing anything."

"He can take it off by rolling," said Eazor proudly. "My Pa designed it."

"It's very nice," said Kita. I'd like to meet your father."

"He's the leader of The Forges."

"Let's go find him."

They found the big, muscular man at the base of the inn's steps talking to Cowboy and Forrester.

"Pa! Pa! The Commander and the Cat Queen are here!"

The men turned and did a double-take at Snowy.

"I'm Leader Murdoch. Eazor says you solved our war cat problem."

"Well, she did," said Kita, motioning to Snowy. "They captured her and ordered the war cats to bring in all the game and livestock they could."

"Yes, Leader Murdoch. My cats will supply you with game for a year so you can reestablish your herds and fields."

"That's excellent news. We've been rationing our stores."

"Norway's armor is fantastic. Did you make it?"

"The villagers in The Forges made it."

Kita cocked her head confused.

Murdock laughed.

"Most of the villages making up The Forges are underground through those heavy doors in the mountainside."

He pointed to two towering bronze doors.

Wow, those are big. What does it take to open them?

"Since we have nothing to make, we wanted to know if we could outfit the war cats."

Kita looked at Snowy.

"If it's as well made as Norway's. I will call to convince some brave volunteers."

Frostbane roared.

Snowy's whiskers twitched.

"He says bears get armor. He will have the first set, which will be better than any other set."

Kita chuckled as Murdock rolled his jaw.

"We can do it if we can get measurements and have a model to fit the pieces."

Snowy conversed with Frostbane.

"He says he'll give you a bear, but he is first."

"No problem. Beats making what the Crown's demanding."

"The Crown is gone," said Kita.

"That explains the odd signature we received a few days ago. It's not the king's or his advisors."

"Can I see the order?"

"Sure."

He pulled the scroll from a case on his hip.

Kita unrolled it, seeing it was an order for two hundred sets of helmets, chainmail, swords, and shields.

"You have to make this?" exclaimed Kita.

"We have it on hand. Even when we had no orders, we were always busy until I started getting these orders with unrecognized signatures. We're not making anything for them until they send someone to tell us differently. Instead, we'll gladly make the war cats and bears' armor."

Frostbane huffed.

"He and I say thank you," said Snowy.

Curious to see who was signing the orders, Kita snarled in rage.

"I will gut that spineless, impotent slime mold!"

She tore the order in half.

"What is it?" asked Cowboy.

"Cunningham thinks he's king."

"Ambitious son-of-a-bitch," muttered Cowboy. "Kita, get something to eat, and we'll have a leadership meeting to plan our way forward."

K ITA SAT IN A corner, trying to pay attention as Cowboy went over every detail, from food shipments to guard duties to where the animals would be. She knew she needed to know this, but she planned on having other people do it for her.

"Commander, do you have anything to add?" asked Cowboy.

"Ah, I need to talk to the spies in a secure room."

Cowboy chuckled.

"In the Legion, it's known as intelligence, and they're operatives."

"Still spies."

"I'm hoping the spy hunter isn't going to leave a room of bodies."

"No, but I have some missions for them."

"We can use the back room. Everyone else is dismissed. Let's get shit in order. I want to send patrols out in two days."

Kita fell in next to Cowboy as they switched rooms.

"What do you have?"

Kita hid her grin behind her mask. "The spy hunter has been busy."

"Shit, who? I just gave everyone our plan."

"Don't worry. I'll switch out his correspondence later tonight."

The back room was a store room, and everyone found seats on sacks, barrels, or leaning against stacks of crates.

"I know you're busy, but I wanted to get my spies moving. You're our eyes and ears, and we need to know what's happening now."

"General Yang and General Fedorov's people excel at intelligence," said Cowboy, pointing out the two men.

"Excellent. We'll need someone to keep an eye on our enemy spy."

"We have a counteragent?" exclaimed Yang.

"Yes. I've been watching him since I met him. He's a seducer type, and I've frustrated him to no end. He doesn't know how to handle two girls in a relationship. I've strung him along enough, but I want to know who his handler is and what he's passing. I'll switch out the correspondence tonight, but generals, your people will have to watch him when he's not with me."

"Who is it?" asked Zidin.

"Bart."

"Inglorious bastard," snarled Snowy.

"So, from now on, watch what you say around him. I'll let him sit in on the staff meetings, but he's not allowed in this room. Anything sensitive will be kept here under guard."

She looked at Yang and Fedorov.

"We will have a guard at the door—"

"No," said Kita. "That will raise his suspicion level. I want the door locked and a guard inside, ready to slay whoever comes through the door without the right knock."

Snowy raised her hand.

"Can the cats guard, too? They would like the honor and chance to prove their loyalty. They can patrol inside and out, looking for anyone doing something nefarious. A pair can also be in the room if we get an unwanted visitor."

"Sounds good. Now, the part you're not going to like," chuckled Kita.

The men looked at each other.

"I'm the underboss of the Shadow Guild of Leedings, and I want us to work with them and the other shadow guilds."

"This is something you should have run by me first," replied Cowboy gruffly.

"And you would have said no."

"And you're going to do it anyway. We need to meet with your boss on what we and they can and can't do."

"I plan on using them for spying—intelligence—and running a few rings for me."

"They're going to want something in return," said Zidin.

"I know. When we take Leedings, I plan on letting them govern."

"We should talk about this first," said Cowboy.

"I know they'll take care of the people. They know how to govern, maybe not like you're used to, but my dad oversees the commoners in the city, and I want them taken care of. The nobles can rot. I'm not about to put someone who sides with the nobles in charge, and I don't trust. I trust the Shadow Guild."

"We'll need to take a trip to Leedings and talk it through with your dad. I don't want any Legion secrets given away."

"I think they'll be teaching us. They know how to operate in the city without being detected. They have safe houses, and people are always watching. We need to tap into that, especially when we go to take the city."

"Having a group on the inside would be useful, Commander," said Fedorov.

"Yes, the intelligence they can give us will be invaluable."

"They can do more than that. Sabotage, acquire our enemy's equipment, misdirect, and just be in the way. They can track commanders and take out patrols. I plan to use them to full effect."

"I'm not against the idea," said Cowboy, "but we need to chat to see what both sides want. I think giving them the city is a bit of a stretch. It'll need a proper government."

"I'll show you what the guild does when we get there. In the meantime, I can give those who don't know a primer on what to expect regarding how we operate."

I T WAS DARK WHEN the meeting adjourned. Kita held Snowy's hand as they left the storeroom, now the intelligence center. The main room was full of legionnaires and townspeople as they entered.

"Surprise!" everyone yelled. "Merry Birthday, Commander!"

Kita's jaw dropped. She'd known her birthday was upcoming. She hoped to ignore it. Now, there was no escape. Scanning the room, she saw her brother grinning like the cat that ate the canary.

I'll get him back for this later.

"Thank you, everyone. I've been so busy I forgot. You didn't have to throw a party."

"Any excuse for a happy celebration," said Cowboy. "Come. Everyone will want to meet you and Darla."

Kita waded through the crowd of well-wishers and became separated from Snowy. After escaping the crowd, Kita found her dejected girlfriend sitting at the end of the bar.

"What's wrong?" asked Kita.

"No one will talk to me, and they all look at me funny."

Kita took Snowy's hand.

"Come on. No one will look at you funny when you're with me. I know what you need to cheer you up. Hey, barkeep, do you have anything sweet?"

The big man chuckled and reached under the bar.

"I've got something women love."

He displayed a bottle of pink liquid. Filling two shot glasses, he pushed them at the girls.

Kita grabbed hers and shot it back.

Snowy was more hesitant.

"Oh, that is yummy," said Kita. She frowned at Snowy, still holding the glass. "What's wrong?"

"I've never taken a shot before."

"It's easy. Just open your mouth wide and toss it in the back of your throat."

Snowy did and had a coughing fit.

"Wrong pipe," laughed Kita. She hugged Snowy and comforted her. "We'll try again."

"Why?" exclaimed Snowy.

You can't get drunk. Your body metabolizes the alcohol too fast.

Can I get her drunk? How about if I had a bunch at once?

I don't know her nanites, but it might last a few minutes.

"Line us her up a three-shot boat and me a five, barkeep."

The bartender lined up the glasses and filled them with the pink liquid.

"Whatever this stuff is, I have to get it for Dad."

"It's watermelon," said Snowy.

"There's an old guy who runs a still in the woods. He flavors his lightning with whatever he can get. Watermelons are in season now."

"Come on," Kita urged Snowy.

Kita took the shots one after the other, making her head swim.

"Weeee...." She giggled.

Snowy had a tougher time getting the 200-proof alcohol down, but she did.

"Wow, that stuff is potent."

Snowy giggled.

Across the room was a collection of legionnaires and townspeople playing a game.

"Let's go see."

Kita took Snowy by the hand and pulled her over. Turns out it was a drinking game.

Oh, I can make some money here.

"How much to play?" said Kita.

"Commander?" said a sergeant.

"What? You don't think you can outdrink a little girl?"

"Put a coin in the pot. You're four rounds behind."

The sergeant lined the shots up for Kita, and she knocked them back without a thought.

"Next!"

"You're going to be carrying her to her room," a legionnaire said to a swaying Snowy.

"I don't think I can get myself to our room."

"Hey, Snowy, keep drinking the pink stuff. It'll make the night much more fun, and then you can watch me put these guys on the floor."

"Tiny thing like you will pass out in the next round," laughed another sergeant.

"Yeah? Let's find out."

Kita tossed a gold coin from her purse on the pile.

"Winner takes all!"

"B

AM! I WIN," SAID Kita as she slammed the glass on the table. The legionnaire across from her slid off his chair. "Pay up."

Kita collected her winnings with a smile. This was the third drinking game she'd won. She retrieved her gold coin and tossed some silver ones into the pot. She divided the winnings among the other players.

"I don't take money from my legionnaires," announced Kita. "But I will give you a headache in the morning."

Everyone laughed and cheered except for the five sergeants under the table.

Kita found Snowy at the edge of the group, looking bored. She had the bottle of watermelon lightning and was nursing it.

"Are you finished?" the cat asked drunkenly.

"Yeah, I drank them under the table."

"Good. Come on. I got us a room."

"You mean a real bed? How'd you get a bed?"

"Gerald arranged it for you."

"That's sweet of him."

"You know neither of us sleeps much."

"Yeah..."

"So, I was thinking we could use it for other things."

"Are you sure? You really want to?" Kita said as her heart raced.

Snowy nodded with a hungry grin.

Kita leaned in, nuzzled Snowy's ruff, then whispered, "Good. I've wanted to make you scream since I met you."

Snowy's nose turned red. "I've never screamed during sex before."

Kita laughed. "He wasn't doing it right. Come on."

Hand in hand, they went upstairs to the room at the end of the hall.

As Snowy reached for the handle, Kita grabbed her by the waist and spun her.

"I—"

Kita shoved her against the door and kissed her.

"Oh!" exclaimed Snowy when they split. "You don't want to wait until—"

"Nope," said Kita as she went for more.

Snowy found the handle and opened the door. The girls tumbled in, with Kita landing on Snowy.

Kita ran her fingers through Snowy's ruff, feeling the fine, silky fur. She captured Snowy's face in her hands and kissed her.

Kita found Snowy's hesitant tongue. Using hers, Kita coaxed Snowy's tongue into her mouth and stroked it. Gently, Kita sucked out to the tip, making Snowy sigh. Releasing the cat's tongue, Kita ran her tongue under Snowy's upper lip, making the big cat moan.

"Oh, oh..." whined Snowy as the fur on her back rippled.

Kita let go with a smile.

"Good?"

"How...I've never...Oh..."

Snowy quivered as she arched her back and stretched.

"How do you know how to do that?"

Kita laughed.

"I've had sex before and know some tricks. A Champignon assassin taught me."

Snowy's ears went flat.

"I've never had sex with a girl before."

And it shows...

"We all have to have our first time. Don't worry. I can make you scream."

"With the door open?"

Kita giggled, got off Snowy, and closed the door.

Snowy came behind Kita and wrapped her arms around her. She pulled Kita's hood back and tugged at Kita's scarf. "How do I get this off you?" She extended a claw.

"Woah!" said Kita. "Let's not damage my sneak suit. I don't think I can get it repaired."

"It's self-repairing...at least the fabric."

Kita undid her scarf, removed her mask from around her neck, and unfastened her hood. With practiced hands, she undid the belt buckles, slid her top over her head, and dropped it.

Snowy pressed against Kita, making her shiver from the fur.

"You feel awesome. You know what would feel good?"

"What?"

"Feeling your fur against my boobs."

Kita turned in Snowy's arms and rubbed her breasts against the short, fine fur that covered Snowy's chest.

"Oh, meow..."

Snowy laughed.

"You still have clothes on."

"You don't," teased Kita as she put a hand between Snowy's legs, feeling the soft fur covering Snowy's labia.

Gently, Kita stroked Snowy's pussy, making her fur stand up.

"Oh god," exclaimed Snowy.

"I'm not doing anything," giggled Kita. "If you want me to do something, I can."

Kita ran her finger between Snowy's labia, working them apart. When she felt how wet Snowy was, she stroked her clit.

"Oh, oh, oh god..."

Snowy sucked in a sharp breath and put her arms around Kita's neck, resting her head on Kita's shoulder.

"Feels good, doesn't it?"

"What are you doing? I've never felt that before."

Kita cocked her head.

"You've never had someone play with your clit before? Not even yourself?"

"Uh-huh...Oh...Oh...shit...my legs..."

"You've had someone eat you out, right?"

Snowy slowly rolled her head back and forth.

"Oh, well, you're in for a treat."

"There's more?" gasped Snowy.

Kita laughed.

"I don't have a penis, but I know lots of other ways. Come on."

Careful to keep Snowy from falling over, Kita guided her to the bed, and Snowy collapsed across it.

"Oh, my head is spinning."

Kita grabbed Snowy's legs and pulled her to the edge of the bed.

"Eep!" exclaimed Snowy as Kita pushed her legs apart.

"Your job," said Kita as she kissed Snowy's inner thighs, "is to keep your sexy thighs pressed against the sides of my head."

"Huh, why?"

"Because it feels amazing, and it's going to feel even better with your fur."

"I—"

Kita ran her tongue up the center of Snowy's pussy, pushing the labia apart. With the tip of her tongue, she teased Snowy's clit.

"Oh shit...oh shit... oh so many colors..." cried Snowy.

Using her fingers, Kita spread Snowy's labia, and her clit swelled under Kita's tongue, making Snowy moan and gasp. Enjoying Snowy's sounds, Kita took Snowy's clit in her lips and sucked.

"Ah, ah, ah, ah...oh, oh, oh shit...my god, what are you doing?" yelled Snowy.

Kita smiled around Snowy's clit and, while sucking, traced it with her tongue. Snowy made a new set of awesome sounds.

"Holy fuck!" screamed Snowy as her back arched off the bed. "Oh, oh, oh fuck me, oh, oh..."

Let's see if we can crank this up a few octaves.

Using her finger, Kita traced Snowy's hole.

The big cat's back bounced off the bed as she whimpered.

Kita let go of Snowy's clit. "You want me to go in?"

"Oh please, oh please, oh please. It's so good."

Kita resumed sucking on Snowy's clit. As she moaned, Kita pushed the tip of her finger into Snowy. Gently, Kita moved it around, pressing against the warm, soft walls as Snowy's hips moved up and down.

"Oh, come on," pleaded Snowy. "I want to feel you in me."

"Are you sure?"

"Oh, yes. Come on, what do I have to do?"

Kita giggled.

"Just keep making awesome sounds...like this."

With a quick, hard thrust, Kita pushed her finger into Snowy as deep as she could.

Snowy's back arched so only her head and tail were on the bed. The big cat screamed.

Kita thrust her finger in and out.

"Gah, ah, ah...oh, oh, oh shit," screamed Snowy. "Oh, fuck me. Fuck me. Yes, yes, yes..." Snowy screamed as all the fur on her tail stood up. Her back hit the bed, and she shuddered.

Kita took that as a good sign and stopped. "Feel good?"

"I...ah...wha...I...can't feel my legs or tail."

"Are you sure you don't want more?"

Kita stroked Snowy's clit with her finger making her convulse.

"No, no, no, no," gasped Snowy. "I can't take any more."

"I didn't do anything," Kita said innocently.

Snowy lifted her head, but was having trouble holding it up.

"That...that's not true...Oh, my head is filled with fireworks."

Her head flopped back on the bed.

Kita laughed.

"So, when's my turn?"

"I don't even know what you did."

Kita smirked.

"I can teach you. I can't wait to feel your tail on my pussy."

"Give me a minute."

"No rush," said Kita, taking off her boots and bottoms.

Happily naked, Kita crawled onto the bed and cuddled Snowy.

"COMMANDER, I HAVE A message for you," said the guard at the top of the stairs.

Kita motioned for Snowy to go ahead.

"How did I sleep through that kind of party?" Bart shook his head. "You think this little backwater mud hole has a place to get her something special? Maybe we could all go in together?"

"By the Crushing Depths, you're cheap," rebuked Zidin.

Snowy sat at the table.

"No thanks," replied Snowy. "I already gave Kita her birthday gift."

"What's that, a hairball?"

"Sex."

Bart howled with laughter. "You paid someone? Stupid cat. Guys would line up to do it for free."

Snowy smiled and winked.

Bart scoffed.

"Like she would ever sleep with an abomination, if you're in heat, I'm sure one of your cats will knock you up."

"Knock it off," said Zidin.

"What are you going to do about it, big guy?"

Bart grew a fireball in his hand.

Zidin drew Great White.

The liquid around the table floated out of their dishes and circled Bart.

He sneered and extinguished the fireball.

Zidin returned the liquid to its glassware.

"Only because I don't want my robes stained," said Bart. He returned to Snowy. "I don't care what you say, furball. A night with me, and she'll never look at girls again. She won't be able to take her eyes off my crotch."

"My sister is a shrew," said Jeffrey from a neighboring table. "The last man who thought he could tame her bled all over my mother's floor."

Bart shrugged.

"He wasn't the right type. It still doesn't explain what she wants with the walking fur coat."

"Me either, but my sister's always been into weird things."

Snowy pushed away from the table.

"Did we offend the poor kitty-cat?" cooed Bart.

"No. I don't want to get any blood on me. The girl whose afterglow you've ruined doesn't look happy."

Not much of an afterglow. Oh well, we'll just have to practice until she gets it right.

Dusk landed in front of Jeffrey.

"What the stars, Kita!" he yelped.

Bart went white.

Kita flipped onto the table and walked to him. She kicked his dishes aside, sat on the table, wrapped her legs around his chair, and pulled him to her.

Leaning in, she whispered in a sultry voice, "Do you think you have what it takes to keep me going all night?"

Bart nodded.

"Do you have the touch, the caress, and the patience to make me melt?"

Bart looked at Kita hungrily.

"You have no idea what I can do."

"Can your tongue move and touch me in ways I can't imagine?"

"My tongue is a miracle worker."

"Can you make my body quiver and shake from orgasm to orgasm?"

Bart grinned.

"Of course I can."

"Can you make me scream your name so long and loud that I'll go hoarse?"

"You better believe it, baby."

"Are you manly enough to fulfill my every need?"

"Your wish is my desire."

"Can you leave me begging and crying for more?"

"You'll love it and want it."

"Will you make me dream about you?"

Bart drooled.

"Are you so sure you're so good that I'll never want to leave you, making it so I can't live without you?"

Bart's face flushed a lustful red.

"You'll chain yourself to me."

"Do you have parts of your body that can touch me in ways nothing else can when your hands, feet, mouth, and piece are busy?"

Bart looked at her, confused. He jumped when she tapped his crotch.

"That's too bad because you're too late. I'll never need you, want you, or think about you. You'll just be some poor, pathetic man with a fake façade. Now go clean up that wet spot."

Kita put her boot on his chest and pushed him over.

Kita sauntered to a red-nosed Snowy. She sat on the table's edge and pulled Snowy's chair to her. Grabbing Snowy's hands, Kita pulled her up, wrapped her arms and legs around Snowy's slender body, and kissed her.

Kita looked into Snowy's eyes and hummed happily.

"I like that. I feel better now."

Snowy laughed.

"I like it too, kitten, but I feel like everyone's staring at us."

"So, let them stare."

Kita kissed Snowy again.

They stayed together until Cowboy coughed.

Kita looked and laughed. Her entire staff stood watching.

Forrester said to Cowboy, "Look at it this way. If the commander's happy, everyone's happy."

FIVE

BRAVE
SARA BAREILLES
THE BLESSED UNREST

A FTER THE NIGHTLY BRIEFING, Kita pulled Jeffrey aside.

"Got some time?" Kita asked after she stepped through the tent flap.

"Of course, Commander," Jeffrey answered with a raised eyebrow and resigned tone.

"Come walk with me then."

Kita took them past the camp's perimeter. A guard detail of war cats followed. Zidin and Sarge brought up the rear.

She chased them away when she reached the top of a hill overlooking her camp.

Kita glared at Jeffrey.

"If you try and screw me, I'll skin you alive."

Jeffrey flinched.

"Call me a monster if you want. the duke already did. But I'm not a monster. I'm a fallen angel. I bring the retribution of the innocent upon the wicked and corrupt. These are my people, and I will defend them from you and those like you. If I have my way, the noble class will disappear."

"You can't rule without the nobles."

"Why not? Other regions do. I just need to find qualified people who can administrate and lead. And I know who to put in charge—the Shadow Guild. No one knows the cities better than them."

"You're out of your mind! They're thieves, criminals, and hooligans. They'll wreck the city."

"Maybe you and I should take a walk through the slums of Leedings and see how badly the noble class has wrecked the city for the majority of the citizens."

"I don't need to see filth and garbage. I don't wallow in swill like you."

'Which is the noble's fault. If they didn't horde the wealth and only care about themselves, Leedings would be a glorious city, and I plan to make it that way."

"You can't rule without the nobles."

Kits scoffed.

"Who said I want to rule? That's a prison without walls. I want the power to do what I want when I want. There are plenty of people qualified to be mayors and run the region. I'll turn it over to the Legion if I have to."

"You're insane."

"Not insane, maybe a little strange. And it's not like we have a king anyway until we free the nobles. I have people looking."

"Then I should be king as the only noble male."

Kita laughed.

"Yes, you can be the last noble king on a sinking ship. I hope you go down with it."

"Wait until people find out who you really arc. If you're lucky, they'll throw you out. When I'm king, I'll lock you in the dungeon."

"Hmmm, most of the people who need to know do. You're not springing any surprises on anyone. They know I'm an assassin, a serial killer, an underboss, and the Angel of Yorq. What surprise are you planning on springing?"

"You're a menace."

"To people like you."

"I'll challenge you for the right to lead."

Kita grabbed him by his breastplate collar and yanked him down to her.

"Don't forget. I'm the one with the army and backing of the largest military organization on The Mass. You barely have a company of soldiers. Do you really want that fight? And if you try to stab me in the back, I'll be waiting..."

Kita vanished. She walked back toward Zidin and Sarge.

"Brainwashed fool," she muttered as she reappeared.

"He's entitled and thinks it brings him power," replied Zidin.

"Power at the tip of a sword is nothing compared to the power I've gained from what you've taught me."

"Applied knowledge is power."

"And I'm just beginning to apply it."

YELLING AND BOOT-STOMPING CAME from the main room of the inn.

Kita stuck her head out of the intelligence room and was surprised to see General Barnoky in armor, covered in dirt and blood.

"There you are!" Barneky bellowed.

"General, glad to see you're safe," Kita said with an even tone as she approached him.

"No thanks to you. You abandoned us. You should be court-martialed and hanged."

Kita glared at him.

"I see they didn't stop you."

"Of course not. I'm a combat soldier and know how to lead my men. I saved the Hub's men and two other outposts without losing a man."

"I'll put you in for a medal."

"Stuff your trinkets. I want more men so I can rescue the rest. You've played commander long enough. Let a real commander do his job."

Kita fought to control her temper.

"General, Commandant Hennessey left to warn you the moment we knew. I've been trying for a week to reach anyone, but I've received no answer. What little field intel I have says the west and the north are destroyed. Those here in the east and south got out."

"You left us to fend for ourselves. That is cowardice of the worst kind. Now give me back my Legion before you destroy what's left."

"*AT EASE*, General!" Kita yelled. "I let you disrespect me once. Keep going, and you'll be a permanent example."

"Little girl, get out of my way."

Barneky pushed Kita aside and addressed the room.

"Listen up, everyone. My name is General—"

Kita grabbed him by his chest protector and threw him over a table. He landed in a heap. She jumped over the table and landed next to him. Pulling him upright, she punched him in the chest.

Barneky flew through the inn's door, past Zidin and Cowboy, hurrying up the stairs. Barneky lay crumpled in the dirt.

Kita slammed through the door and jumped next to Barneky.

"Get up, you son-of-a-bitch!" Kita commanded. "If you want my Legion, you'll have to fight me for it. If you think you're all blood and guts, get your ass up and face me like a man."

Barneky climbed to his feet.

"I won't hit a girl."

Kita stood with her fists clenched.

"You better learn. I'm not the only girl here with the Legion's mark. They come from our sister Legions. You better get used to the idea, *cochon chauvin*. So come on. You beat me, and you can have my Legion."

"Say goodbye to that pretty face."

Kita let him hit her once, setting the tone for the duel.

Barneky wasn't out for a fight. He wanted to break her.

She let him hit him twice more, her face absorbing the wallop the man could throw.

And he's not even augmented. Damn, that last one was one too many. Now my eye's going to swell.

"Had enough, sweetheart? Give in now, and I won't break anything."

"Oh, we're just getting started."

Kita struck with a furious combination of body blows and headshots faster than Barneky could react.

The older legionnaire tried to retreat to get his arms up, but after several punches, he gave up.

Delivering her final uppercut, Barneky flew through the air and landed in a watering trough. With a dark scowl, Kita grabbed his hair and yanked him up.

"You think you have what it takes to kick this little girl's ass, old man? *DO YOU?*"

Barneky didn't say anything.

"This is my Legion. It was never yours. Understand?"

Barneky sneered.

Kita shoved him underwater and held him there until he flailed his arms.

She yanked him out.

"Do you understand?" Kita yelled.

Barneky sputtered a few curse words.

Kita dunked him again.

They repeated the process four more times until Barneky relented.

"I understand," he sputtered.

"About damn time," said Kita. "Go report to Commandant Hennessey and beg his ass for a job. Pray he has something. Now get your sorry old man ass out of my sight."

Kita found the street packed with onlookers.

Zidin, Cowboy, and Forrester looked worried.

"Anyone else?" Kita yelled. "Forrester? Cowboy? Anyone else want to take a shot? Now's your chance."

I think their hearts have stopped.

"Fine, then get back to work."

Now, where the blazes was I before that fool interrupted me?

K ITA SAT ON A chair backward, listening to her generals' report.

"We've put together an estimation of our enemy's troop strength. Most of the soldiers around Yorq died at Razor's Pass, so there aren't many, and Cunningham has brought in Arconian mercenaries to swell his ranks."

"Arconians?" Kita cooed, looking at Zidin.

"We're outnumbered almost four to one. We could get more troops if we freed the earls and dukes Cunningham holds hostage, but we'd still be at a disadvantage. The ravager armies have infested the Yorqian tubes. We have no idea how many there are."

"Chang, your men picked up Bart's trail?"

"Yes, Commander. He passed several scrolls to a rider. We trailed them to a house in the nobles' quarter of Leedings. We have it under surveillance."

"Good. I was able to change out his correspondence. Nothing critical yet—biographies on the leadership, troop strength—because we don't have a plan, he doesn't have much information to pass on."

"And how were you able to do that?" asked Cowboy.

Kita grinned.

"An assassin never reveals her tricks. And no, I didn't sleep with him."

"Can't he recognize his own handwriting?" asked Snowy.

"Bah, he writes like he's a noble. It was easy to forge."

"His mistake," said Fedorov. "Now we know his safe house and handlers without revealing anything."

"Intelligence we've received says Cunningham is going to move against us," said Yang.

Kita nodded.

"Swat the bee before the fly. Still, we'd swell opposition to Cunningham if we can rescue the earls and dukes."

"How are we going after them?" said Forrester. "We barely have enough legionnaires to defend this place."

"I might just have to go and get insulted," Kita laughed.

Zidin raised an eyebrow.

"You can cancel the contract on your word."

"I know, but if I get insulted, it looks like I had a legitimate reason for canceling the contract. It's not like it'll be hard. Cunningham can't see me without a discouraging word."

"We'd outnumber Cunningham's forces if we could get them."

"I guess I'm making a trip to New London."

"I don't understand," said Forrester.

"I'm the Rose of Arcone," said Kita, like Forrester knew what that meant.

"She is the incarnation of the warrior spirit of Arcone," said Zidin. "Insulting her is insulting the Arconian Nation. Not that she has to. She can cancel the contract on her word. She can also rally the guilds and clans to her to defend Arcone's honor."

"But if I get insulted, it doesn't look like I'm trying to do it for the Legion."

"I don't know about that, but moving the mercenaries to our side would make it a fair fight."

"How does LCOM allow that? No one is allowed to have a private army," said Forrester pointedly.

"I've talked to the commandants, and we've come to an agreement."

"What will we do with Cunningham once we have him?" asked Snowy.

Cowboy fidgeted with his hat.

"We'll have to rescue the nobles and have them declare who should go on the throne. That should be our first step."

But I want to get the Arconians. Sigh. I guess Cowboy knows best.

"Alright," said Kita. "Someone get Barneky."

"Are you sure?" said Snowy.

"He's a soldier and won't pass this up."

Barneky was found and brought in. Cowboy pointed to a stack of crates for the legionnaire to sit on.

"What's this, my court-martial?" he said, looking around the room. "It's supposed to be by my peers, not your flunkies."

"Still have that fighting spirit, General?" said Kita. "Good. You're going to need it."

"You brought me in here so you can whip my ass again for your lackeys' entertainment? Go ahead. I'm not afraid of you."

He puffed out his chest.

"Don't flatter yourself. You're here because you will lead the combat part of our next mission."

Barneky gave Kita a dubious look.

"Why me?"

Kita leaned back and grinned.

"You rescued over three hundred men and led them to safety. I think that qualifies you to be a combat leader. The mission is dangerous and deep in enemy territory. It comes with the added complication of keeping VIPs alive."

Barneky rolled his jaw with a contemplative look.

"Alright, little girl, I'll lead the mission for you."

Kita raised an eyebrow.

"That's kind of you, General, but let's get two things straight. First, let's work on your vocabulary. Let's swap *Little Girl* for *Commander*. How's that sound?"

"Yes, Commander," Barneky ground out between his teeth.

Kita kept her face neutral.

"Keep working on it. Everyone else has gotten used to it. Secondly, I'll be in charge of the mission. You're in charge of the combat team."

Barneky's eyes narrowed.

"And what will you do besides being in my back pocket, Commander?"

"My team and I will do the more delicate tasks, like getting you in and freeing the VIPs."

"What makes your people more qualified than the men I choose?"

"Now you see me. Now you don't."

Kita turned invisible.

Barneky slightly moved the corner of his mouth. "That's impossible. What the blazing suns are you? A devil?"

Kita laughed and returned to normal.

"Just think of me as someone who's just more technologically advanced. Fair warning, General: I take information security seriously. Call it my professional paranoia. If I find a leak, I will find out who."

Kita flourished Dusk.

"I get it. Is there anything else I need to know about?"

"Right now, we need to work on a plan."

"THIS IS SO GROSS," whined Bart. "Who lives in such squalor?"

"I do," rebuffed Kita.

Snowy made a disgusted face.

"It's not bad. Just watch where you step. Remember, here, no one asks questions, and no one remembers anything—unless you're a certain well-dressed shaper who is obviously out of place. You should feel happy we're here. Otherwise, you'd be mugged."

"I thought you were a noble?" said Snowy, her whiskers and ears drooping.

"I am. That doesn't mean I was a good noble. Nobles are the worst, just better dressed."

"That alone makes them better," Bart said condescendingly. "These people are trash."

"It's a crime for a commoner to insult a noble, you know," chided Kita.

The group followed Kita through the maze of passages of the Leedings slums. The streets were more like tunnels as the buildings grew up and over them. Some places were so narrow that Zidin had to turn sideways. She stopped before a faded red door with a shingle that said SWORD AND DAGGER.

Kita pushed through the door.

"Mom! Dad! I'm home!" Kita yelled across the inn.

She hurried down the landing to hug Glen. She hopped up on the bar, and the pair took turns tapping with a finger. Tapping on the bar top was a way of communicating, and Kita told her dad about her adventure.

Barb came from the kitchen, an old lady who looked like everyone's favorite grandmother.

"Kita! I was sure they'd taken you for good the last time."

"Ah, Mother can't keep me locked up for long."

"What's with the new tattoo? It's pretty, but not you."

Kita laughed.

"True. But I can make it appear as I need. It's my marking for my Arconian guild."

"So, Marie finally did it," said Barb.

"You knew?" exclaimed Kita.

"We knew something was supposed to be transferred from mother to daughter. She never said what."

"So, I'm now the emissary for the Arconians and the personification of the fighting spirit of Arcone. I don't understand all of it, but Zidin—" she motioned to the elder— "is supposed to be my mentor and guide for Arcone. But there's even more...."

"Oh?"

"I've been named Commander for the Legion of Yorq."

"Ho-ho!" exclaimed Glen. "Our little Kita has hit the big time."

"I, ah, was hoping you'd help me."

"Anything you need, love," said Barb. "Aye, it's so good to have you home."

"I'm hoping the Shadow Guild and my Legion can work together. I've got some great spies ready to work with us."

"We still need to talk about this before you go charging in like a bull," said Cowboy.

"Meet Commandant Gerald Hennessey, my advisor and mentor for the Legion."

"How are you, sir?" Cowboy offered a hand to Glen and Barb.

Glen stroked his beard.

"And what do I get out of the deal?"

"I'm hoping you'll govern Leedings when we take it."

"That's quite the offer.... if you can follow through."

"I'm building an army now. I also need the thief's help getting into Earl Maybrow's plantation."

"That's a tall order."

"Snowy and I are going to case the walls and buildings to see how best to get in. Once we find the VIPs, we can start the rescue mission. The thieves and I will open the gate for the combat team and rescue the VIPs. The combat team will load and take the VIPs to our camp."

"I think we can do that," mused Glen. "I'll send Pen and Reg with you to scout. You can devise a plan after you see the lay of the land."

"Thanks, Dad."

"You and your friends can have the rooms upstairs. Your room hasn't been touched."

"I'll make sure I have people following you and watching your back. Maybrow's men have been extra aggressive lately."

"He sides with Cunningham."

"Must we stay here?" muttered Bart.

Three big men stood up from playing cards and approached the mouthy shaper.

"Problem with the establishment?" said one.

"Back off," said Bart, growing a fireball in his hand.

One of the men waved his hand, and a strong gust of wind blew the flame across a table.

"The King isn't the only one with shapers," chided Kita.

"It's just not what I'm used to."

"You're free to hike to the commercial district...if you can find your way out of the slums before you're mugged."

"I can take care of a few muggers."

"Remember, they come from behind."

"Who's the dandy?" asked Glen.

"Bartholomew Jackson Van der Hoost the Sixteenth, rock and fire shaper in the service of his Majesty, the King of Yorq."

"Hard to be in the service of a dead man," mocked Zidin.

"We call him Bart," said Kita as she tapped out what happened between them and that he was a spy.

"Well, you're free to sleep outside," chuckled Glen.

"Why don't you get settled in?" suggested Barb. "I'll cook something, and it'll be ready shortly."

"Alright. Thanks, Mom."

"Good to have you home, love."

"I, ah, brought home some, too," said Kita, pulling Snowy beside her. "This is Snowy, Queen of the War Cats, and my girlfriend."

"Going to have your hands full," chuckled Barb. "Glad to meet you, Snowy. If you need anything, don't hesitate to ask."

Snowy smiled nervously.

"Can you make sure her food is raw, Mom?"

Barb chuckled.

"Save me the time to cook it. Go pick your rooms. I'll call you for supper."

COWBOY CALLED IN EVERYONE to talk about their missions in the city.

"So, why do you call them Mom and Dad, and this your home?" demanded Bart. "I thought you were a noble."

"I am a high noble. This is where I came when I didn't want to be at Arbol. They adopted me and taught me about being a thief and how to survive."

"But why the slums?" Bart lamented.

"Because we'll have people watching our back, any authorities enter, and we'll know in minutes, and we can move around unseen. You stick out like a sore thumb."

"So, what was the tapping about?"

Filthy spies.

"Nothing but a game Dad and I play to teach me how to deal with distraction and do two things simultaneously."

That sounds good.

"When are you leaving to scout?" asked Cowboy.

"Why does the alley cat get to go? You can't hide that ugly mug."

"Because she can keep up with me, knows how to hunt and be quiet, and her spots are better suited for the city."

I can't wait to gut him.

"We all have things to do, so let's get them done," Kita ordered, annoyed.

E VEN AFTER DARK, THE side streets were crowded. Kita easily pushed her way through, but Snowy drew wards and stares. When one sailor drew a knife, Kita gave her girlfriend her half cloak to hide her face and body.

Turning down a side street, Kita followed the twisting path to a door with several tough-looking men standing around.

"What do you want?" asked one when Kita stopped.

"Best be moving on," said another.

"I'm here for the lollie," said Kita.

"Kita!" the men laughed.

"That password is old. The new one is shiny and silver."

"Dad didn't tell me. Come on."

Kita waved Snowy through the door.

Shelves and cases were filled with jewelry, statues, artwork, weapons, trinkets, tools, furniture, and rare animals. Oil lamps lit the neatly laid out merchandise.

Snowy examined a few things and ogled others. She paused at the jewelry.

"These are pretty."

Snowy held up a set of silver bangles and an armband.

"You want them?"

"I'm sure they're expensive, and I don't have any money. It's ok. It's fun to look."

She smiled disappointedly.

"Give them here."

Kita took the jewelry and walked to the back of the store, where a grizzled old woman sat going through a crate.

"What do you want?" the old woman barked.

"These, you old bat."

"Who the suns has got the nerve to call me that?"

The old woman turned, saw Kita, and sneered.

"Oh, it's you. Thought I was rid of you, scallywag. I told you never to set foot in here again."

"Only about a dozen times. I can't believe you're still upset over that lamp. I know you got a better than fair price. All I wanted was what was fair."

"You blackmailed me."

"Not blackmail. You called it leverage when you were teaching me how to deal."

"I did, but you weren't supposed to use it on me."

"All I wanted was two more gold. Not my fault it ended up being ten."

"You're too good to be wasted doing whatever you're doing. You could make a fortune running this place. The offer still stands."

Kita smiled.

"My reply still stands. I want to be outside doing stuff."

"Your loss, kid. Let me see what you've got."

Kita handed the jewelry over.

"You've got good taste. These are from the Kremlin Silver Works. I'll give you a discount for everything—ten gold."

"No way. Two gold and fifty silver."

"I'm not giving it away," croaked the old woman. "Seven-fifty."

"What? I could get ten sets for that price. Three gold."

"Get out of my store. You're robbing me."

"Come on, Snowy," said Kita, "she's not serious about selling this stuff. I'm sure the old man at the docks will want to deal."

"Four gold and fifty silver. That's my final offer!" the old woman yelled.

"Sold," Kita said happily. "Charge it to Glen. I'll pay him back for it later."

"What? That wasn't part of the deal! His accountants will screw me further."

"Not my fault you didn't say I couldn't pay for it on credit."

"Rotten child, get out of my store."

The old woman pointed to the door.

Kita laughed and led Snowy outside. There, she traded jokes and barbs with the protection.

"That was unpleasant," Snowy said, her ears flat against her head.

"Don't worry. She'll calm down. Nothing bad will happen, I promise. Now come and put them on so I can see," said Kita impatiently.

Snowy slid her arm into the armband and put a bangle on each wrist and ankle.

You know what would really be a turn-on?

Kita removed a bangle from around her ankle and clamped it on Snowy's tail.

"I hadn't thought of that," Snowy said as she swung her tail back and forth. "I like it. They're so pretty. Thank you."

Snowy kissed Kita and hugged her.

Kita winked at her girlfriend.

"Anything for my girl."

"**W**ELL, THIS SHOULD BE easy," chuckled Kita as a bar came loose from a set blocking a drainage ditch through the plantation wall.

The plantation was outside of Leedings, a few miles on a large estate. The wall around the house showed Earl Maybrow was a little paranoid.

Kita carefully removed enough for them to crawl through.

"This will make a great infiltration point," said Kita as she replaced the bars.

Scanning the grounds, Kita didn't see any roving patrols—just a guard by the front gate and on the porch.

Kita reached into her pouch and put a pinch of diamond dust on Snowy.

"That'll keep you from being seen in the shadows."

"What is it?"

"Something they make in The Orient. It costs a fortune, but it's worth it."

They checked the perimeter and walked the grounds. It was everything Kita expected to find—a stable, barracks, a kitchen, a shed of farm equipment, and a water cistern, but no guards. Checking the barracks, Kita discovered the garrison asleep.

Must not worry too much about unwanted visitors.

They returned to the house. It was two stories with columns in the front holding up a balcony.

Kita motioned for Snowy to watch her step on the wraparound porch. She didn't want something to squeak.

Finding a window unlocked, Kita used Dusk to lift it open until she could get her fingers underneath. Checking inside, Kita heard footsteps.

"They've got roaming guards inside," she whispered to Snowy.

Slipping through the window, Kita checked the house doors and hallways for traps but found none. A pair of guards stood by a door in the hallway.

They're pretty confident in themselves.

Kita didn't approach the guarded door but noted where the prisoners were being held.

Looking upstairs, they located nothing of interest and no guards.

Kita motioned for Snowy to follow her back outside. Slipping through the shadows, they crawled through the drainage ditch and returned to the city.

T HEY RETURNED BY THE third bell, after finding the plantation guard lax.

"Since we're here early, I'm going to take a nap," said Snowy.

Kita tucked her in and took the opportunity to snuggle.

Kita awoke to a board *creaking*. She remained still as someone moved across the room to the desk, then left through the window and locked it from the outside.

Kita moved Snowy's tail from around her, checked the desk, and discovered a note.

It's odd that the intelligence people would leave me correspondence. Maybe they didn't want to wake me.

Opening the note, it was written in assassin symbols.

This didn't come from my people. What assassin is after me?

The assassin who did leave it left a single instruction to follow a trail of symbols to a meeting place.

Great. I don't want to do a treasure hunt.

Kita didn't want to alert the others. She left a note beside Snowy, hoping the others would understand the trail she would leave them. She kissed Snowy and left via the window.

The assassin's trail wasn't hard to follow, leading Kita to the wharf and an old wool warehouse.

Whoever planned this wants me to find them.

The lower level was dark, and Kita opened a door to a rickety, old staircase in the back. Another symbol adorned the stairs' base, directing her upstairs.

Not wanting to play into her adversary's hands, Kita climbed the staircase wall to the ceiling. She pulled a loose board free and slid it aside. Crawling onto the roof, it was as dilapidated as the rest of the building—loose, missing, or broken boards were exposed by the missing shingles.

Kita carefully placed each step until she reached the roof's peak. Crawling, she made her way to the back of the building. Large sacks of wool were stacked, making a ring.

Kita's heart stopped when she saw a woman in purple armor waiting for her.

Sarah. What do you want with me? This can't be good.

Kita retraced her steps back to the center of the room.

I hope the floor is sturdier than the roof.

Kita located a large hole and slipped through. Dangling, she dropped onto a board that cracked under her weight.

The sudden noise startled Sarah, as did Kita's appearance.

"I know I trained you well, but you've improved. Excellent. I was afraid this would be over quickly."

Sarah's sweet Champignon accent caused Kita's breath to catch.

I didn't realize I missed it.

"I thought I'd taught you better than what they reported. I think whoever wrote that report should have his throat cut."

So, you're the one getting Bart's reports.

"It's been a long time, Sarah." The lump in Kita's throat made her force the words out.

Sarah played with her dark, wavy hair. "It has. It's too bad you're covering that precious face. I was hoping to get to see it."

Kita pushed back her hood and lowered her scarf and mask.

"You've found employment with the Shadow Guild. That'll make some of the other assassins unhappy. But you've gotten more beautiful since the last time I saw you."

"What do you want?" demanded Kita.

"When did you become all business? You used to be fun and do anything but work."

"People grow and change."

"Yes, they do. You've become a very important person."

"Just a small-time thief and assassin."

"That's not what I heard. Rumor has it you're the Commander of the Legion of Yorq. That is an important person, and being important has advantages and disadvantages. One disadvantage is that you can make enemies who have the wealth to hire us."

"You're implying someone put a contract out on me?"

"Yes, I thought you should know. It's the least I can do. I don't want it to become between us."

Kita's heart froze.

"You took the contract?"

"Stars, yes. This will carve my name in stone as one of the biggest and best big-game hunter assassins. My reputation will soar. But don't take it personally. It's business. I thought I'd give you a chance. I owe you that."

Sarah smirked.

"Don't be so sure of yourself," Kita whispered.

"Come on. Speak up. I know facing death is hard, but do it with some dignity."

Sarah's harsh words stung.

"I'm not the same assassin you trained," said Kita, unable to hide her sorrow.

"Then this shall be interesting."

Sarah drew her sword and dagger.

Kita unsheathed Dawn and Dusk.

"Those are gorgeous. I've been meaning to get a new set. Do you mind if I have them? You won't need them."

Sarah spun her dagger in a flashy flourish.

"You can have them when you pry them from my cold, dead hands."

"If that is your condition. I promise to put them to good use."

As they circled, the floorboards creaked.

Sarah lunged.

Kita blocked, but her heart wasn't in it. She felt tired and weak.

Sarah's blows came hard and fast, finding their targets as Kita could only offer token resistance.

Sarah kicked Kita, knocking her to the ground.

Kita curled up, coughing.

Sarah looked down, disgusted.

"You're worse than before! Pathetic! I'll skin whoever gave me your report."

I did.

Kita pushed herself to her knees and hung her head.

"I can't do it. Not you, anyone but you."

Big tears fell from her eyes.

"What are you blubbering about?" demanded Sarah.

"I love you. I won't fight you."

Dusk and Dawn clattered on the floor.

"You silly little girl," Sarah scoffed. "You think I loved you? Now that's pathetic. Sorry, little Kita, but you're just a toy. You had a great body and were fun to sleep with because you did whatever I said. I fed you crap so you'd keep coming back.

"I taught you to be an assassin as a bet. Kita Logine, daughter of Duke Logine of Arbol, the assassin. It was too funny and too good to pass up. You're a joke to the rest of the assassins. I never loved you. You were willing to please, and a good way to pass the time."

"You meant everything to me," blubbered Kita as big tears fell off her chin.

"You meant nothing to me. I barely tolerated you, let alone loved you," Sarah said, rolling her eyes.

"No...no, don't say that," Kita said around sobs.

"Oh, yes. Now, get up and fight like I taught you. At least die with dignity, you pathetic noble bitch. Stop blubbering like a coward. Assassins don't cry when they're about to lose. They fight to the end. You say you're an assassin. Prove it. Put your feelings aside. Prove me wrong. You noble assassin joke."

Kita pushed herself to her feet, fighting the tears. She tried to wipe them away, but more came.

"I told you I don't love you, so stop crying!" Sarah yelled. "You want me to tell that thing you're sleeping with you died crying? Would it help to tell you I've got a contract on her, too?"

Oh, you shouldn't have mentioned that, sweetheart.

The red aura closed around Kita's vision, and her tears stopped. Humiliated, Kita's heart broke, releasing a violent sticky black tar that bubbled up from the ring in her chest, ignited by her fury.

"Don't you touch her," Kita said in a voice that made Sarah step back. "Or I'll skin you alive."

"That's a new threat," cooed Sarah.

"It's not a threat. Your screaming will be music to my ears." Sarah smiled.

"That's the fight I want to see. Come on and show me what you've got."

Kita flashed forward, leaving four long cuts through Sarah's chest plate. Kita spun to the left.

Sarah fumbled blocking the whirlwind attacks, and a series of gashes appeared up Sarah's arm.

Kita moved around Sarah, slashing and stabbing her armor and bringing Dusk down on Sarah's dagger, shattering it.

Sarah collapsed to the floor, blood leaking from her armor.

Kita kicked the defeated assassin across the room.

Sarah struggled to her knees.

"I told you I wasn't the same person I was before," said Kita.

"I believe it now," Sarah whispered as she coughed up some blood. "Will you let me die with my head up?"

Kita nodded and helped Sarah to her knees. Kita raised Dawn.

Sarah looked into Kita's eyes.

"I love you and always have loved you. You know that, right?"

Liar.

Kita brought Dawn down.

W HEN THE OTHERS ARRIVED, Kita sat cross-legged, cradling Sarah's head.

"Oh, *kitten!*" Snowy yelled as she pushed past Zidin to rush to Kita's side.

Dropping to her knees, Snowy tried to pry the head free.

"Kita, it's ok. I'm here."

Kita clung to Sarah's head like her life depended on it.

Snowy hugged Kita and held her tight.

"It's alright. Please, drop the head and let me hold you."

Snowy stroked Kita's cheek. With her other hand, she pulled the head from Kita's grasp. Taking Kita into her arms, Snowy held her and sang.

Kita was asleep in a minute.

K ITA AWOKE LIKE SHE had a bad dream. But she knew it wasn't.

What's Snowy going to think? I hope she doesn't leave me. Is she even still here?

She remembered Snowy tucking her in.

Kita pushed back to the green and gold Arbol comforter and scowled. Her room was perfectly set up to alert her if something was amiss. Now, everything was everywhere.

Finding her clothes, she set up her room. The activity helped calm her and gave her something to think about besides Snowy and Sarah.

Finished, she descended the ladder to the second floor and the guest rooms. She didn't feel like dealing with anyone and sat on the top step of the stairs, listening to the conversation downstairs.

"My cats wouldn't hurt anyone. They were only doing bad things because I was a prisoner. They're loyal to me."

"How are they getting along without you?" said Glen.

"A few follow me around. I'm sure there are some in the city. More are in the mountains waiting."

Barb raised a nervous eyebrow. "They're in the city!"

"A few braver ones might be, but I haven't seen any. I'm sure they'd come out of the shadows if I went outside and called."

Glen laughed.

"Sounds like my men. So, how long have you and Kita been together?"

"Ah—"

"Yeah, why don't you tell us, alley cat? I've been wondering that myself," Bart injected.

"Uhm, well..."

"Well, are you or aren't you together?"

"I said she was my girlfriend."

"Do you love her?" Bart said, raising an eyebrow

"Well...it's early, and I'm still getting to know her. She takes some getting used to."

Bart pointed behind Snowy to the stairs. Kita stood with tears streaming down her face. She turned and fled upstairs to her room.

"Wait!" Snowy yelled and ran after Kita. She reached the hatch too late as the lock clicked shut.

Kita threw herself on the bed, sobbing.

No one loves me. Not Sarah. Not Snowy. Not my family. I'll be alone forever. What did I do to deserve this? What's wrong with me?

"Kitten, let me in. Please. I'm sorry. I can explain. Please let me in. I'm so sorry. Please, Kita..."

Snowy knocked on the hatch as she pleaded. When Kita's sobs didn't diminish, she returned downstairs.

S NOWY ENTERED THE INN through the front door. Cowboy, Glen, and Zidin were at the bar. Glaring at everyone, she handed Cowboy a few pieces of paper containing her scouting report and disappeared upstairs.

"She's really upset, isn't she?" Glen said to Cowboy.

"I can't blame her. I wish she wouldn't camp out at the foot of the ladder."

"Kita was always good at throwing a tantrum. I feel sorry for Snowy. That jackass set her up." Glen frowned at Bart.

"I should have caught it. I was too busy reading to listen until it was too late," Cowboy growled.

"Not your fault, son. He caught us all looking the wrong way. I wish you'd let my men take him out back and beat some sense into him."

Glen tapped his fingers on the table.

"Kita says he's not to be harmed."

"Kita's not interested in him, is she? She's not trying to have both?" Glen said, looking concerned.

Cowboy snorted.

"Her interest in him is purely professional. Hmmm, you can help. Kita has him pegged for a spy. Our intelligence people are watching him, but yours should as well."

Glen sighed.

"I can't believe she's going through all this for a spy. It's not worth the hassle."

"I don't know. She's learned who his handler is, and that's what she wanted. She might have planned to oust him, but this business with Sarah and Snowy got in the way. I don't want to make a move against him without her."

Snowy came downstairs and went into the kitchen. She came out with a whole chicken. She sat in the corner and took a bite out of the bird.

"That is disgusting," Bart yelled when he saw Snowy eating.

Snowy ripped a big chunk off the chicken and swallowed it.

"You are a disgusting flea-infested alley cat that shouldn't be around decent people."

Snowy finished the chicken and cleaned the blood from her fur. As she cleaned her face, rock encased her.

"Let go of me!" Snowy yelled.

Cowboy and Zidin rushed Bart. Zidin tackled Bart while Cowboy aided Snowy. The Arconian yanked Bart off the ground and slammed him on a table.

The rock receded from Snowy.

Zidin pulled his arm back to hit Bart.

"Let him go," Kita whispered over the yelling and noise.

Everyone looked to see an exhausted but furious Kita.

"Snowy, I want to talk to you," Kita said sternly.

Snowy stepped forward, her long tail draped over her arm.

"Have fun, alley cat. Try not to say anything too stupid this time," chided Bart.

Snowy lashed out with her claws. She ripped three gashes across his face, and his eyeball bounced onto the floor.

"You mangy gutter whore! You took my eye!" Bart screamed as he clutched his face.

"You'll live," Kita said flatly and led Snowy upstairs.

Kita barred the hatch and looked at Snowy.

"I'm sorry," they said together.

"You don't have anything to be sorry for. I opened my big mouth."

"You were set up. Hearing it hurt, but that's not why I've locked myself in here. I'm sorry for that. I hate that I made you wait.

"Please, don't be mad at me. I thought I was over Sarah, and seeing her again brought it all back. I loved her, even though she didn't love me. My heart broke all over again. I've been up here trying to pull myself together and get over her. You don't deserve that, and I understand if you want to leave."

"Kitten, we all have our first loves and have a special place in our hearts for them. Even if Gerald is an ass, I still have feelings for him, but I no longer feel the way I do about him that I do with you."

"You don't hate me?" whispered Kita.

"I hate that you wouldn't talk to me for three days. At least tell me you're alright. I care about you, and causing you pain hurts me. Sarah will be a distant memory soon enough. But I'll be here if you need to cry or a hug."

Kita hugged Snowy and put her head on the cat's shoulder.

"I can't believe she would do that to me."

"People change, and you are a big target for our enemies. We're going to have to be more careful. No running off into the night without us."

Kita frowned. 'Yeah, I messed that up."

"Why don't we go downstairs and get you something to eat. We can see if Bart has found his eye."

That made Kita giggle.

"So much for the perfect face."

SIX

FALLEN ANGEL
THREE DAYS GRACE
HUMAN

S NOWY AND KITA CAME down the stairs hand in hand. Kita had a devilish face that froze the others in the inn in place. They stopped at the table where Bart was playing with a deck of cards.

"How are you fixing my face?" he demanded when he looked at the girls.

"I can't," said Kita with a grin.

"You fixed the alley cat. You can fix me."

"That would require a walk back to Razor's Reef. But you're on your own for that. Those that know what to do are busy...and I've been very busy."

Kita walked around the table to stand next to Bart.

"I've come across some interesting correspondence."

"I didn't know you could read."

"Even noble girls are taught to read and write. I want to know who wrote these."

Kita dug into her belt and pulled out Bart's notes. She laid them out in front of him.

"Anyone could have written this. It looks like you have a spy."

"I do."

Kita grabbed Bart's arm and pinned it to the table. She reached up his sleeve and pulled out several scrolls. Opening one, she set it down next to the others.

"Looks the same to me."

"My personal observations, nothing more."

Kita kissed Snowy on the cheek.

"This seems to upset you."

"What do you want, other than being lewd in public?"

"I want....I want...I want to clean out the rats and pigeons, so to speak."

"Going to put the disgusting furball to work?"

Kita's smile became villainous, causing Bart to pause.

"No. I'm here for you. Did you really think you could hide from an assassin?"

"You have nothing."

"I took this scroll off an assassin who took a contract on me. How do I know who wrote it? I did, and I swapped yours for mine. Believe me, Sarah was furious at getting such an inaccurate report."

"I'm in the service of the king. Touch me, and you'll be hanged."

"Cunningham doesn't have that kind of reach, and James is dead. Who's going to protect you?"

Bart lit the cards on fire.

"The only thing worse than a spy is a traitor," cooed Kita. She jumped on the table and grabbed Bart by his fur collar. She yanked him so they were face-to-face, his feet trying to touch the floor.

"Did you think I would let a spineless spy operate under my nose? I knew what you were the second I laid eyes on you. I've been playing you from the beginning. I sacrificed the one person I care for to keep you thinking you were getting somewhere. Now I'm done with you."

Kita dropped Bart in a heap. She jumped from the table, grabbed him by his perfect hair, and dragged him out of the inn.

She pulled him through the muck and excrement of the alley to an open courtyard. Kita let Bart go.

The shaper stumbled to his feet.

"I will—"

Kita kicked him in the chest, sending Bart crashing into the stone wall of the courtyard.

He slid down the wall and landed in a heap.

"Get up!" Kita taunted while drawing her swords. "You said you could beat me. Now's your shot."

Bart stumbled to his feet.

"Assassin bitch, I'll kill you! I'll skin the cat and make a coat when I'm done."

Cowboy's hand moved to his revolver.

Bart grew a fireball and hurled it at Kita.

She batted it aside with Dawn.

The ground shifted under Kita's feet. She jumped, grabbed a hanging sign, and flipped onto it.

A string of fireballs came at her.

Jumping, she caught an empty sign pole and swung to a ledge above Bart.

A flame lance dislodged Kita from her perch. She leaped and bounced off a wall to a window ledge.

Bart created a wall of stone between them.

Kita drew Midnight and fired an arrow that shattered the wall and hit Bart in the shoulder.

As Kita landed on a ledge, a pair of fireballs exploded on her, sending her tumbling.

That bastard singed my hair.

Landing with a *thud* on the stone-covered ground, Kita's body was encased in rock.

"I told you I was better than you, bitch. I'm going to enjoy torching that pretty face off. Anyone try to save her, and I'll torch you too."

Bart yanked the arrow from his shoulder and cauterized the wound.

"I'm more curious to know what she'll do to you," said Cowboy with a revolver aimed at Bart.

"When I'm done with this gutter trash, I want my coat."

Zidin brandished Great White as Cowboy turned into his flaming demon.

"You want the girls, you've got to go through us."

I can survive this, right?

Funny time to ask that question. Ah, depends on what he burns. You should be fine, but you'll look like flame face.

Bart aimed an uninjured hand at Kita, and flame splashed across her face.

Kita screamed as the courtyard filled with the smell of burning flesh.

"What a waste of a pretty face," chided Bart. "You should've respected your betters. Goodbye, Kita."

The laughter came as a whisper, then grew louder.

Bart stopped his flame to find Kita's face gone, only her miscolored bones.

The laughter became deeper, sinister.

"It's impossible," gasped Bart.

"Don't think you're getting out of this alive, son," said Glen as he came up next to Cowboy. He had a squad of bruisers and thieves on the roofs with him.

"Bring it, old man. You're all dead. I'll get my commission, the contract money, and the gratitude of King Cunningham. It'll be a triple payday."

Bart laughed.

Kita punched through the rock, stood, and brushed the dust from herself.

The mouths of Kita's companions fell open.

"Now, you're getting it," said Bart. "Took you long enough to recognize my greatness."

Snowy pointed behind Bart.

"Like I'm falling for that."

"Hee...hee...hee," Kita said in a sinister, airy voice.

Bart gulped as he turned to Kita, her bones reflecting the firelight. He backed away until he felt the tip of Zidin's sword in the middle of his back.

"What the blazes are you people?"

"Shapers," said Cowboy, "just more advanced than you."

"She should be dead!"

I can't see.

And your eyes won't regenerate. I need to get you to an autodoc for that.

So, I'm blind?

Yep.

Being without her eyes was a disadvantage, but assassins trained in the dark learning to use their ears to locate their target.

Kita grabbed Bart by the throat and pulled him to her so he could watch her slowly regenerate. When he whimpered, she slammed him on the cobblestone.

"Someone get me some rope and a board," Kita whispered.

A bruiser approached her.

"Here you go, boss."

Kita took the items in her free hand and dragged Bart through the slums to the city's main square. They arrived in front of the towering statue of the first king of Yorq. He stood with a shield and sword, pointing his people forward.

Using Bart's blood, she wrote TRAITOR on the board and tied it around his neck. She'd climbed the statue before and had little trouble carrying Bart to the outstretched sword. She tied a loop in the rope and tossed it toward the end of the sword. It took a few tries, but she got it.

"You've been more trouble than what I got out of you. Now, you're going to swing."

Kita shoved him off the arm.

Bart's scream died when the rope caught, leaving the shaper swinging in the breeze.

Kita climbed down and was met by the others.

"It's been a long time since we swung someone from His Majesty," chuckled Glen. "Are you alright? Do you need your mom to bandage you up?"

"It'll grow back—quicker than most," said Cowboy.

"My eyes won't," said Kita.

"That's a problem. I know you can echolocate, but we can't have you on the mission."

"I'm going, even if I have to stay with the wagons."

"I need Darla to help infiltrate the house. She's the only one who knows how to get to the hostages."

"I'll have the thieves and legionnaires to watch over me."

"We'll talk about it. We still have a lot of planning to do."

"**G**LAD YOU MADE IT, General," Cowboy said to Barneky when his platoon arrived.

"Two days in the bush have left us chomping at the bit, sir."

"Good. A flare will signal you to attack and bring the coaches and carts to load the VIPs. Kita's thieves will open the gate."

"Can they be trusted?"

Kita scowled behind her mask. She had a bandana over her eyes.

"I trust my thieves," Kita said tersely.

"What happened to you?"

"Commander, you must have forgotten. I did away with Bart, but not before he took my eyes."

"Not as good as you thought," Barneky laughed.

With a flash, Dusk was against Barneky's throat.

"I may not be able to see you, but I know where you are."

"Ok, we don't need a scrum here," ordered Cowboy. "Barneky, take Kita and wait for the signal."

"I'm not going?" exclaimed Kita.

"You're no good in a fight," said Barneky. "Too much noise and commotion."

"He's right, kitten," said Snowy. "Don't worry. I know how to get into the basement undetected. We'll need you to calm the VIPs and explain what's happening."

"Fine. I'll be waiting," Kita grumbled.

KITA VAULTED THE PLANTATION wall after slipping away from the coaches. She landed in a cacophony—men yelling, metal on metal, and the occasional explosion—blinding her.

Barneky's voice rose above the din. She followed it, knowing he'd take her where she wanted.

"This is the last of them," yelled Zidin.

"What the hell are you doing here?" demanded Cowboy in the eerie voice of the demon.

"I thought I'd be more help here than calming frightened nobles. Where's Snowy?"

"I don't know. She was the last one out. We don't have time to look for her. We need to go before the city guard arrives."

"What the bloody moons happened?" demanded Kita. "We have to go get her."

"Mission first," said Cowboy. "We have to get the VIPs to safety. General, get the coaches and wagons moving."

"Yes, sir."

"Fine, you go," ordered Kita. "I'll find her."

"There's no way I'm letting you go in there," said Zidin. "She'll find her way out and knows how to get back to the inn."

"Not good enough!" Kita yelled. "Without her, I'm dead. Take your pick."

"No."

"Fine."

Kita pulled a smoke bomb from her belt and spiked it on the wooden porch stairs. She dodged Zidin's attempt to grab her and ran into the house's open door.

She dragged her hands along the walls, searching for doors. When she found one, she checked underneath. She knew she'd found the basement when she found one with a draft.

She opened the door cautiously and gently put her foot on the warped loose top stair. The board gave a little under her foot.

I'm not getting down there silently that way.

Instead, Kita crawled along the wall.

She landed on the compact earth floor.

"Snowy?" whispered Kita.

There was a deep rumble of laughter, then the sound of a UEE door closing.

What has found us?

Whatever it is I bet it has Snowy.

We need to find the door.

Kita had a map in her head from her scouting expeditions, so there were only so many places big enough for a door in the wall. Most were facing the wrong way from where the laughter had come from, leaving her with two.

The door is going to be hidden. You'll have to find the control panel.

How do I do that?

You'll feel the difference, and it'll be about chest-high. You'll need to push it to shut off the camouflage.

Kita searched the first section but found nothing.

She moved through the stacks of crates, barrels, and furniture covered in sheets to the second area. Searching with her fingertips, she found a bump and pushed it.

Did it open?

No idea. Feel for a pad.

I feel keys. What's the entry code?

Four-nine-six-three-nine-five.

Kita entered the numbers and heard a door open.

Using her hand, she found the opening and went down the passage.

Where are we?

"Where I am god. Welcome to the colony ship—my ship."

"I don't understand."

"When I crash-landed on this rock, the ship broke into sections to soften the landing. Most are now buried underground. We're in the Legion section. There are

some good toys in here. On the ship, I have control over everything."

"Where'd you say that from?"

"A speaker on the wall. I have a wireless connection with the ship. I'm anywhere and everywhere. The thing that has Snowy is chaining her up in the fighter bay. I don't want to alert him we're here, so I'm keeping the ship off until we get there."

"How do I get there?"

"Follow the clicking sound."

A click came from in front. She followed it through the ship until they reached a giant cavern.

"We're in the Legion hangar bay. I'll have to see about freeing this ship piece. The interceptors would send Cunningham's forces running.

"That would be great."

"Here, I'll show you one."

Kita found a large piece of metal that was sleek and smooth.

"Those things coming off the sides are wings, the holes in the back are the engine, and the bulb in the front is the cockpit for the pilot—the person who controls the interceptor."

Clicking her tongue, Kita found many interceptors lined up in rows.

A door opened at the far end.

"Uh-oh, I found Snowy. She's chained to one of the lifts."

The rattling of chains and a garbled scream from Snowy were all Kita needed. She rushed to Snowy and removed the gag.

"Kitten, you have to get out of here. It's a trap."

"My wayward junior commander. I knew you'd come for this one," said a deep growl.

"He's some kind of monster!"

I guessed that.

Kita drew her swords and lunged at where the deep growl had come from. A heavy hand hit her, sending Kita sideways, crashing into a piece of equipment.

Discombobulated, Kita lost her mental image of the room. The *thuds* of Angus' footsteps coming toward her didn't help.

She sprang to her feet, ready to take on whatever Angus was.

"Kita! Look out!" cried Snowy.

Kita wasn't sure which way to jump. Her hesitation allowed Angus to grab her.

Agnus flicked Dusk and Dawn from Kita's hands.

"What do you want with me?" demanded Kita.

"Your body," Angus growled.

"Already taken, and you're not my type."

"Don't worry, you won't be in it. The power bestowed on you is a waste. With the Legion and Arcone armies, I can conquer The Mass. I've waited a long time for this."

"You can't have known I was getting the roses."

"I've known your mother for a long time. She told me about her children and her plans. I just had to get you in fighting shape. I suggested you learn the sword. I bet Sarah she couldn't seduce you and teach you to be an assassin."

He sounded big with lots of teeth.

"I'm over Sarah, so that won't help you."

"I thought you'd want to know before you die."

"I'm no good to you dead."

"On the contrary, your dead body will be perfect. Your abilities will be a nice bonus. With your body, I will find Omega, conquer everything, and rebuild the UEE utopia that once was."

"Let me guess, you plan to rule over it?"

"Of course."

"As me?"

"I have lots of bodies. The condition of your body doesn't matter. You'll be cast aside like the trash you are."

"Have to kill me first."

He squeezed her as Snowy screamed for Kita.

Kita's bones may have been unbreakable, but that didn't mean they couldn't be popped out of place. Several of her ribs poked through her chest. She gasped from the pain and lack of air. A moan escaped her when her spine dislocated, and she hung limp.

I hoped to hear Snowy's voice when I died, but not like this...

"**Hello, Dave,**" said Omega.

"Omega! Alpha! Capture him!"

Sleepy, so sleepy...

KITA AWOKE SCREAMING ON the floor. She was on her elbows and knees, and the area between her shoulder blades hurt worse than getting her roses. A weight pulled on her back as a burning sensation went up between her shoulder blades.

When the burning and pain stopped, she flopped on her side and moaned. She realized she had her eyes, but could see in every direction.

What happened to me?

"Omega?"

"**Oh, you're awake. That's good. Angus is getting tired of playing with my robots.**"

"What happened?"

"You died. I got you to the hangar's emergency trauma autodoc and repaired the damage."

"My chest hurts."

"You were crushed to death."

"Why is my back heavy?"

"A little surprise for you. Pull one around and see."

Kita reached behind her and found black feathers. She pulled them around her. She flexed her back, and her wings opened.

"I...you gave me wings?"

"You are a fallen angel. Now you look the part. I was also able to add photoreceptors to your skin, allowing you to see in all directions. My computer will control how much you see when you want."

"This is going to take some getting used to."

"Since we're in a machine shop, welding nanites were available, and I installed them in you. Now, your hands will be hot enough to melt metal. The heat can also be channeled through Dusk and Dawn."

"I can't wait to try that."

There was a series of *thuds* on the door.

"Angus wants in. I will open the door when you're ready, and you can obliterate him. Dave—Angus—was one of the worst officers on the ship. I don't know why Sven hired him."

Kita didn't know what the AI was talking about and, instead, opened and closed her wings to get used to them.

"Can I fly?"

"That didn't take long. Yes, you can."

"How?"

"Think about the direction you want to go. You don't fly by your wings like a bird. In your feathers are gravity wells that do the heavy lifting."

Up.

Kita rose off the deck.

Left.

She glided to her left until she hit the wall.

I guess I need to say when to stop.

Kita moved around the room, learning to fly. After a few crashes and wild tumbles, she glided around the room without a problem, all while Angus beat on the door and yelled at Omega.

Next, she drew her swords and practiced some basic maneuvers and strikes. She then added tumbling and her unique sword form.

"I wish the room were bigger. I guess I'll go with what I got. Open the door."

Kita opened her wings and took up a fighting stance, expecting Angus to charge in.

Omega opened the door, and Kita burst out laughing. Angus was a behemoth.

"Run out of bodies to snatch?" chided Kita. "Ravager isn't you."

"Omega's more powerful than I thought," contemplated Angus.

"You have no idea."

"Interesting choice. The fur does offer protection from my swords, but your agility sucks. Omega, if you please."

The red aura filled her vision.

Kita flashed forward, putting her shoulder into Angus' gut, throwing the behemoth across the hangar. He landed hard against an interceptor wing with a *crack*.

"Did I break something?" asked Kita as Angus struggled to stand.

You can ignite your swords if you flourish them fast enough.

The behemoth charged the Angel.

Kita heated her hands and flourished her swords until they burst into flame.

Kita grinned as Angus thumped toward her. "Are you fire-proof?"

Angus ignored the question and swiped with his claws.

Kita glided around the strike and cut off the arm.

Angus roared.

Kita thrust her sword into Angus's fur out of curiosity. To her delight, the hair ignited.

Angus thrashed as the fire engulfed him.

"I will have Omega, and I will take you!" Angus yelled as the fire overtook him until he was a pile of ash.

Kita poked through it, looking for something valuable, but found nothing.

"Kita!" Snowy yelled.

Kita glided over to Snowy and snapped the chains. The war cat fell into Kita's arms.

"Are you alright?" Kita asked, wiping tears from Snowy's fur.

"I was so scared. How are you alive? And wings?"

"Omega healed me and gave me some new abilities. Like flight." She rose off the deck.

"That is incredible. I've never seen anything like it."

"Are you alright?"

Kita motioned to the raw skin where Snowy had pulled against the chains.

"I'll heal. What's important is that you're healed."

"I would like to point out that all the machining and manufacturing equipment is missing."

"That's a mystery we're not going to solve now," said Kita. "We need to catch up with the others."

"Or you and I can spend some time together," suggested Snowy. "The boys can handle it."

"What do you have in mind?"

"Omega, is there a bedroom in this section?"

"Ah, no. Just sleeping quarters for the crew."

Kita blinked.

"Oh." Her mind hadn't gone there. "Who says we need a bed?"

"The deck is uncomfortable," protested Snowy.

"Who says I was thinking of the deck?" Kita cooed as she slipped her arms around Snowy.

She grabbed the war cat by her butt and lifted her onto the wing of an interceptor. Leaning in, she kissed Snowy.

"Now you're the right height."

"For what?" asked Snowy.

Kita pushed Snowy's legs apart.

"This and more..."

When you're finished, I have some nanites for Snowy...

"**T**HESE ARE INCREDIBLE," SNOWY said in wonder. "How did you make them?"

"**I've been saving them for a rainy day. I was going to give them to Kita, but I decided that after Angus took you, you needed some protection. I've also made your skeleton like Kita's, and it made your claws metal.**"

Snowy extended her claws.

"Wow!"

"You also have mirroring—you can create up to seven holograms of yourself, generate a small electrical charge, better communicate with animals, freeze enemies with a touch, and phase—you can move up to six feet using the fifth dimension. I just need you to get in the autodoc."

I'm going to have to get phasing.

"Wouldn't these be better for Kita?"

"Love, I want you protected so this never happens again."

"I'm going to need time to practice."

"We've got time. I need to practice flying, too."

"SO, HOW DID THEY get the machinery out of here?" asked Kita, looking at a cleaner section of the deck where something used to stand.

"I have no idea. I do know they tunneled in."

"How'd they get inside? Not the way we came."

"Through the environmental shield. It was down because the ship piece was on low power."

"Like rats that burrowed in and stole it all," muttered Kita.

"It's too bad too. I could've made some useful things."

"Maybe we should follow and see where the tunnel goes," suggested Snowy. "The war will end before it begins if we have Legion equipment."

"That's a good idea," said Kita as she buckled on her weapons harness.

Kita took Snowy's hand and followed the line on the floor to the tunnel.

Snowy examined the rock.

"This was cut using laser bore machines. Only the colonists would have those."

"So, this was grand larceny way back," said Kita.

"But who did it? La Forge, Red Legion?"

"Maybe we'll find out at the end of the tunnel."

The tunnel was wide enough for Kita to glide while Snowy stumbled over the uneven floor.

"Why is the floor so damn bumpy?" snarled Snowy after tripping the tenth time.

Kita looked. There was a deep ripple in the floor that appeared often.

"Some geological formation of the lava? I don't know. But I can carry you if you don't want to walk."

"That sounds good," said Snowy.

Kita picked up the cat and glided down the tunnel. She guessed it was going toward Leedings. They came to a brick wall.

"Where are we?" muttered Kita. She knew the Leedings sewers and was unaware of any bricked-up passages.

"Dead end?" lamented Snowy.

"Not necessarily."

Kita struck a brick and knocked it out of place. Two more strikes, and she had a hole big enough for her head. She looked inside and raised an eyebrow. It was the Leedings sewers. She pushed a few more bricks out of the way to let them through.

Kita picked up a brick and raised an eyebrow. Whenever this was bricked up, it was a long time ago, judging by the slime, mold, and nastiness on the brick. It was no wonder people missed the hole. The crap covering it was so thick you couldn't tell.

Maybe Dad knows.

"Come on," said Kita, offering her hand to Snowy. "It's a bit of a walk to the inn."

As Kita told Snowy the story of the Angel of Yorq, she guided the war cat through the sewers and stopped at a wall. Not as covered as the one they'd come through, but enough that it hid underneath.

Hitting a latch, a door swung open. It was a short passage with a ladder at the end. Kita climbed the ladder and pushed open a wooden hatch in a dark part of the inn. She climbed out and helped Snowy out.

"Hey, Dad," said Kita, coming up behind him.

"Kita! Where did you come from?"

"The sewers. Are you aware of any bricked-up passages in the Essex part of the sewers?"

"I can't say that I do. What did you find?"

"Nothing." Kita tapped on the counter to tell him what she found.

She explained it was a Legion facility that had been robbed. She was still puzzled about how they moved the heavy machinery through the sewers. Glen offered to send a search team down as well as guards. Kita wanted it bricked back up to keep scavengers and Cunningham's forces out. Glen agreed to that.

"What happened at the plantation?"

"Angus took Snowy, and I had to go in and get her. He killed me, and I was resurrected with these."

Kita opened her wings to the astonishment of her parents. She then hovered off the ground.

"Kita! What did they do to you?" exclaimed Barb.

"They were a gift that helped me defeat Angus."

"How'd they do it?" asked Glen.

"I'm not sure. I was dead at the time. I know I woke up to the pain."

"They...whoever did it, worry me. What if they do it to someone else or turn a poor soul into a ravager?"

"I'm not a ravager," laughed Kita. "It's just me with ten pounds of feathers."

Glen rubbed his beard.

"Sounds and looks like you, you knew how to get here. Still, from what you told us, there are clones in the world. Come prove to me you're who you say you are."

"My word is not good enough?" protested Snowy.

"Don't worry about it," said Kita. "Test of loyalty isn't unheard of."

Kita glided over to the bar, sat, crossed her legs, and let her wings hang off the back. Kita tapped her finger in a coded message only her Dad would know.

"Congratulations, dear. They do look stunning."

"Yes, love, they're striking," said Barb.

"I need a few people for a private mission," Kita asked Glen.

"What's the mission?"

"I'm going after Bart's handler."

"Fool should've left town after he swung. He has to know the Guild is coming for him. What do you want?"

"I need to stake out his residence. I figured Stinger and Jackle could help."

"How long do you plan to watch?"

"A few nights. Long enough to get the duck and ducklings routine down."

"What about me?" said Snowy.

"This is professional work. It's a hardened target."

"I gathered information about the plantation."

"I read it. It was good for a beginner. But this is not a Legion smash-and-grab. This is an assassin mission."

"You're going to assassinate him?"

"Yeah."

Snowy folded her arms and pouted.

"You can hang out with Mom or visit your war cats."

"I will not let you cast me aside."

"Believe me, girlie, it's for your protection," said a bruiser who had come over when Glen challenged Kita.

"Protection from what?"

Glen cleared his throat.

"Constables, spies, guards...It's dangerous out there. Leave it to those who know what they're doing. They've done more than one mission."

"I am not a child or a first-year lab tech. I stalk prey all the time in the mountains."

"In the mountains. The streets of Leedings are way different."

"Are you going to let him talk to me this way?" demanded Snowy.

Kita was caught flat-footed but knew there was only one answer, and Snowy wouldn't like it.

"As the underboss, yeah, I am. My dad is correct. The city is different than the mountains. You might—"

"The answer is no," said Glen. "I only send the most experienced on this type of mission. If you want to learn, I've got some simple missions you can go on led by experienced thieves."

"I am not some cub going on her first kill."

"You kind of are," retorted Kita.

"You're going to take his side?" Snowy yelled.

"It's nothing personal. Go hang out with your war cats. I'll be done in a few days."

"I will not let you dismiss me as common rabble."

"Snowy, I'm sorry. But it is the best thing. If you want, I can teach you some stuff so you can go on the next mission."

"I can't believe you would do this to me."

"I'm sorry. I don't want to see you get hurt."

"How does one get hurt watching a building?"

"For starters, you stick out," said a thief.

"Maybe at night," offered Kita.

"No, and that's final," said Glen.

"Harrumph," said Snowy as she stuck her nose in the air and draped her tail over her arm.

The war cat stomped upstairs.

"You have your hands full with her," said another thief.

"You think she was the Shadow Master," said a bruiser.

Kita sighed.

"I guess I'll go talk to her. Maybe we can find—"

"No," commanded Glen. "She stays out of the operation. The rest of us will keep an eye on her."

"Should I tell her *I'm sorry?*" Kita asked Barb.

"I've never met someone so entitled in my life. Don't say sorry. She should be apologizing to you."

"I guess I'll see if I can calm her down."

"Your choice, but she needs to learn she's not even good," said Glen.

Kita sighed, having read Snowy's notes she passed to Cowboy. They were amateur at best.

"I'll go talk to her. I don't want her mad at me."

"If you don't stand up for yourself, she'll walk all over you," warned Barb.

Kita bobbed her head slowly.

"I'll try again to explain why she can't come."

She glided down from the bar toward the staircase.

"Shiny feathers, little tuna," said a thief as Kita went by.

He made her smile.

She went upstairs to the ladder leading to her room. When she went to open the hatch, it was barred. Kita banged on it.

"Hey, let me in," Kita yelled.

I guess I'm not the only one who can lock herself in a room.

"Snowy! Let me explain!"

Kita growled as she pushed against the hatch. It gave some. *Snowy didn't dog it down. She just moved the dresser over it.*

She put her shoulder to the hatch and pushed using her superior strength to knock the dresser over, and the hatch opened. Kita stuck her head into the room. Snowy was sitting on Kita's bed, legs drawn in and tail wrapped around her.

"Snowy! I promise it has nothing to do with you personally—"

Snowy grabbed Kita's bear and hurled it at Kita's head.

Kita caught her bear, but the act enraged her.

"That's *my* bear and *my* bed!"

Kita floated into the room and squeezed her bear warmly. "Sorry, buddy."

She set the bear on the overturned dresser.

"This is my stuff! I didn't permit you to be in here or to abuse my bear. If you refuse to be reasonable, you can have a room downstairs."

"I'm your girlfriend. What's yours is mine."

Kita frowned.

"It's not...but whatever. I was thinking of letting you come to learn, but now, you can stay downstairs."

"You can't kick me out. It's my room, too."

"Please, Snowy, don't be like this. I know you have skills I don't, and we'll someday need. I won't stand in your way. Why are you standing in my way to do what I do?"

"You're going to leave me here for days! Alone!"

"I tried offering alternatives. Only a handful of girls can do this, and I'm one of them. This is what I was trained for. Would you rather I be back quickly or have to take extra time watching out for you?"

"I want you to treat me like your girlfriend, not some common thugs."

"My thieves are not thugs. They're highly trained at what they do."

"That's not an excuse not to take me."

Kita sighed.

"Will a few kisses now and promise lots more when I get back help?"

"Humph," huffed Snowy. "You'll have to do better than that."

"Ah....what else is there?"

"To be treated how I'm supposed to be treated. I'm your girlfriend. You should treat me better than anyone else."

"I do. But that doesn't mean you're qualified to go."

"I did your job when you locked yourself in your room. No one complained about my reports."

I don't know why Cowboy didn't.

"I promise when I get back, I'll take you out and treat you right."

"You better come back with something shiny."

Bloody moons. Maybe I can pinch something from the handler's house.

"I, ah, sure. Whatever you want."

Snowy got off the bed.

"Then I'm going to see my war cats. They know how to treat me right."

She stomped past Kita with a dirty look.

"I'll be back in three days."

She jumped down the hatch, leaving Kita to hug her bear tightly. She made the bed and placed the bear on the pillow when she finished. Afterward, she went downstairs.

"Are you alright, love?" asked Barb. "Snowy left in a huff."

"We came to a resolution. She's going to see her war cats."

"A couple of days without her might be good for you. I know girls like her. They'll abuse you."

"I think it's my fault. She wants me to treat her better. I promised her a night out and something shiny when I finished."

Barb scowled.

"She's using you, love. It's not your fault. You need to do your job, and she has to respect that...especially if she wants you to respect her."

"I don't want to lose her. I just found her. If I treat her better, she'll come around."

Barb sighed.

"You have to learn the hard way."

SEVEN

SIGN OF THE CROSS
IRON MAIDEN
THE X FACTOR

K ITA LANDED ON THE edge of the tile roof of Bart's handler's residence to minimize her silhouette in case someone looked out a window at two bells past midnight. She was invisible, but she didn't want to take chances.

Most homes in the city had thatch or wooden shingles, depending on what the owner could afford. Tiles were for merchants and nobles. They also made getting in harder. Thatch she could spread and slip in. Wood always had a loose board. Not tile. But there were ways in.

Kita floated down to where the rafters rested on the wall's top support. There was always a gap between the rafters, allowing her to crawl through.

Finding a hole she thought large enough, she stuck her head in, but her wings wouldn't fit. They caught on the tiles. She grabbed her left wing and pulled it around her, and wiggled partway through the hole. She then did the same for the right wing. Once she had the top of her wings through, she slid in without a problem.

The ceiling was made of thick wooden timbers, too thick to go with her initial plan of removing one. Now, she had to find the attic access. Creeping around the empty space, she found the attic access. She opened it a fraction to check for traps or alarms.

A single string attached the access to something. Kita cut the string, slowly opened the access hatch, and ran her hand around the edge to ensure there wasn't a secondary trap.

This guy is a paranoid type. It seems odd for a young politician trying to get into court.

Kita opened the hatch and crawled onto the ceiling, then closed it silently.

Kita cautiously crossed the ceiling to the handler's room. Moving down the wall, she tried to open the door handle but found it locked. Kita took her lockpick from her belt and picked the lock upside down.

It wasn't hard. She only had to turn a set of tumblers to unlock the door. The security was in the intricate key and notch design. The key had to fit through slots to turn the tumblers. Once they were laid over, the latch would release.

Kita slipped through the door and closed it.

While surveying the room, she noticed it was smaller than it should have been. A set of bookshelves were on an interior wall. The bed was across the way, with her target snoring loudly. A small table was in the center of the room. A dresser with a necklace tree held several pendants and rings.

Snowy will like one of those.

Kita crawled along the ceiling like a spider until she was above the handler. Taking a vial from her belt, she pulled out a length of string soaking in a potent poison made by Barb. Slowly, she uncoiled the string until it was above the target's mouth. A few drops fell from the saturated string.

To make sure, Kita carefully poured more poison onto the string. It ran down and fell into the handler's mouth. As Kita recovered her string, she listened for the handler's breathing to stop. He convulsed, and his head lolled to one side.

Kita flipped down from the ceiling. Curious about the missing space, she tried several places she thought might have a switch. When she found nothing, she resigned herself to checking the bookshelf, studying the dust and marks on the wood. When the shelves provided no clues, she checked the books, starting with the most obvious.

She found fingerprints in the dust on top of a large book. Kita pulled on it gently. There was a click, and the neighboring shelf opened.

Use your finger to see and make sure it's empty.

Kita stuck her finger around the corner. The room was empty but full of scroll cubbyholes. She entered the room and pulled a scroll from its rack. Looking it over, it was information on the Duchess of Trent's affair with the Earl of Campbell.

Pulling some of the other scrolls, she found information on various people.

He's not a handler trying to get into Cunningham's court but an information broker.

This was a person you came to when you needed dirt on an enemy. He'd collected information on most of the nobility from the number of scrolls.

Kita didn't have time to read them all, but her intelligence group did. Finding a scroll tube and a case, she loaded as many scrolls as possible. She scanned the headings of each scroll to see if it had anything to do with Cunningham, his plans, or interests.

When she finished, she'd taken a third of what the information broker had.

I'll let those who find it sort out the rest—going to be some interesting days in court.

Kita body slung the tubes. The case would be difficult to get out, but she'd find a way.

On the way out, she pinched a pendant with a large ruby.

She went to the bedroom window. She undid the lock, took a string, and tied it to the latch. Opening the window, she looked down to ensure the guards were busy elsewhere.

As she struggled to fit through the window, voices came from the path below.

"You going to share that?" a voice demanded.

"I found it. Go get your own."

"Like you can drink all of that. Give me a swig."

Kita was half out of the window.

Oh, please don't look up.

She freed her left wing, floated against the wall, and turned invisible.

Below her, the two guards arguing over their booze walked down the path and around the corner.

When they were gone, Kita took off over the city toward the inn.

N O ONE WAS AWAKE when Kita arrived, so she took her prize upstairs to her room. To her surprise, Snowy was sleeping in her bed. Kita raised an eyebrow but cleaned her kit, ensuring all her bombs and other gear were ready.

Not being tired, she went downstairs to find something to eat. Snowy was waiting for her as she came out with three plates of food.

"I take it you were successful?" said Snowy grumpily.

"I was, and I brought the intel people interesting things to look at. How were your cats?"

"Fine. I came back two days ago to wait for you."

"Why would you do that?"

"Because I was hoping you'd be done early."

Kita looked sideways.

"I said it would take three days. We had to be meticulous. This wasn't an easy job."

"You could still have taken me."

"Well, I'll take you on the next one. Oh, here I pinched this."

Kita pulled out the ruby pendant.

"Did you steal this?"

"Ah, he was dead, so no."

Snowy frowned.

"It's nice, but the chain is gold, and my bangles are silver."

Kita smiled.

"No problem. The Guild has jewelers. We can get a silver chain or mount it to a bangle."

"I'd need more to match."

"Ah, I'll see what favors I can call in. Don't worry. We'll find something."

"You need to think more about when you give a gift."

"Alright. I didn't know what you liked."

"I like things that match, are expensive, and prestigious. This is none of those."

"I'll do better next time. I still want to take you out. I know a great restaurant not far from the inn."

Snowy sneered. "You're going to take me to some slum?"

"It's nice, clean, and the food is excellent."

"You're the Commander of the Legion of Yorq. You should be taking me to the nobles' quarter."

Kita rubbed the back of her neck. "I don't know how well received I'd be."

"If you dressed the part, no one would question you. Instead, you dress like a hoodlum."

"Thief or assassin, there is a difference."

"Not that I've seen."

Kita scowled.

"I'll take you out and show you the difference. I'm hungry. Come tell me about seeing your war cats, and I'll tell you about my assassination and what I found."

KITA SAT IN A back corner, reviewing the scrolls and papers she'd taken from the broker. She divided things into four piles. One that pertained directly to the Legion and Cunningham, a pile for her intelligence to investigate further, some for the Shadow Guild, and useless political and personal information that no longer existed.

At the bar, thieves came and went, talking to Glen. After a visit, he came over.

"Finding anything good?"

"I've got a stack for you. More than a few people are talking."

"Hmmm, I'll have to send a reminder about that."

"Here."

Kita gave him the Shadow Guild stack.

"I'll probably have more later."

"That might have to wait. Reports say some general has taken over your Legion and kicked all my thieves out."

"Bloody moons. Who could that be? None of the generals from the other Legions would do that. Where the hell is Cowboy? He shouldn't let that happen."

"Sources say everyone in your camp thinks you're dead. Zidin went to join some Arconians, and Cowboy left to track Angus."

"It's been four days! They should wait at least a week to declare me dead. Guess I'll gather my stuff and go straighten this out."

"You need some muscle or thieves?"

"No. This is strictly Legion business. I need to show them I'm the commander, not a puppet of the Shadow Guild."

"THIS IS SO MUCH fun!" exclaimed Snowy as Kita carried her toward The Forges.

"You haven't flown before?"

"I have been on shuttles, but nothing like this."

Kita smiled, excited to see Snowy happy.

As they approached, Kita dropped lower so as not to be seen. In doing so, she attracted the attention of a bear in armor. It stood on its hind feet and roared.

"Is it upset?" Kita asked Snowy.

"No, he wants us to land."

"Alright." Kita spiraled down and landed next to the brown bear.

The bear and Snowy growled and grunted at each other.

"He says Frostbane wants to see you."

"No problem. Where is he?"

"The bear says he's coming."

Kita took Snowy's hand and gently tugged, thinking it would be a good impromptu date to see the meadow.

"What?" said Snowy, pulling her hand back.

"I thought we'd walk around the meadow while we waited."

"Seen one, seen them all. Take me flying instead." Snowy said something to the bear. "I told him we'd be flying over the meadow and would come when Frostbane arrived."

Kita picked up Snowy, flapped her wings, and rose into the air.

Snowy seemed more interested in the view than talking, and Kita didn't want to upset her.

Kita admired the view, too. She'd never flown this high, always staying close to the ground so she could see what was happening.

A deep roar announced Frostbane's arrival.

Kita banked toward him and landed before him, putting Snowy down.

"Damn bears ruin everything," Snowy muttered.

"Hey, Frostbane," said Kita. "Why are you out here and not in camp?"

Snowy translated.

"He said an old man kicked them and the war cats out."

"Who would do that? Not Forrester. I've got some old men, but none that would throw the bears and cats out. Something doesn't smell right, Frostbane, can you tell your bears to look for Cowboy? I'm not sure where he is."

"He says they've seen him heading toward Leedings. Once we're done with the bears, we can write a message, and my cats will take it to him."

"I don't know what's going on, and I'm not about to walk into a trap. You and Frostbane can go to camp. Tell them I'm alive and see what comes out of the woodwork."

"You're going to put me into a trap?" grumped Snowy.

"No. Once I figure out what's happening, I plan to land and take command. I hope that if the men hear I'm alive, they won't back this old man."

Snowy explained the plan to Frostbane.

The big bear scooped up Snowy, put her on his back, and then trotted toward camp. Kita turned invisible and followed from the air.

WHEN SNOWY ARRIVED IN the village, guards patrolled intersections in full armor and carried light rifles. A nervous guard stopped her.

"What is going on? Where is General Forrester?"

"Who are you?"

From the man's accent, Kita could tell he wasn't from the Legion of Yorq.

"I'm the Junior Commander of the Legion of Yorq."

Kita stifled a laugh from above.

"Excuse me, Commander. They are at the inn."

"Why is everyone at arms?" Snowy asked curiously

"You'll have to ask the generals."

"Ok, take us there."

Snowy slid off Frostbane and followed the legionnaire through the village to the inn. All the legionnaires she saw were not from the Legion of Yorq.

Forrester met Kita at the stairs to the inn.

"Mighty glad to see you," said Forrester. "I hope Kita's not far behind."

"We were separated after she freed me. What's happening?"

"That fool Barneky thinks he's in command of the Legion of Yorq and the whole damn operation."

"We've already had one shootout. Right now, the other legions have the Legion of Yorq encircled."

Kita swore to herself.

I can't disappear for three days without a mutiny. This would never happen to Angus, and he'd disappear for months.

"Without Commander Kita, we have no legitimate successor to the legion of Yorq."

"Before we split, Kita made me her junior."

"You have proof of that?"

Kita pressed her chain of command into Snowy's hand.

"I have her chain."

She held it up.

"Well, you're the closest thing we have to being legitimate. More than Barneky."

"We'll present you to the Legion of Yorq. Everyone knows you were with Kita."

"Cowboy can set this right. I have the animals out looking for him."

"Yes, he said he had some business to attend to. Come inside, and we'll plan our next move."

Snowy clipped Kita's chain to her ear as she followed the general.

E SCORTED BY A GUARD detail, Snowy, Forester, and several other generals from sister legions entered the Legion of Yorq camp. At the main tent, Barneky waited, grinning like a hawk. He had his guards flanking him.

I hope they don't have to shoot their way out.

"So, Forrester, come to give me what's mine?"

"At ease, General," snarled Snowy.

"I concur," agreed Forrester. "You are not a general staff member, nor are you in command of the Legion of Yorq. We have the rightful successor."

"We don't know if Angus is dead."

"We have first-hand reports from Commandant Hennessey That Angus died in the tubes fighting elves. Kita is the legitimate commander. In her absence, her junior can take command. You are not her junior, just a general."

"First I've heard of her taking a junior. Don't tell me it's the alley cat."

Snowy stepped forward and flicked her ear, shaking the chain of command. "She did choose me right after she rescued me and killed Angus."

"Forrester said he died in the tubes," scoffed Barneky, acting as if he had caught the others in a lie.

"Angus is a body snatcher. If he is killed, he can move to a new body. This time, he was a behemoth."

"Bull. Forrester, get out of the way and let a real general take charge. I'll have New London and Cunningham captured in two weeks."

"If you want my legion, General, you'll have to take it," challenged Snowy. "Or are you afraid of getting your ass kicked by two girls? Unlike Kita, I don't like keeping morons around. You just complicate things."

Snowy snapped her claws out, causing the legionnaires with Barneky to raise their weapons, and the guard detail's rifles met them.

Alright. It's time to end this before it gets out of hand.

Kita rolled over, dove for the ground, and landed hard, making a shallow crater with a *boom*. As the dust cleared, she stood, arms crossed, glaring at Barneky.

"I won't be keeping this moron around. You'll hang for this."

"What cockamamy pageantry is this?" demanded Barneky as Kita opened her wings.

"I'm the Angel of Yorq. Why wouldn't I have wings?"

"The Angel of Yorq really is an Angel!" a man with Barneky exclaimed.

"I am. Now, why are you here? Tell the Legion I want everyone formed on the parade field in an hour."

Some of the men with Barneky looked at him.

"Eh-hem," prodded Kita.

"Yes, Commander," they mumbled as they left with the others.

"You're dead," snarled Barneky.

"No. That's just you believing what you want to believe. I've been gathering intelligence on our enemy."

She held up the scroll cases, then turned to the guards with Forrester.

"Take Private Barneky into custody. He can get his sentencing later."

Four guards moved to detain the new private, but Barneky drew a light pistol and aimed it at Kita.

"I'll make sure you stay dead," he snarled.

Kita flashed forward, striking Barneky in the chest. He tumbled backward, landing on his back. She walked over, stepped on the hand holding the pistol, and put the other on his chest.

"Angels are more than wings, private."

She leaned down, heated a finger, and pressed it against Barneky's forehead.

"The mark of the condemned. We'll see how many join you."

"You don't have the stones to hang me or my men."

"*My* men that you led astray. I hoped giving you a combat command would earn your trust and loyalty. You did a good job with the VIPs. It's too bad you chose this route. Oh well. You can be replaced. Someone find Major Thorne. I think he's the next highest-ranking officer. Take him away."

The guards lifted Barneky to his feet.

"General Forrester, I assume you can find a place to hold him until this is over?"

"Yes, Commander. We'll put a guard detail on him."

"Good. Tell Generals Yang and Fedorov I need them to interrogate the entire Legion of Yorq to root out all those who supported Barneky after I give them a chance to surrender."

"I'll get their best interrogators."

"Good. Where is Cowboy?"

"He left when you didn't return. Said he had some business to attend to. I've already sent a group out to find him."

"And Zidin?"

"He left, too. He heard there was a group of Arconians in New London. Not sure what his motive is or if he'll join them."

"We need to find them, especially with the Arconians in Yorq. We don't want to be fighting an ally."

K ITA STOOD ON A platform with Snowy, and Generals Forrester and Thorne. Barneky, under guard, stood at the base.

Thorne called the Legion to attention.

Kita stepped forward and opened her wings.

"For those who think I'm dead, take a long look. Not only am I *not* dead, but I've gained wings as the Angel of Yorq. In my absence, I killed Cunningham's information broker and stole as much intelligence as possible.

"Now, I know some of you are loyal to Private Barneky. He successfully led you out of the tubes and rescued the VIPs. I understand why you'd trust him. But this time, he's led you astray. I'm not without leniency. If you step forward now, you'll be interviewed, and if it is found that you have only followed, I'll be forgiving and lenient. If I have to root you out, I will not be lenient. This is your chance. Prove your loyalty to me or Barneky."

Once the first few stepped forward, large groups joined them.

After the last stragglers had joined the formation, Kita turned to Forrester.

"Interrogate these men first, then do the rest. Anyone who should be here, but's not, can join Barneky in the stockade."

T HE MERRY JINGLE MADE Kita's head snap to the door. She darted over just as Cowboy pulled it open.

"You've got a lot of nerve coming back," she chided playfully.

"I went to see what our enemy was up to. And I'd finally gotten worried that something had happened to you. So, I thought I'd better take a look. Then I heard rumors of a girl with wings in Leedings. Figured it had to be you, so I high-tailed it there."

"I was gone so long because I went after Bart's handler and found a treasure trove of intel."

"Good. We'll see what matches. Where'd you get the feathers?"

"My inkling."

"Your inkling does good work."

I'd like to see him do better.

"We should compare notes and see what Cunningham is up to. Why is the camp on lockdown?"

"Yes, we should compare," said Kita, "but I need to explain about Barneky and his mutiny."

Cowboy raised his eyebrows.

"I'd believe it from him. I—"

General Fedorov appeared next to Kita, waiting to be noticed.

"Yes, General?"

He handed Kita a scroll listing the names of the leading mutineers they'd uncovered.

She looked at Cowboy, unsure of what to do.

"What is it?" he asked.

"They've found twenty-one people guilty. I can't hang twenty-one legionnaires. The rest will hate me."

Cowboy touched Kita's wing and gently pulled her aside.

"Then we don't. Here's a command lesson for you. A little sympathy and leniency go a long way. Put them all on the noose, but at the last second, reprieve the sergeants. Barneky and the officers are the ones who need to hang, as they're the leaders. This way, you hold your officers accountable and show the men you're not without mercy, nor do you favor the officers. You'll gain the men's loyalty and eliminate the troublemakers."

"I'm not bad for hanging the three, am I?"

"No. You're not being wicked. Stupidity is what's going to kill them. If Barneky had sent out a search party and confirmed your death like you did Angus', then it wouldn't be a criminal offense."

"They shouldn't have to die for stupidity."

"For some, like Barneky, that's the only way he'll learn."

Kita stood with Snowy and Cowboy in front of the twenty-one men to be hanged. As the commands were given, the condemned stepped forward onto the trapdoor, and an executioner from a sister Legion set the noose and placed a black bag over their heads.

Kita glided to the first man.

"Sergeant Garth, you understand your crimes and your sentence?"

"Y-yes, Commander. I'm sorry, Commander. If I'd known you were still alive, I'd never have gone along."

"I understand, Sergeant. And you are forgiven but must still pay for your bad judgment and crimes."

"Yes, Commander. I understand why."

"Good luck to you in the next life, Sergeant. I hope to see you there."

Kita went to each man. Most apologized and agreed they would never have joined if they'd known she was alive.

"You're going to ruin my Legion," Barneky snapped.

"My Legion," Kita corrected. "And your death will win me the hearts and minds of my men. A little sympathy and pageantry go a long way."

"You're not hard enough to kill us all."

"I am, and I promise you'll die slowly. The only thing worse than a spy is a traitor. I slow-hung a spy. Now, I'll do it to a traitor."

Kita reached around and repositioned the noose so it wouldn't break Barneky's neck when he fell.

"This is cruelty and savagery," yelled Barneky, but no one came to his defense.

"I've broken their loyalty to you. Now, I will gain their loyalty by simple mercy."

Kita stepped back to the front and nodded to the execution team. The steps were called out to the beating of a drum. She called a halt as the executioners moved to their levels for the final order.

She went to Sergeant Garth.

"Sergeant, as the power vested in me as Legion Commander, I hereby commute your sentence."

Kita removed the bag from his head, tears streaming down the man's cheeks.

"Your punishment will be to take the place of the executioners. You will pull the lever that may or may not kill the leaders of this mutiny."

After unbinding his hands, Kita waved him to the executioner's position.

Kita went down the line of sergeants, commuting their sentences and having them take the executioners' role.

"Commander," said a sergeant, "I won't kill them. I'd rather die with them. General Barneky saved me, and I believe he's better for the legion than you."

Inwardly, Kita sighed.

That makes four.

"If that is your wish, I will grant it."

Kita replaced the hood and moved to the officers.

"Captain Kildraw, I will *not* commute your sentence. As a leader of the mutiny, you led my legionnaires astray. I can't have disloyal officers or officers who act against better judgment. Good luck in the next life."

Kildraw pressed his lips together and bowed his head. "You'll bring ruin to the legion."

"With your death, I will make it stronger, loyal, and follow my orders. Goodbye, Captain."

Kita explained her decision to the other officer with tears in his eyes, then moved to Barneky.

"I knew you couldn't kill us all."

"I don't have to. I believe only you should hang, but as your counterparts have said, they'd rather follow you. So they are, to the end of a rope. I hope you're happy getting good men killed. I understand loyalty, but not stupidity. You made a stupid choice and now, you'll pay for it."

Kita drifted backward out over her legion.

"Pull the levers," she ordered.

There were four levers, so no one would know who killed the men.

The trapdoors opened, and the four men fell. Three had their necks broken when the ropes went taut. Only Barneky was too stubborn to die. He kicked his legs, swinging back and forth. When he finally stopped moving, Kita landed on the platform.

"Today we've learned a hard lesson—including me. I know some of you think this is unfair, that they didn't deserve this fate. But in battle, there can be no question who is in command. Barneky's crime was mutiny, but also stupidity. And we all know that stupidity on the battlefield will get good legionnaires killed. This includes questioning your superiors. I hope you all understand the lesson and apply it. The Legion of Yorq is no longer in containment. You can return to your duties. You're dismissed."

Kita returned to Cowboy and Snowy.

"You should have hung them all and sent a stronger message," grumbled Snowy.

"I know compassion has never been your strong suit," said Cowboy, "but she's gained their loyalty in sparing those men. Anyway, killing twenty-one men would be a waste. We need every man we have. I'm sure as hell glad you're not in charge."

"If I'd been in charge, there would have been no mutiny. I would have killed Barneky the first time."

"And kill a hero to most of the legionnaires. Kita did the right thing. She waited until her adversary made a mistake. Killing Barneky when he first arrived would cause more problems."

Then why do I feel like I lost?

K ITA CAME DOWNSTAIRS IN a foul mood and found Jeffrey in deep conversation with Earl Caezul.

I forgot Merc was one of the nobles we rescued. I wonder what he wants with Jeffrey?

Kita approached the pair.

"Merc, I hope you're finding the Legion's hospitality to your liking?"

"Kita! My, your brother didn't do your wings justice. They're magnificent."

She opened the left side to show off her feathers.

"I'm sorry your return has been marred, but the nobles stand ready to help in any way we can."

Jeffery scowled.

"It's been a long few days, but nothing I can't handle. I hope you and the other nobles are settling in. We need to solve who will be king before going further."

"Unfortunately, adding more nobles just escalates the conflict. Neither side has a viable candidate and are not military men, just political hacks. Those savvy enough to handle the throne are too old to lead an army."

"Did all the military men die with the king?" Kita asked, surprised.

"Yes, your brother is one of the few with youth and military experience."

"So, elect him. He'll be a happy puppet for you and the others."

Jeffrey turned red. "It won't work. It'll look like the Legion is putting me on the throne."

"So, what if I am? Fine. If you don't like it, I'll take my army and go clear my tubes. You can figure out how to beat Cunningham and where to get an army.

"Since when does the Legion back away from its commitments?" asked Caezul.

"My duties are to keep regional conflicts from spilling over. We're only involved in this civil war because Cunningham attacked us. I thought I owed it to my region to help. But if the nobles can't get their heads out of their asses, find yourselves a new army."

Kita spun on her heel and went to find Snowy. She was ready for bed.

E XHAUSTED FROM THE DAY, Kita held Snowy's hand as they went upstairs to their room. Kita flopped down on the bed, staring at the ceiling, anxiety gnawing at her.

"Why are you on the bed in your sneak suit? I don't want dirt in the sheets."

"I'm exhausted."

"So, go to bed."

Kita stood and undid her weapon's harness.

"Did I do the right thing?" she asked as she removed her scarf and mask.

"You should've hung all of them. They deserved it. Showing compassion is showing weakness. The Legion will be weaker, and others will try. Killing them all would have sent a message that you're strong, powerful, and not to be trifled with."

Kita flopped down on a chair.

"That's not what Cowboy told me."

"He's a senior researcher playing Legion. He doesn't know what it takes to be great. I'm Gaia's best researcher, and you don't reach that level without work, dedication, and self-sacrifice. Gerald also has no idea how to judge talent, or he would have put me in charge of his lab."

"Cowboy told me a little compassion can go a long way. The men I spared would be grateful and loyal, and the rest of the legion would see I'm merciful and hold everyone to the same standard."

Snowy scoffed.

"The standard you set so far led to mutiny."

"Maybe. There might have been some people who still couldn't get over the fact that a girl is the commander. Maybe I should have done something to them...made an example of someone. Punishing people for what they might do doesn't seem right. Just because they don't like me, doesn't mean they should be put in the stockade."

"You'd avoid a lot of trouble if you did."

Would I? Or would I have made it worse?

Kita stood and lifted her mask and hood. She fixed her scarf as she walked to the door.

"Where are you going?" demanded Snowy.

"I'll be back. I need to go ask the general staff a question."

"I think most are in bed."

"I'll find somebody. Don't worry. I won't be long."

"You better not be. I want a cuddle."

"I'll give you all the cuddles when I get back."

"What are you asking?"

"Just a nagging question on logistics."

Snowy waved Kita away.

Kita left the room and went to the first room on the right. She knocked on the door, and Cowboy answered.

He had his duster and hat off, but not his banana. His boots were next to the bed.

"Sorry to bother you, but I need guidance."

Cowboy raised an eyebrow.

"What's up?"

"You said killing the officers and Barneky was the right thing. Why do I feel like the bloody moons over it? And Snowy said not killing them all shows weakness."

Cowboy grunted.

"Darla's not a great one to take advice from. I hate to tell you this, but she's conceded and a leech who uses others to gain stature. I know you like her, but she will be a handful. Same as you're going to be a handful for her. Your rambunctious, opportunistic nature is going to drive her crazy.

"I'm not saying the two of you won't work, but it will take some compromise for both of you. I'll warn you, she's great at playing the victim."

"She hasn't done that yet."

"Darla's still in the early stages, trying to learn to manipulate you. However, you don't seem to be the type to fall for that. Why did you pick her to be your junior?"

"I didn't. She took it in the grand tradition of thieves and assassins."

"Not making her earn it plays into her modus operandi. I made that mistake. Seems now, so have you. But don't worry, I'll help whip her into shape."

"I don't need to watch my back, do I?"

"No. She's not that type. She needs someone, or in the case of the war cats, something to take care of her and treat her like royalty. At least, that's what she wants."

"I have no problem with her being my junior. I'll just have to watch her and ensure she treats the legionnaires correctly."

"Don't get me wrong. She's brilliant and could be an asset in planning attacks, but I wouldn't pick her to run people."

"She'll have to learn."

"If you can, you'll be the first."

Kita pressed her lips together.

"She's not trying to use me, is she?"

"Of course she is. But if you worry about whether she loves you, she does plenty. So don't worry. But if she ever gets out of hand, get me. I know how to put her in her place."

"That doesn't seem right."

"I wouldn't be harsh or physical. I know what to say to talk her down. I hope you'll take notes, and I don't mean to scare you, but you should know what you're getting into."

Kita made a contemplative noise.

"You do love her?"

"I...I don't feel love. I don't feel a lot of emotions. I care for and adore her. I think she's smart and could be a great asset. I do like her a whole lot."

Cowboy grunted.

"Anti-social. Not surprised."

"What does that mean?"

"Nothing, just a description of who you are. No different than me being an egotistical ass. You're going to have to decide if she's worth keeping around."

"She's nice to have."

Cowboy laughed.

"She is that. I hope you two can make it work."

"I want to make her happy."

"Once you learn the rules, it's not hard."

"Yeah, expensive, prestigious, and matches."

"Sounds about right."

"So, I did the right thing? I'm not showing weakness?"

"You did the right thing. Your command will be stronger for it. Like I said, it'll show the men you can be lenient and you'll increase loyalty."

"I need to spend time among them and get to know them like I knew my thieves."

"That's a good idea. Being seen helps the men get to know you. You're well on your way there. I heard about the drinking games. Shows you're not afraid to get down to their level."

"Busy day tomorrow. So what do you have for me?"

Cowboy chuckled.

"I was going to grab forty winks. You should do the same."

Kita nodded.

"Night."

She went back to her room and found Snowy in bed. With a happy hum, Kita undressed, slid in next to the cat, and cuddled her.

EIGHT

KINGS AND QUEENS
AVA MAX
HEAVEN AND HELL

As Kita exited the intelligence room, she found Cowboy, Jeffrey, and a few other nobles waiting, including Earl Caezul. In a hurry, she wasn't in the mood to chat.

"What do you want?" she said sharply.

"We have come to a consensus on who we wish to put on the throne," said Caezul.

"Congratulations. I hope he's a happy puppet."

"They've chosen me, Kita," said Jeffrey.

"Lucky you. Take it to General Forrester. I don't care as long as I have a body."

"Kita, stop," ordered Cowboy.

He motioned for the Angel to follow him into a side room. Kita huffed but didn't have a choice.

"What's the matter?" said Cowboy. "With a new king, we're moving forward."

Kita sucked in a breath as a mixture of rage and anxiety mixed in her chest.

"My Legion disintegrated when I was gone. Angus could leave for months, and I can't be gone for three days."

"Barneky was in a unique position that he had the respect and loyalty of some of the men. That doesn't make him any less of a fool. Proving you can command will earn you loyalty and respect. The discipline parade proved that. My sources tell me the men think highly of what you did. Don't forget you're still young and inexperienced at running a Legion. You've used some tricks from the Shadow Guild, which've worked. I won't tell them that you can metabolize alcohol as fast as you can drink it, if you don't."

"What does that mean?"

"It means you break down the alcohol faster than it can take effect on your body. You'll find it hard to get drunk."

"I figured that much out."

"Don't worry about your legion. General Thorne is smart, has field experience, and knows how to lead. Some time working with Forrester, he'll be an excellent general who can keep things together when you're gone."

"I just never want to have to do that again."

"I won't say it won't happen again, but it's your choice on how to handle it."

Kita sighed.

"Maybe I need to recruit some girls. There's too much—"

"Testosterone," Cowboy laughed. "Might not be a bad idea, if you can find some that can fight."

"I'll train them. They just have to be willing."

I

N THE INTELLIGENCE ROOM, a few new faces joined Kita's staff. Kita gave them the same security brief she gave everyone else.

"I need a status report from Jeffrey and Snowy."

Jeffrey stood up.

"The forces of Yorq are gathered in three locations. This locale is too far away to be a deterrent to protect most of our estates and states. We would like to petition that the entire force be moved to a more central location. The forces stand ready to defend at this time."

Kita looked at Forrester.

"The Legion forces are ready, save the Legion of Yorq."

Snowy went next.

"All the animals available who want armor have been outfitted. They're ready to move at a moment's notice, but food will be a problem. The farmland doesn't have enough wild game to support them, unless they want to give up their livestock."

"We can't starve our own people to feed these furballs," said one of Jeffrey's advisors.

Snowy gave him a dirty look.

"We could move the animals as close as possible and call on them when needed," said Cowboy. "We can take as many as we'll need for the camp. The rest can stay nearby in the forest or hills."

"That's acceptable."

"What about us?" said Murdock.

"We won't abandon you," said Jeffrey. "We'll leave a detachment of soldiers here to guard The Forges."

"Some of the animals will stay as well," said Snowy as she glared at Jeffrey's advisor.

Murdock nodded.

"What is the next step, Commander?" said Cowboy.

"While you're moving to the new location, I will pull the Arconian forces away from Cunningham. I'm not sure how long it will take. I'll need to go to New London."

"Who's going with you?"

"No one. This is an Arconian matter, not a Legion or Yorq one."

"You should go with someone—for your protection," said Cowboy disapprovingly.

"I'll have Sarge. He's always played that role." Kita turned to Yang. "Do you know where Zidin is?"

"No, Commander."

Cowboy shook his head.

"I will go with you to cover your back."

"Don't forget we'll have the Shadow Guild thieves and our operatives."

"All the better."

Kita folded her arms.

"You're coming whether I like it or not, aren't you?"

"Yes. Last time you went alone, you didn't show up for a week, and most people thought you were dead."

Kita huffed.

"Fine. It means it'll take us longer to get there. I was going to fly."

"That isn't advised. The last thing we need is to spook the locals," said Jeffrey.

"You know how hard it'll be to sit in a coach with these?"

"We all have limitations."

Kita rolled her eyes.

"General Fedorov, I'll need to send a message to Glen and let him know I will be in New London."

"No problem, Commander. I can have it on its way as soon as it is written."

"Good, then dismissed."

S NOWY GRABBED KITA'S HAND and pulled her up to their bedroom.

"What's the matter?" Kita asked, confused and resentful of the pulling as she shook out her arm.

"You're leaving me again."

"I know. But this is an Arconian matter."

"But you're still bringing Gerald."

"He didn't give me a choice."

"And what if I didn't give you a choice?"

Kita sighed.

"You're my junior commander. You're supposed to take over when I'm not around."

Snowy's ears and whiskers stood up.

"I'll be in charge?"

"I expect you to spend time with Forrester and Thorne learning to lead. You're in charge, but they're in command. You'll oversee the camp's breakdown as the Legion moves to its new location."

Snowy looked starstruck.

Maybe this wasn't such a good idea.

"Remember, you're a commander, not a queen. You have obligations to the legionnaires, just as they do to you. I expect them to be cared for and treated properly. They're not serfs or lab students or whatever else."

"Of course I'll treat them as they're to be treated as long as they treat me like I'm their commander."

"If they don't take it to Forrester or Thorne, let them deal with it. You're to observe and learn. Leave the command decisions to the staff."

I hope repeating that makes its way through. I don't want a problem when I get back.

"I'll be perfect."

"Alright. I shouldn't be gone more than a week."

Snowy tugged on a whisker, greed in her eye.

"Don't worry. Everything will be ready when you get back."

Kita smiled.

"I know you'll do well. Just—"

"I know, let Forrester and Thorne make the command decisions."

"Good. I've got some time if you want to cuddle."

A glint appeared in Snowy's eye.

"Or you could do what you did last time."

"I don't think I have time for that."

"You're the commander. Everyone waits on you."

"I guess I can do a quicky."

"**C**OMMANDER, WE HAVE A problem," the covered supply wagon driver called as they approached the gates of New London.

Kita and Cowboy were sitting in the back with a load of lettuce.

"What's going on?" said Cowboy.

"They're searching the wagons, and I don't see a spot to let you out."

Kita pulled back the front flap. The gate was fifty yards ahead with guards on the towers and others patrolling or checking carts. Kita ducked inside as a guard guided the wagon to a parking area with a line of wagons.

"How did they know we were coming?" Kita hissed at Cowboy.

"This probably has nothing to do with us. Cunningham's being paranoid."

A pair of guards arrived to question the driver and searched the wagon.

Kita looked at Cowboy.

"What do we do?"

"We might have to shoot our way out."

"Let's leave that as a last resort."

"You have a better idea?"

"Turn into your demon and sit there with your shotgun. I'll lie in the back as close to the tailgate as possible. You distract them, and I'll make them forget."

Kita extended a barb to illustrate her idea.

A guard came to inspect the cargo. He undid the tie downs and lowered the tailgate, exposing Kita.

Bloody moons.

The demon whistled to get the guard's attention. He jumped in surprise and backpedaled. Pushing with her wings, Kita lunged upward and grabbed a fistful of the guard's chainmail. She jabbed the barb into his overweight gut.

"We're only carrying lettuce," she commanded, then let the guard go.

The second guard, alerted by the noise, came to investigate.

"Everything alright?"

"Everything's fine. Just lettuce," said the first guard.

"What was the bang?" the second guard demanded.

"I...I don't know."

"Tell the guard to stick his head around and look," Cowboy whispered to the driver.

"I've got some bad hinges on the tailgate. Take a look if you want," the driver said with just enough of a mixture of calm and fear.

The guard grabbed the tailgate and yanked.

Cowboy pulled him in like he was inspecting the cargo. Kita injected him and gave him his instructions.

"The tailgate looks fine to me. You're free to go," said the guard after being released.

The driver snapped his reins, and the wagon made its way through the massive stone gate of New London.

AT AN INTERSECTION, KITA and Cowboy disembarked from the wagon.

She led them through the narrow passages of the New London slums. Some were so narrow she couldn't fit and had to detour into neighborhoods that weren't under Shadow Guild control, and she wasn't sure she wanted to be in them. Eventually, she found their destination. A shingle above the door said WANDERINGS in faint yellow and gold paint.

Inside had a warm and inviting vibe similar to the SWORD AND DAGGER in Leedings. Large casks of ale were behind a bar run by a tall, thin man. Tables full of patrons sat around an open fire pit.

Kita approached the barkeep.

"What can I do for you?" he said.

Kita put her hand on the counter and tapped.

"I'm looking for a place to stay."

"You're not one of my thieves."

"Glen sends his regards."

The tall thin man laughed.

"Is that little Kita under there?"

Kita pulled back her hood and lowered her mask. "How are you, Bull?"

"City's gone to shit. Surprised you could get in. Cunningham has guards posted everywhere and has sealed the sewers."

"I hope to fix that. I heard he hired a bunch of my mercenaries. I plan on taking them back."

"These aren't Glen's men, they're Arconians."

"I know and I'm their Rose...queen. I plan to take them out of the city and join my forces near Leedings."

"That would leave Cunningham with barely enough to secure the area around New London. What forces do you have?"

"I'm also the new Commander of the Legion of Yorq. I have an army of legionnaires waiting to make a move."

Bull whistled low.

"Glen wasn't kidding when he said you were the ambitious type."

"Just making the most of opportunities that present themselves."

"Well, you get the city back, and I'll be forever grateful. If you need rooms, take your pick—food is on the house. I'll waive the pet fee. You just need to pay for what you drink."

Kita smiled.

"Thanks. We'll get settled in and start looking for the Arconians."

"There's a big group watching the west curtain wall gate."

Their tapping also revealed two other large gatherings of Arconians.

Kita waved Cowboy over.

"This is my associate, Cowboy. He's been advising me on Legion matters. You haven't seen a big Arconian with a bald head, face like a shark, and carrying a giant sword, have you?"

Bull laughed.

"They're all big. I haven't heard of any with that description, but I'll have my thieves keep an eye out."

"If you find him, have them tell him the Rose is in the city, staying here. He's my Arconian advisor."

"Will do. Nice to meet you, Cowboy."

"Likewise. Hopefully, we'll turn the tables on Cunningham and drive him out."

"You've got our support. I'll have a detail follow you. I'm not about to explain to Glen how his little tuna got arrested or worse."

"That'd be great."

"Feel free to settle in."

Kita led Cowboy up a flight of stairs to a balcony lined with doors on one side.

"I thought we'd explore the city—if you're up to it?"

"It's been a long journey and I'm old—but not that old. Give me a few minutes."

THE MOON WAS HIGH in the sky as Kita and Cowboy approached the inner curtain wall gate. The gatehouse portcullis was down.

Through it, Kita could see Arconians mixed with soldiers wearing yellow crane smocks.

"There they are," Kita whispered to Cowboy.

"How are you going to convince them you're you?"

Kita swept off her hood and lowered her scarf and mask, then made her roses visible.

"Help me lift the portcullis."

They picked up the gate and slipped underneath.

"This better work or we will have to fight our way out."

No one had seen them yet. Stepping partially into the light to keep her wings hidden, Kita drew Dawn.

"Warriors of Arcone, your rose calls you to my sword."

Everyone turned to look.

A large Arconian, almost the size of Zidin, approached bearing an axe and shield. He slung them on his back and said, "Marie, is that you?"

He stopped in front of Kita and inspected her roses in the firelight.

"My, the years have been kind to you, lass. Your brother misses you."

"You're...you're talking about my mother?" gasped Kita.

"Are you Marie's daughter?" said the Arconian.

"Yes. My name is Kita Logine of Clan Mackay. I'm the new Rose."

"Crushing Depths be praised!" he exclaimed. "Clanfolk, our rose has returned! And that makes me your uncle. I'm Xeen."

"Mother never said she had a brother...or a sister. I met Neka."

"Where is she?"

"I don't know. She was creating a diversion so we could escape the castle from Cunningham's men."

"Where's Marie?"

"My...my mother is dead. Cunningham's men killed her as we escaped."

"That barnacle-covered barracuda! He's got the nerve to hire us after he kills the Rose's mother? This means war!"

Kita held up her hands.

"I already have war plans. I need you and the rest of the Arconians to leave New London and join us in the south near Leedings."

"On your word, the contract is cancelled."

"Do it."

"Are we to serve the new King of Yorq?"

"A, kind of. Me actually. I'm also the Legion Commander of Yorq."

"Not the same legion we were sent to destroy?"

A lump formed in Kita's throat as tears welled in the corner of her eyes.

"Yes."

"They march now. I'll send a runner to turn them around."

"Can...can you do me a favor and bring any legionnaires home?"

"Of course. Your legionnaires are our brothers and sisters. We'll bring them home."

"I'll go with them," announced Cowboy.

"Xeen, this is Cowboy, my Legion advisor. He can get you into the outposts and get the men to follow you."

"What's going on over here?" demanded a knight.

Kita stepped fully into the light, letting the firelight reflect off her feathers. "Taking back what's mine!"

"You're under arrest."

A rock clanged off the knight's helmet.

"Commander Kita is under the protection of the Shadow Guild, Captain Santos!" Yelled a thief from the top of a nearby roof.

"Nobody move," yelled a legionnaire holding a light rifle. His squad gathered on another rooftop.

"You're outnumbered, Captain," said Kita. "Surrender and you won't be harmed."

"Capture the legion commander, kill the rest!" Santos ordered Xeen.

"Our contract with Cunningham has been canceled. Warriors of Arcone, protect the Rose!"

What ensued could only be considered a scrum as the Arconians attacked the soldiers in close-quarters combat. From above, bolts and knives rained down from the thieves as the legionnaires fired their light rifles.

Kita found herself blocked by Arconians who wished to protect her.

Cowboy turned to his demon and fired his revolvers at the foot soldiers who exited from several doors.

A bolt hit Kita in the arm. Annoyed, she glided up to the crossbowmen, yanked the crossbow from him, then shoved it into him, causing him to backpedal and fall off the wall's far side.

Kita flourished her swords until they burst into flame and charged down the wall walk, dispatching crossbowmen. The men turned to flee, but Kita glided over them, cutting off heads and landing in front of the remaining soldiers. She grabbed the first soldier by his smock and tossed him from the wall. Kita spun and took the remaining three's heads.

It ended as fast as it began.

Wounded Arconians applied their healing balm, while the soldiers left alive were put out of their misery as revenge for Kita's mother.

"Is everyone alright?" Kita asked Xeen.

"A few dead. We'll send them to the Crushing Depths. Otherwise, all injuries are being attended to."

"Kita, give me an emissary to help me with the Arconians headed for the tubes. You and Xeen rally the Arconians and lead them to the camp."

"Xeen, do you have someone who can go with Cowboy?"

"Aye, but you'll be hard pressed to catch them."

Cowboy whistled, and his horse appeared.

"As long as they don't mind riding on the rump, we can catch them in a few hours."

"Jim is one of our senior leaders," said Xeen.

Cowboy mounted his horse and helped Jim up. He flicked the reins, and the horse galloped through the portcullis lifted by the Arconians.

"Do you know where the other groups are?" Kita asked Xeen.

"Aye. We should go to them and gather your warriors. Then we'll go to camp and move it to yours."

THE LINE OF ARCONIANS stretched for miles. Leaving the city was easy, as Cunningham didn't have the forces in and around the city to stop them. Kita's name was never mentioned, only that the new Rose canceled the contract for a better deal elsewhere.

As they went, Xeen introduced Kita to the clan and guild leaders. The people were jubilant over her sudden appearance, and everyone wanted to meet her.

Kita did her best to talk and greet everyone, but the familiar pain in her chest appeared after a few hours. The more people she met, the more her responsibility grew and weighed on her.

Finally, after meeting with the parrot guild, she could take no more.

"Xeen," Kita said in a shaky voice. "I need to go." She spread her wings and flew toward a hill with a rocky outcropping. She sat, trying to bring the fire in her chest under control.

Xeen climbed the hill and approached cautiously.

"Are you alright, lass?"

Kita looked up with a tear in her eye.

"I don't think I can do this. I can't be responsible for more people. The Legion is hard enough...but an entire nation? I have no idea what I'm doing with the Legion. How am I going to rule a nation?"

"You don't lead the nation, at least, not like a queen. You're the personification of the fighting spirit of Arcone. You lead us into battle and direct the Arconian ship's sails. The clans and guilds take care of the day-to-day governing. In a clamshell, you give us direction, and we decide how best to get there. The elders make sure our vision and how we proceed follow Tradition."

"I don't think I like this Tradition part."

"The elders are there to make sure Arcone's best interest is at heart. You can consult them about your vision, and they will guide you."

"I thought that was Zidin's job?"

"Aye, it is. But they speak for the Nation. Zidin is there to ensure you understand and carry out your duties as Rose."

"We're off to an auspicious start. But I just have to steer the ship and look pretty?"

"I would substitute fight for pretty, but yes."

"I think I can do that. As long as I don't have to maintain the ship."

Xeen laughed.

Kita sighed.

"I need to sit and rest. I'll catch up when I'm ready."

"Are you alright?"

"Just overwhelmed. That helped. Now I need time to digest it and see how it fits in with the rest of my plan as Legion Commander."

"Take all the time you need. We've a long way to go."

AFTER GIVING THE ARCONIANS a place to camp next to the Legion camps, Kita escorted Xeen into the village center, looking for the headquarters building. Kita stopped a patrol to ask for directions. The tiny town had an inn, schoolhouse, and temple. The inn was the headquarters, the schoolhouse was the secure intelligence room, and Jeffrey and the nobles took the temple.

The inn wasn't as nice as the last one. It was made of mud brick, wood, and a thatched roof.

Kita pushed open the door into a dark and dingy room with dirt floors. A small bar was in one corner, and the Legion staff had commandeered the tables.

Her arrival didn't go unnoticed. Cowboy called the room to attention and saluted her.

"What's this for?" asked Kita.

"Respect for one helluva commander, Commander."

"All I did was march with the Arconians."

"And that's part of it. You sending me and them to the tubes allowed us to rescue seven hundred men from five outposts. You're a hero."

Kita frowned and shook her head.

Cowboy put a hand on Kita's shoulder.

"What's the matter? Come talk to me."

The quiet room watched them go into the back to two bedrooms.

Cowboy closed the door.

"What's the matter?"

Tears trickled down Kita's face.

"It just proves I should have gone in earlier. I could have rescued more."

"We couldn't go any sooner. We didn't have the manpower. Those Arconians know how to fight. They didn't blink, facing down the ravagers. You, taking the Arconians, gave us the manpower we needed to rescue those we could. Now, we're in a good position to defend against an attack and challenge for the throne. Those legionnaires sacrificed themselves so we can win."

"How can I justify sacrificing them without telling them why? How can I live with that? They died not knowing why they were being attacked and why help wasn't coming. And that's my fault."

Cowboy shook his head. "They were legionnaires. They knew their duty—to defend the tubes at all costs. They weren't going to hole up and wait for rescue. Legionnaires are not scared farmers with pitchforks. They are professional soldiers. You belittle them by denying them their duty."

"They had no reason to die down there. Who gains from their deaths? Only me and my stupid plan. It makes me as bad as Cunningham and Angus. I can't be like that."

Cowboy sat Kita on the bed. "Is that what this is about? You're afraid you will end up like them?"

"I am like them." Tears trickled down Kita's face.

"You are not like them. Those are evil, despicable men. You're not. What sets you apart is that you're trying to make up for your wrongdoings. Same as me."

"It hurts so much."

"I know it does. Now come, you look exhausted. Everyone will be here in the morning. We've commandeered the town. This can be your room."

"I am exhausted, but I have to get Xeen and the Arconians introduced and integrated."

"Leave that to me."

"Where's Snowy?"

"Pouting over in the Legion of Yorq's camp. When I arrived, she'd set herself up as queen. I had to put a stop to it, and I read her the riot act."

"She was supposed to be learning from Forrester and Thorne." Kita flopped onto the bed. "One more thing to worry about. Tell her I'm back and I could use a cuddle."

Cowboy chuckled.

"I'll send her. We'll see what mood she's in."

The door *clicked* as Kita fell asleep.

KITA AWOKE TO SHOUTING from a heated argument. She turned invisible and slipped out the door to listen.

"Where is Commander Kita, Commander? She should be here for these meetings," said Forrester.

"She's sleeping," said Snowy.

"I know you're together, but you need to keep that separate from your duties," said Jeffrey. "She's the theater commander, for stars' sake. She needs to quit being coddled and perform her duties."

"Kita is not being coddled," grunted Cowboy. "She needs sleep. She's been running for weeks nonstop. And the way her body functions when she does need sleep, she needs a lot. I'll tell her what we discussed. And when do you think she was being coddled? I know you slept last night. Are we coddling you?"

"I'm talking about yesterday afternoon and all those other times she's fallen apart. No one tells her to deal with it and grow up. You just run to hold her hand."

"You're mad I put her to bed? She's just added another thing to her plate with the Arconians. She's young and learning. Her body may be nearly indestructible, but her mind is not. It needs rest, just like yours. You've had years in the military, she's had a few months. Cut her some slack."

"She would learn her jobs faster under the stress," said Snowy.

Cowboy's eyes narrowed at the two.

"Have you ever seen what happens when she gets stressed? Last time, she killed a field of ravagers. That's her final release valve: killing things. What happens when there is no enemy for her to kill? I like to think she's found a better way with Darla."

"She needs to be here!" Jeffrey said, slamming his hand on the table.

"Be here for what?" Kita said, appearing into the room.

"For major command decisions!"

"I thought that's why I had you."

Kita motioned at the group.

"What are you doing up?" Snowy demanded.

"I couldn't sleep after you left, and I slept on a wing funny. Oh, and I'm hungry."

Kita went to the breakfast bar, grabbed all she could carry, and set her dishes down on the paperwork spread across the table the men were using.

"So, what is this major command decision that my presence is so desperately needed that you can't decide without me?" Kita said around mouthfuls.

"It's not that we can't decide," said Forrester. "I think King Logine is more concerned about you learning why we concluded what we did."

"You can't explain it to me afterward, so I don't have to listen to you argue for two hours? Speaking of learning, where's General Thorne? He was supposed to be learning from you."

"He's taking care of your Legion since the Commander and Junior Commander are too busy."

"Is that what you think?" said Kita. "I made her my junior because she's also my girlfriend? That we're dumping our responsibilities on you, General Thorne, and the rest?"

"Don't answer that, General. Kita, calm down," said Cowboy.

"General, when I got here, I said there were two people who could argue with me. That's Cowboy and Zidin. If you don't like something I've done and don't have the stones to bring it to me, then take it to them.

"Cowboy hasn't questioned my decisions. I expect Snowy to do as I did, follow me around, and learn. Did you know there is a manual for every position in the Legion, including the commandant? Yet none for commanders. I get to make it up as I go along.

"If you think I'm not paying attention to what goes on in my command, you're mistaken. I have a lot of time on my hands at night. I go through the reports and logs in headquarters. I chat with the night guards to see how things are. I study manuals and update boards. I am not back here goofing off.

"I'm going to chalk this morning's little tantrum up to the added stress of the Arconians arriving. Here's your next order. I want to move on New London in three days."

Kita folded her arms and glared.

"Lady Rose, I hope I can make it on that list as qualified to argue with you," said Xeen.

"As long as you're not questioning how I handle my legion. You have a suggestion?"

"Yes. We move on Leedings instead. Its defenses are much weaker."

"What do we gain by taking Leedings?"

"Cunningham's forces need more supplies than the capital can produce, and they import through Leedings. If we cut his supply route, it will weaken his forces in New London."

"Wouldn't we cut them off if we siege the capital?"

"There is no navy to block the port of New London. We must think of our supply lines. Leedings would give us a port and the money the city generates. This way, when we attack New London, they will not be at full strength, and we will be stronger."

Kita nodded.

"Makes sense. Fine, we leave in three days."

Xeen raised a hand. "Give us two weeks to train with your armies. Even that small amount will give us an edge over the soldiers guarding the city."

"Can we afford to wait that long?"

"Cunningham has made no moves against us," said Forrester. "I'm sure he's trying to compensate for losing the Arconians. It'll take time to import more mercenaries, if Cunningham can find them. If he can't, his only strategy will be to wait until we're closer to the cities to keep his supply line short."

Kita looked around the table. "Does anyone have a problem with this?"

Everyone shook their heads.

"The more time we have, the better we'll be," said Cowboy.

"Ok then, make it happen. Forrester, Jeffrey"—Kita drew Dusk and picked up a piece of meat with the flat of the blade—"when I get stressed, I get deadly. And I don't care who I take it out on."

The meat was cooked, burned, and then charred to dust. Kita blew the dust away.

"Come on, Snowy. Let's go have a look at our Legion that we've been ignoring because I'm too busy being coddled."

"THEY SEEM TO BE getting the hang of it," Kita said happily, as messages were sent to a unit using the new flag system under development.

Forrester grunted.

Kita frowned. Forrester had refused to say anything since the morning at the inn. Concerned, she pulled Cowboy aside.

"I wouldn't worry too much about it. It won't affect how he does his job. He is too professional. You did make him look bad by calling him on what he said. You heard the whole thing?"

"So, what if I called him on it? He was wrong, and I told him. I heard the argument and listened. I didn't appear earlier because I wanted to know the grievances. He crossed the line when he went after my personal life—what little there is."

"You have to remember these guys have worked hard to get where they are. They have big egos. Forrester is better than most. Making them look like fools, deserved or not, in public, makes it worse. You could have walked away or, better, sent him away—it helps reestablish who's in charge of whom. Understand?"

Kita nodded.

"He had no business going after Snowy and my relationship."

"I know, but it's one of the few handles people have on you. When there isn't much, they'll grab what they can. You'll have to get used to defending yourself."

A Legion runner approached and saluted.

"Yes, what is it?" Kita said while returning the salute.

"There's a man at the camp entrance asking to speak with you. He's come with a dozen rather unsavory-looking men. He told me to show you this if I found you."

The legionnaire took a ring from his pocket.

"He said you'd let him in. We weren't going to, but one of the intelligence officers said to take it to you."

Kita took the ring. It had a stylized S and M carved into a simple gold signet ring. It belonged to Glen, but he wouldn't part with it unless it were a dire emergency.

"Problem?" said Cowboy.

"Glen wouldn't be here if it weren't serious. I'll go find out what he wants. You stay here and keep an eye on things."

Kita took off and flew to the main gates of the camp. Glen and his men waited while Arconian and Legion troops surrounded them. Kita landed in the center.

"At ease," she ordered. "You can go about your business. These men are with me."

The legionnaires left. The Arconians stepped back but refused to go. Mentally, Kita shrugged. She didn't want to argue with them.

Kita handed the ring back to Glen.

"Dad, what's wrong?"

Dad looks very old all of a sudden.

"They've taken her."

"Mom?"

"Yes."

"When? How? Where?"

"They took her two nights ago. We fought them, even killed two Mongulesian, but they grabbed Barb and disappeared. The men traced her to the Tower of New London. I'm afraid they'll kill her if we try to rescue her. I hoped you could get her out."

That was the politest You Owe Me *I've ever heard.*

"Of course I'll help. Tell your men I'll meet them at the Wanderings to go over how we'll get her out."

Glen nodded.

"Good. Do they know where she is in the tower?"

"No."

"Then I'm off. Cowboy and Snowy know who you are. They'll take care of you."

Kita gave instructions to the Arconians to take Glen to Cowboy. With a large flap, she lifted off.

NINE

DEAD AND BLOATED
STONE TEMPLE PILOTS
GRUNGE!

K ITA LANDED IN THE middle of the tower and whistled to get the guard's attention. When they turned, thieves came over the walls and backstabbed them.

She put her hand over the lock on the hatch and melted it, then went down the ladder and searched the level. Shaking her head to the other thieves that Barb wasn't there, they went down a spiral staircase to the next level.

Kita dispatched the surprised guard with a throwing knife. The thieves checked the cells, but they didn't contain Barb. None of the prisoners were guild members, so Kita left them.

On the second level, they found Barb. Kita melted a large lock that hung on the door. Inside, the plush room was worthy of a noble bedroom, just with bars on the windows. Barb sat in a chair with a chain shackling her wrist to the wall. Kita waved the men to Barb.

"Kita, is that you?" said Barb.

"Don't worry, Mom, we're here to get you out. Deek, get her out of those chains. I—"

"Hey, Boss. We've got trouble coming," a man in the hallway called.

Kita stuck her head into the hallway and heard the *clank* of metal and *thud* of heavy footsteps coming up the stairs.

"We need to go," Kita said to everyone.

Deek came out with Barb.

"Up the stairs," said Kita as she drew her swords. "I'll hold them off while the rest of you escape."

At the other end of the hall, the wall collapsed with a *crash,* revealing a large metal disk as tall as Kita. A humming noise came from the device as an invisible force pulled Kita toward it. Any free metal was pulled along with her. Unable to resist, Kita slammed against the disk, held fast, and unable to move.

I guess there are drawbacks to metal alloy bones.

One of the other thieves came back.

"No, go! Get Barb out of here. This was a trap meant for me. I don't want anyone else stuck."

The thief nodded and hurried down the stairs after the others.

The other doors in the hallway opened, and guards dressed in leather and carrying clubs exited. Cunningham stepped out of the door nearest Kita with a man wearing a hood.

Did I see something flicker?

"Well, well," said Cunningham, "The Master was correct. Our little Katrina Logine can be caught if you have the right trap."

"Cunningham, you snake! Let me go so I can kill you!" Kita snarled.

"Interesting choice of words, my dear. May I introduce you to my advisor, Serpentine."

The other figure removed his hood, revealing a man with solid black eyes and green scales covering his face. A long, thin tongue darted out when he opened his mouth, and two curved fangs unfolded.

"You're more of a snake than he is."

Kita spat at Cunningham.

He slapped her face.

"Think of that as your first lesson in respecting your betters. Though we might finish an earlier lesson."

Lustfully, he ran a hand down Kita's armored front and between her legs.

"The Master gave specific instructions not to touch her or do anything that might set off her berserking ability," Serpentine hissed.

Cunningham's lip curled.

"I guess I'll have to get my fun in other ways. I have a lot planned for you, Kita. How much pain can a fallen angel take? I've brought in a specialist just for you. But first, Serpentine would like to take the Master's share of the prize."

Serpentine pulled a syringe from his belt and drew a large vial of blood from Kita's arm. When he finished, a block of ice encased the syringe. He tucked the frozen vial in a bag.

"Get her downstairs and tell Dmitri to be ready for a visitor."

Cunningham kissed Kita's cheek.

"You'll be begging for me before this is over."

Kita gnashed her teeth.

"I'll die first."

The guards wheeled Kita down to the basement, attached to the disk. It was a bumpy trip down lots of stairs. They took a confusing route through the prison's basement and delivered her to a small room with a set of odd-looking tools laid out on a bench. More hung on the wall behind it. She was left alone to study them.

AN OLDER MAN, WHO looked like someone's grandfather, entered the room. His overweight stomach was hidden under a heavy leather apron. He had a happy face, but his hard eyes made Kita worry.

"Hello, my dear," the old man said with a warm smile. "I have the privilege of working on you."

His smile resembled the smile grandfathers gave their grandchildren to reassure them.

Kita didn't find it reassuring.

"You're Dmitri?" Kita said, trying to calm her nerves.

"Yes, I am Dmitri the Dismemberer, as those who find my work disturbing call me. Others call me Dmitri the Deliverer for being able to extract what I need from a subject."

"And what are you to extract from me?"

"That's the curious thing. I am to extract nothing, just cause pain. Normally, I'd scoff at such a meaningless task—any idiot can cause pain. I took the job after they described your unique abilities. It sounded like an interesting challenge."

"I bleed like everyone else. I don't know if I can scream as loud as some."

"Not everyone can heal as you do."

"That only goes so far."

"I guess we'll find out how far it goes, won't we? If you pardon the intrusion, I have been instructed to remove as much of your clothing and weaponry as possible. My employer is interested in keeping it."

"Well, since you were nice enough to ask, feel free," Kita said sarcastically.

The old man worked diligently to remove what he could.

Ugh. His hands feel old and leathery. He could have warmed them.

"Now, my dear, this is going to hurt," Dmitri said as he picked up a set of spikes and a hammer. He placed a spike over her hand and struck it with the hammer.

In retaliation, Kita heated the spike. The temperature climbed fast enough to burn Dmitri badly. The spike melted, and the hole in her hand closed.

"Impressive, but this is not a two-person game."

Whistling, Dmitri went to the workbench and came back with a hooked knife. He grabbed her left breast, and Kita screamed.

D MITRI WAS GONE WHEN Kita awoke. Pain ebbed and flowed through her body. She struggled to remember what had happened, though a part of her was glad she couldn't. A whistle from the hallway sent shivers down her spine.

Dmitri entered the room with his reassuring smile.

"Ah, good, you're awake, my dear. You have quite the pain tolerance. Let's have a look at you."

Dmitri studied Kita.

"Well, it looks like things regenerated. The ear and other fleshy parts I expected. The hair and fingernails are a surprise."

The removal of Kita's hair hurt her vanity more than her body. She was furious over her missing nipple.

How long is it going to take to grow back? I don't want to be lopsided for Snowy.

"I understand you have a unique skeletal structure that's said to be indestructible. I think we should test that assumption. What do you think?"

"To the bloody moons with you," hissed Kita.

"Such language from a beautiful young thing. Your mother must not have taught you your manners. Let me reinforce the lesson."

He grabbed a knife, pliers, a spreader, and a wood block from the bench.

THE FAMILIAR WHISTLE WOKE Kita.

Dmitri came through the door, smiling.

"Awake, my dear? Good. This morning over breakfast, I was thinking you're the first person I've ever worked on with wings. I've plucked a few chickens in my day. I wonder if it's the same."

Dmitri puttered around his bench before approaching with a pair of pliers. Kita whimpered before he started.

"Now, now, no need for that yet. Let's have a look at you. Hmmm, interesting. Regeneration has slowed. I would have expected the areas from our first session to be healed. The newer areas have only started to close. Interesting."

That's because I'm getting hungry, and I can only heal so much at once, jackass.

"Shall we start plucking?"

K ITA COULDN'T REMEMBER WHEN the tears stopped flowing, but she couldn't cry anymore. She begged him to stop and kill her, but it only came out as an airy wisp.

Her body gave up and stopped regenerating as her stomach ached from hunger.

Images of Cunningham visiting several times stuck in her mind. Kita didn't remember anything after that. She floated in and out of consciousness, unable to process what was happening to her.

S OMETHING ROUSED KITA FROM her unconscious state.
A guard stepped away with a vial of smelling salts.

She strained to focus. Dmitri's tools were gone, and Cunningham stood before her with a sick smile.

"Money well spent. Don't you think? I had to buy him a whole new tool kit to work on you."

Kita tried to answer, but she couldn't form any words.

"No need to answer. Dmitri has left you in quite the state. Would you like a look? He said you'd developed a way to see without your eyes. The Master will find this most interesting."

A mirror appeared in front of Kita's face. She didn't have the consciousness to react. Her mind couldn't put what she saw into any relational context. The creature in front of her couldn't be her. Any distinguishable features on her face had been removed. Whatever it was, it wasn't her.

"I had hoped for a better reaction. No matter. Dmitri has done all he could. Now, I get my turn. I hear you like to slow hang traitors—like the spy you left in Leedings. I thought it would be a fitting punishment for you. I understand you have metal or whatever bones, so breaking your neck isn't a problem. You have twelve hours to think about your mistakes in life before you swing."

K ITA AWOKE ON A platform attached to the disk, overlooking a crowd. A noose around her neck didn't cause alarm. Someone was talking, but she had no idea who or why. The blue sky was filled with fluffy, white clouds. She liked it.

It seems like forever since I've seen it.

In the front row, a group of hooded monks bowed their heads, chanting. The guards pushed everyone in the crowd back, but not them.

Who are they?

Kita's stomach rumbled and ached. She wished she had something to put in it.

Aren't the condemned supposed to be given a last meal? Condemned— I'm condemned, aren't I? I'm going to die.

Tears burned as they fell down her face.

I'm not ready to die yet. There's something important out there for me...I wish I could remember what it is...

Whoever was talking finished, and the executioner moved to the lever, waiting.

Cunningham confronted Kita.

"Such a waste. Pity. You're as much a fool as your father. Though, according to him, killing you would do him a favor. I'll catch up with him sooner or later. Not that it matters. Arbol is in ruin, as is most of the region. It's good to be king."

He laughed and waved at the executioner.

"Drop her."

The lever was pulled back with a *clack*, and Kita fell.

She jerked to a stop when the rope went taut. The weight of the electromagnet caused her neck to stretch. Kita gasped for air as the rope dug into her.

A gunshot echoed through the square.

Kita fell to the ground.

The monks in the front row collapsed into one and jumped under the platform. A hand with a long claw appeared and touched the electromagnet. There was a loud *pop*, and Kita slid into the monk's arms.

The monk looked at Kita and whispered. "Don't worry, kitten. We'll get you out of here."

Snowy dashed through the crowd as disguised guildsmen attacked the guards. In the chaos, Snowy pushed through the crowd to the courtyard's exit. She handed Kita up to Cowboy on his horse, Nightmare, and jumped on the back.

With a snap of the reins, the horse galloped through the New London streets.

Shadow Guildsmen stationed along the route kept the way clear to the main gate. Bells tolled in Cowboy's wake as guards ran to shut the main gate's portcullis.

Cowboy spurred his horse faster and barreled through the opening as the portcullis crashed closed behind him. As he galloped through the countryside, a plume of dust signaled Cunningham's knights were in pursuit. He rode to a large thicket, slowed Nightmare, and picked his way through the woods. Cowboy stopped at the far side of a small clearing.

The sound of hooves crashing through the thicket announced the arrival of their pursuers. Cowboy drew a revolver as Snowy hopped off and bared her claws.

The pursuers trotted into the clearing and confronted Cowboy and Snowy.

"Surrender the girl and we'll kill you quickly!" yelled the lead knight.

"Come and get her!" Cowboy yelled back.

"You heard the fool, men—"

A rock clanged off the knight's helmet. From the underbrush, hundreds of angry Arconians, bears, and war cats fell on the pursuers.

Cowboy exited the woods and galloped back to the Legion camp.

KITA HOVERED IN AND out of consciousness. Different voices came and went. Some would stay for a long time and talk to her. Others would say a few words and leave.

K ITA, ON THE EDGE of consciousness, listened as a man and woman spoke.

"My men found her swords and sneak suit in a room in the castle's basement. The room was worse than a slaughter-house. A pile of body parts and flesh must have been hers. My men brought back the bones. We aren't sure if she needs them or not."

"Thanks," said a sweet voice. "Her bones will speed up the healing. Any word on the person who did this?"

"Not yet. We're kicking in every door in New London and checking under every rock outside. We'll find him. No one can hide from the Shadow Guild for long. What do you want us to do when we catch him?"

"I don't know if she'll want first crack at him. I know I do, you do, and there's a list a mile long. Bring him here. If she's awake, she can decide what to do with him."

Kita drifted back to unconsciousness.

K ITA AWOKE AND TRIED to ask for water. The words wouldn't form in her mouth. Something was missing, and she wasn't sure what. She tried repeatedly, but the person looking at her didn't move. Frustrated, she went to sleep.

V OICES BROUGHT KITA AROUND. Something was pressing on her arms and legs. People appeared near her head, and they had something in their hands. They touched her face, and it hurt. Hands grabbed her mouth and forced it open. She tried to resist, but she was too weak. They shoved something into her mouth and down her throat. Scared, she slipped away.

A RASPY VOICE IN the darkness brought Kita back to the edge.

"They've sent forces to the estates under attack. How's she doing?"

"Better, I think," said the sweet voice. "She has lots of new growth. The feeding tube was a good idea. The body has absorbed the bones Glen brought."

Glen—the name was familiar. A friend or family member? A lover?

I wish I could ask, but I'm too tired. Maybe later.

Kita drifted back to unconsciousness.

T HE BLACKNESS FADED AS Kita floated to the surface. She burst into consciousness like a swimmer coming up for air. The world came into focus. She was alone, and something was causing her to gag.

With stiff arms and deformed hands, she reached to her mouth and found a tube. She pulled it out, causing her to gag more. She was missing body parts that should be there. Her left-hand fingers were missing or partially there. On her right hand, half of her palm was gone.

What else am I missing?

She caught on a weird tube in her arm when she tried to sit up. Pulling it out with her stumpy fingers hurt, and it only came out in one direction.

Kita slid to the edge of the bed. Standing for more than a few seconds was tiring. Her legs didn't want to hold her, and she kept teetering to one side.

She sat on the edge of the bed. Looking down, she discovered half of her left foot was gone, and she was missing toes on the right. When she tried to stand again, she tried to compensate for her missing foot and fell to the floor.

I need practice. I will master this.

She kept trying until she could walk around the room without stumbling. Tired, she sat on the bed and scratched an itch on her face. It hurt.

There was a small mirror on the wall. Kita walked to it.

What she saw was not what she thought she should look like. Both her ears were deformed. Her lips were gone—along with most of her teeth. A nub was left of her tongue. Large scabs covered where her roses used to be. Only two holes remained of her nose. Her short and patchy hair hung plastered to the side of her head.

Was I turned into a monster?

A new sensation triggered a new need. She was hungry. She made her way to the bed.

Glad to see you're awake. Standing and walking are impressive for someone in your condition. The tube was for food. It's in that machine next to the bed. Unscrew the lid and eat it all. It'll speed up your regeneration.

Kita traced the tube to the machine. It took a few tries, but she unscrewed the lid. Inside was food. It didn't taste good, but she drank the entire container anyway. Exhausted, she climbed into bed and fell asleep.

A SET OF VOICES came to Kita in a dream.

"I found her like this. Do you think she got up?" said a sweet voice.

"How'd she get the feeding tube and IV out? She doesn't have any hands," said a raspy voice.

"The food mixture is gone. I think she got up and was hungry."

"That girl doesn't know when to quit. Let's let her rest. Maybe the next time she gets up, she can talk to us."

"Ok. I'll bring more food and leave it out for her. Healing takes a lot of energy."

The voices left, and Kita drifted off into the ether.

K ITA AWOKE WITH A start, her mind alert. Sitting up, she examined her body. Her left hand had all five fingers, but nubs on the right. Kita's feet were nearly whole, only missing a few toes on her left foot. Encouraged, she slid out of bed and limped to the mirror.

Her face showed improvement. She had a nose. Gone were the scabs on her cheeks, and her eyelids were back, though her eyes remained gone. Her ears looked almost human, and her lips were nearly complete. Opening her mouth, she found a few teeth and most of her tongue.

She tried to speak, but could only make a few sounds. After practicing, she could say whole words.

Good enough for now.

On a dresser sat her sneak suit and weapons.

A chill went up her spine, and fear tingled in her nailbeds. The familiar ring of pain formed in her chest as panic gripped her.

I can't do that again. I can't. The pain is too much. Look what it's done to me.

She collapsed into a corner and clutched her head. Her body tensed, and she couldn't breathe. She couldn't open her mouth, her jaw clenched, keeping her from crying for help.

Kita wanted out but was trapped in a forever-deepening pit of despair. She wanted to die. That was a way out, a release. But her body refused to move, unable to end the torture. Instead, she sat, letting the fear race through her head as the pain in her chest felt like it was going to explode. *Please stop, please. I'll do anything...Anything...I won't touch a sword again...I'll give it all up...Just make it stop.*

But the panic attack refused to relent. As the panic grew, she hyperventilated until she could get no air and passed out.

K ITA CREPT OUT OF her room carrying her sneak suit, kit, and weapons. She wore a peasant girl's dress she found in a drawer.

In the center of the inn were Cowboy, Snowy, Forrester, Jeffrey, and several other generals standing around a table looking at a map with colored blocks positioned around it.

Jeffrey saw her first and laughed. "I never thought I'd see you wear that. About time you recognized your place."

Everyone turned to look at Kita.

"Kitten! What are you doing up?" Snowy exclaimed. "You're not done healing. Go back to bed!"

Kita shook her head. "I'm done," she whispered.

"Done? Done with what?" said Jeffrey. "We've barely started taking on Cunningham."

"With these." Kita dropped everything, letting it clatter on the floor.

The room went silent.

"I'm sorry. I can't do this anymore."

"What do you mean?" said Cowboy gently.

"I'm leaving."

"Leaving?" demanded Snowy. "For where? Why?"

"My body, mind, and heart are broken. I can't do it anymore. You said there are spots of great beauty around The Mass. I'd like to see them. I'll start at Razor's Reef. Part of the beauty is watching its creation, right?"

"You can't leave," yelled Snowy. "What about me?"

"Yes," added Jeffrey. "You can't abandon your responsibilities just because the enemy wins a battle."

"You don't need me. Everyone does better without me. All I bring is trouble, misery, and pain. I'm sorry. I hope someday you can forgive me."

Kita trudged around the stunned group and opened the door. The cool night air hit her as she spread her wings.

"Damn that girl!" Snowy screamed in frustration. "We bust our asses to get her out of that city and now she wants to quit." She stomped to the door.

"Take it easy," Cowboy demanded, grabbing her arm. "Her spirit's crushed. Cunningham didn't have to kill her to take her out of the fight. If she leaves, we lose. Come on. Will go and get her back."

"You can't leave, not now," demanded Jeffrey. "We've got people strung out all over. She'll come back on her own."

Cowboy shook his head.

"She won't, and you're going to have to. Forrester can take charge of the Legion in my and Darla's absence. We're only running small actions right now, and we're winning. We'll be back in a week. Stick to the plan. Now, the longer we stand here jawing, the farther away she gets."

A tear fell from Kita's eyes as she flapped her wings and took off.

K ITA DANGLED HER FEET in the cool water of Razor's Reef. The water was clear to the bottom, and colorful creatures had taken root on the spire. A school of tiny fish nibbled at her toes. They tickled, making her giggle.

In the distance was the visitor's center. No longer were the tops of the spires barren. Plants had grown. Not very high, but Kita recognized some from her mother's room.

Mother said she came from islands. Were they like these? Is that where those plants came from?

The whinny of a horse made Kita jump and fall in the water. Swearing, she pulled herself out.

What is a horse doing out here?

You have visitors.

Kita looked toward the horse and saw Cowboy and Snowy dismounting. Cowboy looked sympathetic in contrast to Snowy's glower.

"What do you want?" Kita said, shaking the water from her wings.

"We've come to bring you back," snarled Snowy.

"Easy, Darla," said Cowboy firmly. "We've come to talk about what happened, how it affected you, and what we can do for you."

"Omega already fixed my eyes."

"I see." Cowboy laughed.

Kita cracked a small smile at the joke.

"I can't do it anymore. I'm tired of pain and death."

"Kitten, those are a part of life," said Snowy. Her sour expression faded somewhat.

"I know. But how much do they have to be? I can't take any more. I'm tired of hurting. I just want it to go away."

"So, you ran away from a little pain? You didn't even talk to me or anyone about it."

"Does this look like a little pain?" Kita shrieked.

"No. It looks like a lot," said Cowboy.

"It doesn't give you an excuse not to talk about it or run away," said Snowy.

"You don't know. You weren't there. You'll never know the suffering, agony, and heartbreak."

"That's true," said Cowboy. "But we're your friends—one of the things friends do his help each other through tough times. Whatever happened, we'll listen and comfort you. We'll do our best to make you feel better. But Darla's right. Quitting isn't the answer. It'll just let the pain fester and never leave. Talking to us will ease it and make it fade away."

Kita burst into tears.

"It hurt so much, and there was no escape or end. He kept coming back and talking in that fatherly voice, like he was playing with a grandchild. And whistling," Kita shuddered, "always whistling. All I want is for the torment to end."

"The physical torment is over," said Snowy. "We know the psychological recovery will take longer, but you're nearly healed physically. You need to move on."

"That's what I'm doing," growled Kita.

"You're dwelling on it. That won't make it go away, only make it worse."

"I agree," said Cowboy.

Snowy took Kita's hand and sat her down on the edge of the spire. She motioned for Kita to put her feet in as she dipped her paws. She put an arm around Kita.

"I thought you were mad at me," whispered Kita.

"I'm mad you left without talking to me. That doesn't mean I don't care about you. And right now, you need a hug and to be told things will get better and the worst is over."

Kita burst into tears and buried her head on Snowy's shoulder.

"I'm sorry I couldn't take it. I thought I was stronger. That I could take any amount of pain."

"You did take the pain and showed your strength by recovering. I'm impressed with your will to live. From what Glen told us about what they found, it would have killed anyone else. You are strong. Stronger than you realize. I'm proud of you for surviving and not giving up. I...I love you, and seeing your hurt makes me hurt."

Cowboy shook his head.

"I love you too. From the moment I saw you."

"You just like the tail."

Kita laughed through her tears. "It is epic."

"Will you return with us? If nothing more than to sit in the headquarters, watch, and listen."

"I'm not ready for that. I want to stay here for a while."

Snowy let out an annoyed sound.

"You know what? You're just like your mother. But instead of ten years of fighting, it's only taken you a few months to give up."

Cowboy's eyebrows went.

"W-what? I am not my mother!" Kita said angrily.

"She ran away from being Rose, isn't that what you told me? You're running away from being Rose and Legion commander."

"I'm *not* my mother."

"Then come back. You don't have to fight. You can just sit there. But, regardless, I'm not staying. I have a Legion to command."

Cowboy rolled his eyes.

"But...but...what if it happens again?"

"Believe me, Glen has his thieves kicking over every rock in Yorq looking for Dimitri. He'll be found, and you can have your revenge. Let that fuel you and override the self-doubt."

Kita hung her head.

If I stay here, I'll be safe.

You don't know that. There are sharks in the water.

If I go...I don't have to fight. I don't even have to lead. I don't want to lose Snowy. And I'm definitely not like my mother...or am I? I ran away from my responsibilities. If I stay and dump the Legion on Snowy and leave the Arconians...my responsibilities...I am just as bad as her. I'm better than that.

What would Dad say? We lose. We heal. We fight. We keep trying. Because defeat is not an option. We have a responsibility to those who have put their trust in us. I have a responsibility. And I have friends and family who care for me. I can't let them down. I'll prove I'm not my mother.

"I'm not my mother," Kita said firmly as she stood up. "I won't abandon my people. I won't disappoint Dad."

"Glen?" said Cowboy.

"Yeah. He'd sanction my replacement as underboss if I abandoned the guild."

"Pretty harsh, but so is quitting."

"He taught me that I shouldn't play the game if I can't take it. This...this is all part of a bigger game with higher stakes. But when I do get my hands on Dimitri, well, he'll take days to die."

"An eye for an eye, eh?" chuckled Cowboy.

"Please. Revenge is what I want, but I want him to suffer in ways he's never dreamed of."

Cowboy whistled low.

"So, can we take you back? And get you out of that dress?" said Snowy.

"Yes. First thing I'm going to do is slap Jeffrey."

T HE INN'S DOOR BANGED open as Kita stormed ahead of Snowy and Cowboy. During the flight back, her brother's words haunted her, but it was more than a comment about the dress. She was no different to him than Gio, Natali, and the other servant girls he'd abused. She'd championed their protection, but she'd never been able to strike at the source. Until now.

Kita stomped toward her room.

"Got her back?" laughed Jeffrey. "I see you got her to accept her station in life."

"I'd tread lightly," said Cowboy. "I don't know what she's pissed off about."

"She's always mad about something."

Kita took off the peasant dress and laid it on the bed. Her sneak suit, kit, and weapons were neatly placed atop the dresser. She dressed. Meticulously buckled the buckles, fit the fabric around her wings, and ensured her belts were tight. She strapped her utility belt on and finally her weapon's harness. She raised her mask, tied her scarf, and raised her hood.

Kita opened the door to Jeffrey's roaring laughter. She tossed a concealment bomb on the table, filling the room with dense white smoke. Kita jumped on the table and used her wings to disperse the cloud as Cowboy opened the door.

She looked down at Jeffrey and glared.

"Let's get one thing straight. The servant girls are better than you'll ever be, and you owe them for your transgressions. I've helped care for the children you sired for years, but I couldn't stop the source. I bet if I weren't your sister you'd have tried to rape me. I bet my being your sister wouldn't have stopped you. Only the duchess did. The duke protected you from me, but he's gone. And now, I'm the fallen angel and I'll deliver the retribution of the innocent."

Jeffrey laughed.

"The stupid games you play."

Kita kicked him across the face.

Jeffrey landed on a chair and fell to the floor.

"How dare you?" he roared. "I *am* king!"

"And who put you there? You're a puppet on a string."

Kita glided down and kicked the chair out of the way.

She dropped, driving her knee into his breastplate, denting it. She grabbed his head and punched his face.

"You're a sick, sick bastard."

"Sick creep," said Snowy.

As Kita spoke, she rained down blows.

"Those girls deserve a better life, and I'll give it to them. When I'm finished, there will be no nobles, no king. The people will be cared for and not just there for your disgusted looks and to slave over you because you're too lazy to pick up a log and throw it in the fire. The girls are not there for your gratification. They're people. They deserve a good life—one where they don't have to live in fear of you. The duke called me a monster, but you're the monster. I'm a fallen angel, and I promise to make this world better and kill people like you."

"Don't!" said Cowboy. "We need him for the time being."

Jeffrey coughed and spat up blood.

Kita stood, turned, and kicked Jeffrey.

"I would remember who made who," Cowboy said down at Jeffrey.

Kita turned to the nobles in the room.

"You're living on borrowed time."

"You need us to rule," said Cauzul.

"There are better leaders in Yorq than the nobles—the Shadow Guild, for starters. I'm sure a few nobles can be rehabilitated as good administrators. There are good people who will share my vision. I just need to find them."

"You're not queen," said another noble.

"No, I'm the Legion Commander. I have a similar role according to the previous commander. And it's not like you can stop me."

"Don't make an enemy of us."

"I've been an enemy of the nobles since I was sixteen. You're either with me or against me. My vision of the future is one where all are equal. No class division, no sick noble scum like my brother. You know my position. Become useful or not at all. Right now, Cowboy says you're useful. Make sure you stay that way."

Kita turned away from the gaping nobles.

"I'll let you smooth things over," she said to Cowboy.

He laughed.

"Come on, Snowy. Let's go see my Legion and the Arconians. I'm sure both will be happy I'm back and healthy."

TEN

DEAMONS ARE A
GIRL'S BEST FRIEND
POWERWOLF
THE SACRAMENT OF SIN

K ITA VISITED THE ARCONIANS first. Everywhere she went, she attracted a crowd.

As Xeen led Kita and Snowy on a camp tour, they came to a practice session.

Kita was impressed. The Arconians lived up to their reputation as hardened warriors that not even serious wounds could stop.

"Lady Rose, would you like to duel next?" asked a woman from the Parrot Guild.

"Sure." Kita had watched the woman work up the courage to ask.

Kita stepped into the ring and agreed to the rules—no flying or shaping.

Sigh, they know how to take the fun out of it.

The woman wasn't a challenge. Kita didn't need anything but experienced footwork and a quick set of blades.

"Thank you, Lady Rose. I have learned much," the woman said when the duel ended.

The first duel brought a torrent of challengers. Kita started with the women and worked up to the biggest men.

"Anyone else?" said Kita after defeating the last man.

The crowd remained silent, and a voice from far back responded, "Aye."

Kita's eyes lit when she saw Zidin. She jumped on him and gave him a bear hug.

"Zidin, I've missed you so much," said Kita with glee.

"And I've missed you."

Kita let go and glided to be eye level with the Arconian.

"I've come back in hopes that I can serve you again."

"Of course, you can. Don't say *serve*, say *help*. I don't own you anymore. Now, everyone, clear the ring. The Great Elder Zidin and I will show you how it's done."

"And the rules?" said Zidin.

"How about none and first to three cuts wins?"

"Somehow this must favor you."

Kita winked at him.

"I'll go easy. I promise."

"That's what I'm worried about."

They faced off and a referee gave the signal.

Kita tried a quick spin and slash, and Zidin countered by punching her in the gut. Before Kita could stand, Zidin charged and hit her with his shoulder. She rolled and jumped over him, dodging Great White. She slashed with Dawn and sliced his shoulder open.

Zidin swept Great White around and struck Kita as she landed. The shark tooth blade left a nasty gash in her side.

Kita launched into the air out of reach. She pulled a throwing knife from her thigh pad and threw it at him. Zidin swung Great White and hit the blade, returning it to Kita. She caught it and stuck her tongue out at him.

Climbing into the air, Kita turned invisible and dove. She changed directions, but Great White sliced into her upper arm, dropping Kita to the ground. She pressed her hot hand against Zidin's leg, rolled away, and revealed herself.

The combatants circled each other.

Kita tried a few faints, but Zidin wouldn't commit.

They rushed each other and clashed in a blur of attacks. After separating, both were bleeding from numerous wounds.

Laughing, Kita counted the cuts on her and the cuts on him. "It's fourteen to thirteen, my favor."

"A burn is not a cut," said Zidin.

"It's an injury, that's what matters. The whole point is to fight like you would in combat."

"You always have to win, don't you?"

"Yep."

The practice matches resumed, and Kita stood with Zidin to watch.

"You've learned a bunch of new tricks," said Kita.

"I learned from you. The battlespace is not just what's in front. It's what's around. I've learned to use my other senses. You make a lot of noise when you fly. Fast feet are also important. So is anticipating where your opponent will be, especially you. You have learned some new tricks as well."

"You like the wings? I got them after I died."

"I do. You're more Angel than human now."

"I guess you could say that."

"Commander Logine? Commander Logine, are you here?" a voice called from the back of the crowd.

"I am!" Kita yelled back.

The crowd opened, and the fight stopped. Snowy escorted Glen and seven men surrounding Dmitri, wrapped in chains.

Kita smiled wickedly.

"I see you found him, Dad."

"We did. The weasel was holed up in a root cellar in some little village in the middle of nowhere."

"Well, Dmitri, we meet again."

"Hello, my dear. It looks like you're recovering nicely."

"Yes, it has been a trying time. So, tell me, what was a nice person like yourself doing in a root cellar?"

"Hiding, of course. It's very unprofessional to order a professional like me hunted when all I did was my job."

"Well, you can always count on the Shadow Guild to be professional. I think only their professionalism kept you alive on your journey here."

"I don't understand why you want me. All I did was provide a service. Nothing more. My employer is who you want."

Kita cocked her head.

"Cunningham will get what's coming to him. And really, Dmitri, is that all it is, a service? You don't choose your clients. You just go where the money is?"

"I have to make a living."

Kita rolled her eyes.

"I see. I'm in a similar line of work. I go where the money takes me for those who can afford me."

"Then you understand."

"Yes, but if I'm caught, I'll be killed. It's a risk of being a professional in my line of work and a torturer."

"And what is your line of work, my dear? Cunningham said you were a Legion commander."

"I am. I'm also the Rose of Arcone, and you've upset all these people over what you did. But by trade, I am an assassin."

The rosy color drained from Demitri's face.

"Yes, the only people who know more about delivering pain than you are girls like me."

"You are truly evil."

Kita laughed.

"Evil and professionalism are not mutually exclusive. There are many evil professionals in the world. Fallen angels are one, for instance."

Dmitri returned a curious look. "You'll have to explain, my dear. How can an evil being hunt other evil beings?"

"You say you work on anyone—evil or innocent."

"I work on who I'm paid to work on."

"Do you show any remorse or ask forgiveness for your actions?"

Dmitri turned up his nose. "That would be unprofessional."

"I disagree. I love to deliver pain to those who deserve it. I enjoy killing. When I finish, I apologize and try to earn my absolution. Why do this? Because I know what I've done is wrong. Do you know what you do is wrong?"

"No, it is not. It is a service people pay well for. It sounds like you're in the wrong line of work if you can't handle the emotional strain."

"No, Dmitri, it separates evil like you from evil like me. Fallen angels are evil, but we work towards redemption and absolution. You're just a twisted sick freak who gets off on causing pain for no other reason than you're paid for it. Your lack of remorse sickens me."

Kita stepped back and flourished her swords.

"Dmitri, you've had your chance to decide your fate. Now it has come to me. How many people have you worked on?"

"I'm not telling you."

Kita touched Dawn against his neck. "How many, Dmitri?"

"Four hundred and sixty-eight, including you."

"That wasn't so hard, was it? Dmitri, I'm not going to kill you. I'm going to inject you with a drug that opens every pain receptor in your body. You're going to experience all those people's pain."

Kita extended a barb in front of Dmitri's face.

"Unlike you, I don't need a tool kit to cause pain."

Dimitri whistled. "I did not see those before. We could have had fun with them."

A ring of pain exploded in Kita's chest as her vision turned red.

"You haven't seen anything yet," Kita roared and slammed both barbs into Dmitri's neck. "Sweet dreams."

"Everyone, get back!" yelled Zidin as he grabbed Kita from behind.

"Let go of me!" Kita shrieked and threw Zidin over the top of her.

"She's berserking," Zidin yelled to Snowy and Glen.

Xeen ran up with a group of Arconians.

Rolling and drawing Great White simultaneously, Zidin knocked Kita's incoming attack aside.

Kita twirled around him, slashing at his legs.

Zidin blocked.

Frustrated, Kita swung harder and faster.

Zidin stuck his arm out, knocking Kita down, and brought Great White down, but Kita rolled away.

She jumped at him, but he caught her with the flat of his blade. Kita hit the ground and flipped to her feet.

Zidin charged.

Kita jumped at him. Twisting to miss Great White, she sliced Zidin's neck and shoulders. Rolling over in the air, she threw a pair of knives. Zidin blocked them, wielding Great White one-handed. Kita flipped over Zidin and stabbed him with both blades.

"We need to get everyone back!" Snowy yelled at Xeen. "This is not a practice fight. This is real and Kita won't stop util she takes on the whole damn army."

Xeen reluctantly agreed.

"Get the warriors back," he ordered his Arconians. "Everyone get back," he yelled. "Lady Rose is proving she's the greatest among us by taking on the great elder."

"You think you can beat me?" Kita screamed at Zidin.

"No, but Snowy and I can. Someone run and get Commandant Hennessey!" he added as an afterthought.

"Kita, stop it!" Snowy yelled.

Kita charged her.

Snowy jumped.

Kita performed a handspring. In midair, she wrapped her legs around Snowy's middle. Flapping her wings hard, Kita somersaulted and opened her legs, throwing Snowy to the ground.

Cowboy raised his revolver from the crowd's edge, and a shot rang out.

The bullet hit the main joint in Kita's right wing. She fell, hitting hard.

Zidin pinned her down.

Cowboy turned into his demon form and shoved his way through the crowd.

The Arconians was becoming unruly, yelling the others were trying to kill Kita.

Snowy electrified her claws and tried to push them back. Cowboy did the same on the other side as Zidin struggled to hold Kita.

Glen ordered his bruisers to help with crowd control, forming a protective circle around Zidin.

Sarge joined, swiping with claws and snarling.

Xeen ran around trying to push the people back and get his warriors to do the same.

Zidin fought to control Kita, but her wings hit him across the head and shoulders.

Roars carried over the sounds of the mob. Frostbane and a dozen bears pushed their way through the Arconians. He stopped beside Snowy, stood on his hind feet, and gave a spine-tingling roar. The rest of the bears encircled the small group.

Screaming and snarling, Kita grabbed Zidin's arm. He yelled in pain but refused to let go as Kita burned him.

Snowy heard the yell, looked behind her, and swore. Leaving her position, she kicked Kita in the face, breaking her hold on Zidin. Snowy grabbed Kita's arms and pinned them to the ground.

Struggling to break free, Kita singed Snowy's fur.

"Stop it!" snarled Snowy. She plunged her claws into Kita's arms.

"Zidin, when I say *now* get off her," Snowy yelled. When Kita slackened, she screamed, "Now!"

Zidin rolled away from Kita.

"I'm sorry, kitten, but it's for your own good."

Snowy electrified her claws. The electricity passed across Kita's metal alloy skeleton like a high-voltage power line. Kita screamed in rage and then in pain until she quit moving. Snowy cut the power, but left her claws in place and waited.

The sound of Kita crying came from under her hood. Snowy let go and helped Kita sit up.

Kita cocooned herself in her wings.

"What's wrong with her?" Xeen demanded.

"It's the other side of the coin," said Zidin. "You don't have that kind of emotional outburst without paying for it later."

"He's right," said Snowy. "It'll take some time for her to calm down. Leave her alone. She's in a fragile state. You upset her, and I'll kill you."

Xeen glared at Snowy.

She returned it with ferocity.

"Everyone, she'll be fine," announced Cowboy to the crowd after turning back from The demon. "She just needs a little time to collect herself. If you could give her some space, it would help."

The bears took a few steps forward, pushing the crowd back.

"Snowy," Kita called in a tiny voice.

Snowy knelt next to Kita—a wing wrapped around her.

"I'm sorry," Kita said through her tears. "I want to go home."

"Of course, kitten. Do you want Zidin to take you?"

Kita raised her head, smiled, and nodded.

Snowy called for Zidin.

He picked Kita up and carried her back to the inn.

K ITA OPENED HER DOOR to listen. She could hear Cowboy and Snowy.

Odd, the inn is so quiet.

She entered the main room where Cowboy and Snowy sat with Zidin.

"Morning," said Cowboy. "Glad you're up. Feeling better?"

"Good morning, kitten. You're up earlier than expected. Are you hungry?"

Kita nodded.

"Yeah. Now that you mention it."

"Help yourself."

Kita went to the breakfast table, but most of the food was gone. Normally, the table was stacked high with food. Her stomach rumbled. She gathered what she could, took it to the table, and ate as fast as she could.

"I know you don't eat as often as you used to, but you could remember your table manners," Snowy scolded.

"Sorry." Kita put the food down and put her hands in her lap.

Snowy laughed. "You don't have to stop. Just eat like you know how. It's not going anywhere. I'm glad everyone else had a chance."

"Where is everyone else?"

"They left."

"What do you mean *they left?*" Kita cried in alarm. "It was over me, wasn't it? I was going to apologize. Did I injure them badly? Where did they go? I can catch them and make it right. I—"

Everyone laughed.

"Kitten, it's ok. Nobody is mad at you. You might want to apologize to Zidin. He took the brunt."

Kita stood and wrapped her arms and wings around Zidin in a crushing bear hug.

"I'm sorry. I didn't hurt you too much, did I? You forgive me, right?"

"You've done worse, and yes, you're forgiven. Please let go. I can't breathe," Zidin wheezed.

"Everyone is following your orders, Kita," said Cowboy. "They're moving to Leedings and left before dawn this morning. Once you're feeling better, we'll catch up to them."

A wailing sound drifted up through the floor.

"What's that?" Kita said, raising her eyebrows.

"That's Dmitri," said Cowboy. "That reminds me. What did you give him?"

Kita sat.

I wish I could remember. What did I give him? Something nasty. Oh, yeah.

"There was a paralyzer and the pain-inducing agent."

"You hit him with both barbs," said Cowboy.

I have no idea what would take that long to inject.

"You told him *sweet dreams*, if that helps?" said Snowy.

Kita snapped her fingers.

"I gave him a long-term dose of hallucinogenic drugs, a psychedelic, and a delirium. He'll be like this for a while." Kita cringed. "Sorry."

"Well, that explains why he hasn't stopped screaming. I wonder what his nightmares look like," Cowboy said with an amused look.

"They probably focus on Kita," Snowy said with a laugh.

"I said his nightmares, not your dreams."

"You're going to be riding Nightmare in a second," Snowy scolded, turning up her nose.

"Speaking of riding, if Kita's ready, we should get a move on."

"Does this mean I don't have time to eat?" Kita said from the kitchen doorway with an armload of food.

A S KITA ENTERED THE large rectangular command tent, everyone came to attention. She released them and found Forrester hanging some maps.

"Commander, good to see you're feeling better."

"Thanks, how are things?"

"Excellent. Each group has claimed its territory under the big top. We should be up and running within the hour. When would you like to send the notification team?"

Kita raised an eyebrow. "The what?"

"The notification team goes under a flag of truce to inform the city that it will be attacked. It'll allow them to think over their options, like surrendering.

"They may decide to send troops into the field against us. If they lose, we take the city. The worst case is that they send troops out, and we still have to siege. Either way it goes, we will have to line up for battle. The stronger our show of force, the better chance of a less violent resolution."

Maybe we don't need a violent resolution. I've got people on the inside.

"Send them in the morning. Tell them they will have two days to make up their minds. You can set the meeting place, right?"

"Of course. It'll be whatever location I select for the battle-field. I can take care of the details. Two days is plenty of time for us to get organized. I was afraid you'd march us straight into battle."

Kita sighed. "No, I only do that to myself."

"Commander," said the door guard.

"Yeah?"

"There's an Arconian group here to see you."

Oh, joy.

"I'll be back," she said to Forrester.

Kita followed the door guard outside, and a group of Arconians waited. The group consisted of twelve individuals. Each wore a dark blue cloak with gold trim. In unison, they removed their hoods and opened their cloaks. Each cloak revealed a wizened face, and the wearer wore the traditional Arconian kilt and kit.

"Who are you?" Kita demanded.

"The leader spoke calmly but sternly, "We are the elders assigned to this contract. We decide the course of the contract and make sure it follows Tradition. Events have kept us from meeting until now, Lady Rose."

"I have been around a while. The camps aren't that big, and I'm easy to find. The big black wings make it easy. It sucks playing hide and seek. I'm trying to run an army if you don't mind."

The leader shook his head.

"You will always be Lady Rose—no matter what else you are. It is not a title you can put on or take off as you please. It is a bloodline that traces from you back to our people's very beginnings."

"That's nice, but I've got more important things to worry about right now."

"We merely wish to talk to you about other things. We feel there's been a miscommunication between you and us."

"Fine, but I get to choose the place. We'll do it in Yorq's camp. Jeffrey is as much an Arconian as I am. The rest of the Arconians have to stay outside."

The leader nodded.

K ITA AND THE ARCONIAN elders met in Jeffrey's personnel tent, full of elegant furnishings, rugs, and a large bed.

The elders gathered at the far side.

Kita took advantage of the tall ceiling and floated while Jeffrey stood beside her wearing his regal attire. Though, he couldn't hide the black eye.

"I'm sorry, Lady Rose, this meeting is for you only. He will have to wait outside," said the leader.

Kita glared at him.

"He's my brother and the son of my mother. He's as much an Arconian as I am. Whatever you say, he has a right to hear. If you dislike it, we're just wasting time."

"Calm, child. This is the first time any Arconians have seen you, and we know nothing about you. Normally, everyone has watched Lady Rose grow from a seed to a flower. You are not a rose, but a rose bush."

"Watch where you stick your hand, I come with a lot of thorns."

"A skilled gardener knows how to work around the thorns to cultivate the biggest bloom," the leader said gently. "You are the rose, the people of Arcone are the thorns, and the elders are the gardeners. Without proper care, the bush grows wild with few flowers. For us to better be able to help you, we must know you."

Kita rolled her eyes. "What do you want to know?"

"We want to know how you came to this crosscurrent in your life."

Kita sighed and started at the beginning. She told of her Proving Ritual, the death of her mother and father, and the escape from the castle. She left out Omega, the Shadow Guild, and kept details of the Legion to a minimum.

"That is an interesting tale," said the leader.

The elders replaced their hoods and cloaks and lined up to leave.

Jeffrey blocked the exit.

"As our mothers' children, we deserve more than that."

"The tale she tells is full of places, people, and deeds," said an elder. "It does not tell us who she is. She could be a crow with its head stuck in a rose thicket."

"My sister is a bullheaded, manipulative killer," Jeffrey said snidely. "Yet, she can talk people into doing anything for her. She would rather be poor than live the life of a noble and consort with thieves and assassins than do her duty and get married and bring strong heirs into this world. Instead, she's taken a female lover."

"That tells us much more than Lady Rose's story," said an elder.

The leader faced Kita.

"You did not mention you had a lover."

"I didn't think any of that was your damn business. Who I spend time with and what I do is my prerogative."

"Love can tell a lot about a person. Even the hardest of stone hearts can melt when in the presence of the one they love. We would like to meet her."

Jeffrey exited the tent and returned with Snowy.

The Queen of the War Cats entered the tent. Her bangles and earrings sparkled in the light. She carried her tail on her arm. Walking with grace, she stood next to Kita.

"Are you the Lady of the Mountain?" said an elder.

Snowy cocked her head to one side.

"That is a name I have not been called in a long time. My name is Snowy."

"Our legends tell of a woman who lives high in the mountains with the war cats. She protects them. To see her was an omen of death."

"Legends are based on truth, but I rescued stranded travelers. If you saw me, it was an omen of life."

"I feel that it is we who are children in your eyes. Tell us, how old are you?" said the leader.

Snowy's eyes narrowed.

"I'm old enough to remember when the land and people were unified. I saw when your volcanic islands were nothing more than bare rock. I can still see where great cities stood. I know whatever questions you have of me are just questions. Like all questions, their significance is fleeting. What do you wish to know?"

"Why do you love Lady Rose?" said an elder.

"You don't choose who you love. You may choose to be with them. If you mean what I see in her that I like, there is a lot. When I first met Kita, I fell in love with her. It wasn't until after I realized that I wanted to be with her.

"Kita is the most amazing person I've ever met. I feel safe and wonderful when she's around. Anything is possible with her. I've grown as she's grown. I know she's young and has much to learn, but she makes me feel young. I love being there to support, help, and reassure her. She has done the same for me. I find her convictions refreshing, and her passion is paramount."

"If you are so long-lived as you say you are, wouldn't it be hard to watch her grow old?" said an elder from the back.

"Kita has nanites like your ancient Arconians. She'll live at least as long as I. Who's to say that if she dies, I will want to continue to live without her?"

"Lady Rose has picked well, I believe," said an elder. "Time will tell if you are the perfect pollinator, but you have our approval."

"For what that's worth, child. Your approval means nothing to me. You are dust in the wind."

"We will deliberate further on what we've heard." The leader put his hood over his head.

"And what exactly are you to deliberate?" Cowboy's eerie baritone asked from the door. His fire cast the room in a new light. He and Zidin blocked the exit.

"Whether Lady Rose's decisions have led Arcone down the wrong path. We know nothing of her, so we do not know why she has made the choices she has. She will always be Lady Rose, of that there is no question. We wonder if her other commitments have clouded her judgment."

Cowboy chuckled. "I've wondered the same thing myself."

"Who are you?" said an elder.

Cowboy returned to his human form.

"I'm Commandant Gerald Hennessey. I'm her commanding officer and advisor. My job is similar to yours. I'm assigned to ensure she keeps with the Legion's mission."

"Has she?" said another elder.

"Yes. She has proven to be committed to her Legion, even willing to throw everything else away —friends, lovers, even herself— to save it."

"How can one person expect to show the same level of commitment to two different groups?" said a third elder.

"I was tasked with evaluating that very question. As you are aware, the Legion does not accept Arconians because of commitment issues. Kita is a unique case. She was drafted and received her markings on the same night. After studying her, I concluded that removing someone so dedicated to her command would be unfair, just because she might be required to represent someone else's interests. What will happen if those commitments collide? I don't know. We will have to trust her."

"The Legion is willing to trust her with a great responsibility. Why?" said the leader.

"With great responsibility comes a great headache. I whisper the Legion's interests in her ear, Zidin represents Arcone's interests, and Snowy represents Kita's personal interests. We believe she will do what is right for all, not just for the Legion."

The leader turned to Zidin.

"Great Elder, you have been guiding Lady Rose for Arcone?"

"Yes, elder."

"Why?"

"To make sure she upholds Tradition to honor her people."

"Has she?"

"No,"—Kita cringed at the answer.

I hope you're listening, brother. Not everyone does as I want—

"She doesn't adhere to Tradition, but she does to the spirit of Arcone. She doesn't believe in honor, but she fights for the innocent. Her skills as a warrior are unmatched. She will be out front leading the charge. Those she commands come first. Often, she's taken way past the point of exhaustion. She has died trying to save her lover. Nothing stops her. Victory is her only destination. I would follow her to the Crushing Depths."

"Even over your own people?" said the leader.

"I have advised and guided all the roses. None before her are like her. She is the future. The people of Arcone have been adrift too long without the guidance of Lady Rose. Just because she wishes to take us on a new course doesn't mean we shouldn't follow."

"Thank you, Great Elder. Please leave us. We wish to confer and make our decision."

Zidin nodded and led Kita and the others outside, away from the tent.

Kita drifted back and forth.

"Bloody moons! I can't believe everything will unravel because a bunch of old dried bones can't see their noses on their faces."

Snowy put a hand on Kita's arm.

"Don't worry, kitten, everything will be fine."

"You heard them. They think I'm unworthy because they didn't raise me. They disapprove of you and think I'm a puppet of the Legion."

Kita slammed her fist on a hitching post, causing it to splinter.

"We can win without them," said Jeffrey. "It'll be hard, but we can."

"It would take a change in tactics," said Cowboy. "If we reclaim the tubes, we'll have the supplies and equipment to defeat the Crown."

"Let them make their decision. Then we can make ours," said Zidin. "Until then, I'll go and get Xeen and some Arconians. They need to hear this decision."

"Same with the Legion," said Cowboy. "I'll get the general staff."

Kita folded herself into Snowy's arms, trying to calm the painful anxiety ring in her chest.

Jeffrey stood by with his advisors, fuming over being kicked out of his tent.

"It'll be alright, kitten," Snowy seemed to pick up on Kita's distress. "The Legion can handle it."

"But how will we fight Cunningham's men and the Arconians?"

"They wouldn't attack you, would they?"

"I don't know."

"They should go home," said Jeffrey. "This is an internal conflict."

"Maybe we can hire them," said Snowy.

"That's an idea," said Kita. "I make the contract, so I could do it cheap."

"Most of the nobles don't have access to their treasuries," said Jeffrey.

"And the Legion's wealth is out of reach, too," lamented Kita. Her anxiety building, Kita split from Snowy and paced.

"Maybe we can get more legionnaires from our sister legions?" suggested Snowy.

"Yeah, I can ask Cowboy. We have almost six thousand legionnaires. That's half of what Cunningham will have with the Arconians."

"Maybe we could pay them to leave," said Jeffrey. "That wouldn't cost as much."

Kita sighed, hating that her future hung in the balance of people who didn't know or understand her.

"In the cities, there's also the Shadow Guilds," commented Kita.

"They're no good on a battlefield," scoffed Jeffrey.

"No, but they can disrupt the enemy's supply lines, communications, and funding."

Cowboy came hustling up with Forrester and the rest of the general staff.

"Did they come out yet?" asked Cowboy.

"No," said Jeffrey, annoyed.

"We've been trying to come up with solutions to make the Arconians go away," said Snowy. "We may need more legionnaires for the other Legions."

Cowboy's eyebrows furrowed. "I can put in the request."

"Can't you order them?"

"That kind of legionnaire movement must come from La Forge himself. We didn't know about the Arconians or the trouble they'd cause when we first planned this."

Out of the darkness came Zidin with Xeen and several hundred Arconians.

"Speak of the devil," said Jeffrey.

"Nothing's been decided yet," said Zidin. "Look out!"

A circle of sparkles forming a portal appeared in the air behind Kita. As she turned, Sarah appeared and slammed her sword through Kita's lower back and out her front. She gasped in pain.

"Hello, Kita. Did you miss me?"

"Sarah?" Kita whispered at the assassin behind her.

Angus with a white ball with blue lights floating next to him appeared in the circle with someone behind him.

"Ding-ding-ring-a-ding!" the ball, Alpha, cried. "The carny always wins. The chip never lies. I told you I was good at hide and seek."

The AI played a merry carnival tune.

"I didn't doubt you," said Angus. "The question was, would she be alone. Sabatha, my dear, do you mind giving us some privacy?"

The healer put her hand up, and a pearly white bubble encapsulated Angus' group and a portal in the air that looked in on some kind of UEE facility.

Sabatha?

A shot rang out from outside, and Snowy slashed the shield, but nothing penetrated.

Sarah jerked Kita to face Angus.

Kita's former commander raised his Arcom, and a red light blinded Kita.

Bloody moons, there goes my Berserking.

I'm going to have to find a way to fix that.

Kita stuck her finger on the end of Sarah's sword and pushed it back.

Sarah leaned into Kita, but wasn't strong enough to overcome Kita's strength.

Lunging forward, Kita turned the fall into a roll and drew her swords. She flourished until they burst into flame.

"Interesting," said Angus.

"Who knew this circus had a fire eater?" Alpha said with a delirious laugh.

"Sabatha," said Kita, her voice straining from the pain, "What are you doing with Angus?"

"We're going to create a utopia governed by logic and reason."

Sarah tried a quick strike, but Kita turned it aside.

She spun, bringing Dusk around.

Sarah blocked with her long dagger and kicked Kita in her wound.

Kita doubled over as fresh blood flowed from the injury.

Sarah brought her sword down on Kita's shoulder, making Kita drop Dawn, extinguishing the sword's flame.

Kita slapped Dusk onto Sarah's exposed leg, burning her badly. Kita jumped and hit the top of the bubble to escape Sarah's retaliation. It was like hitting rock and caused her to tumble. She flapped her wings to catch herself.

When Kita landed, Sarah was waiting. She slashed Kita with both swords across the chest.

Kita struck out with Dusk, but Sarah trapped the flaming wakizashi with her swords. Using her superior strength, Kita pushed Sarah down. The other assassin slipped her long dagger away, causing Kita to slide down Sarah's sword.

Sarah sidestepped and went to stab Kita in the side.

Kita dropped to the ground to dodge the strike. She whipped her legs around, taking out Sarah's. The assassin landed hard on her back.

Rolling up to her knees, Kita said, "You should know better. You taught me that trick," then slammed Dusk into Sarah's forehead.

Kita stood and faced Angus and Sabatha.

"Are you going to bring back every enemy from my past?" Kita chided. "Drop the barrier."

"Step through the rift gate and I won't kill your friends."

"Never. I'll never give myself over to you. I'll kill myself first."

Kita put the point of Dusk against the side of her head.

"I can always make another of you," Angus said dismissively.

"Then why haven't you? You've made the duke and duchess, and now Sarah."

Because the genes I used are too complex for a normal DNA replicator.

"The DNA replicator can't do it, huh?"

Angus's face darkened.

"Drop the barrier."

"Sabatha, push her through the gate," ordered Angus.

The barrier shrank, hitting Kita in the back and pushed her toward the portal.

"Sabatha," pleaded Kita. "I've known you all my life. Don't go with this snake. You're better than that."

"You cause chaos everywhere you go," replied the healer. "You run on pure emotion, the enemy of logic and reason. Your death will make the utopia I crave a reality."

"Please," Kita begged as she was feet from the portal.

"Your death will end your reign of destruction."

Kita held Dusk, which was meant for Angus, but she wasn't going into the portal either.

I wish I could use both hands.

With her off hand, Kita threw the blade, hitting Sabatha in the heart.

The woman gasped and collapsed. The barrier came down, and a white, dimensionless cloud rose above the healer's body. It floated up into the sky and disappeared.

Is that what she meant when she said others are among us? What was that?

"Well, junior commander, another time. There's nowhere I can't find you."

Angus turned, snatched Alpha's ball out of the air, and fled through the portal, and it collapsed behind him.

Kita collapsed to her knees. She was woozy and lightheaded.

"Kitten, are you ok?" said Snowy, running up and kneeling next to Kita.

"Just waiting to heal."

Zidin rushed over, pulling a jar of the healing balm for his sporran.

"Lay her down," he ordered.

As Zidin smeared on the balm, a crowd gathered. The Arconians were upset over Kita. The legionnaires were trying to understand what had happened. Jeffrey stood back with the other nobles, looking smug.

"What happened?" asked Cowboy when Zidin turned Kita on her side to apply the balm to the gash in her back.

"Angus. Somehow, he made another Sarah."

"Called a clone. And the woman?"

"That was Sabatha, the duke's healer. She wanted some kind of utopia based on logic and reason. I guess Angus was going to make it for her."

"Angus said there was no place he couldn't find me. Alpha said something about a chip."

"Forrester, call for a medic and tell them to bring a viewer," ordered Cowboy.

"Yes, sir."

Snowy held Kita's hand when Zidin finished.

"He can't keep showing up like this," said Kita. "That's twice. And how does he clone the people I know?"

"He's gathered your parents' DNA. The other assassin was Sarah?" asked Cowboy. "He must have had some interaction with her at some point."

"Yeah. He bet her she couldn't train me as an assassin."

A legion medical squad ran up.

"I just need the viewer," said Cowboy.

They handed him a tablet with a screen on the front and back. Slowly, he moved it around Kita's body.

"Ah, found our lost cow. It's in your right thigh. Here."

He tapped the spot.

Kita sat up.

"Woah, you're not healed yet."

"How do we get it out?"

"I'll need an autodoc, or we can do it the old-fashioned way and cut it out."

"Get me Dusk," Kita asked Zidin.

Kita took the blade from the Arconian retrieved from the dead healer.

"What are you—"

Kita sliced open her thigh.

"Kitten!"

"Damn girl," yelled Cowboy. "I didn't say right this minute."

Kita dug into her leg, gritting her teeth against the pain. Her fingers found something the size of a pea. With a sigh, she pulled it out and held it up in her bloody fingers.

"What do we do with it?" said Zidin.

Kita squished the tracking chip between her fingers.

"Now, he'll never know where I am."

ELEVEN

ANGEL OF DARKNESS
ALEX C. FEAT YASMIN K
ANGEL OF DARKNESS

A S ZIDIN EXPLAINED TO Xeen what happened, Snowy kept watch on Kita, forcing the fallen angel to sit still long enough to heal.

Cowboy was on his Arcom reporting the sighting of Angus, how he'd arrived, and who he brought with him.

Frostbane, his bears, and war cats arrived and formed a protective circle around Kita.

Xeen knelt next to his niece.

"How are you doing, lass?"

"I'm almost healed."

"I will detail a squad of our best to watch over you. Next time, you may fight more than an assassin, healer, and eel."

"Thanks, but I took care of his ability to find me whenever he wants. Do the elders always take so long to make a decision?"

"They can take days to talk through everything. What are they discussing?"

"Me, apparently. They don't like me as Lady Rose."

"You'll always be the Rose," said Zidin. "They can't take that away."

"It does me no good if they can overrule me at any time."

"Why would the overrule you?" said Xeen.

"I think they don't like that I canceled the contract with Cunningham and brought the Arconians to fight with the Legion. I should send you home."

"That's a bunch of empty clam shells," scoffed Xeen. "Cunningham did more than enough to warrant you canceling the contract."

With Snowy's help, Kita sat up. The wound in her side had closed, but she still received shooting pain from inside. Her shoulder was healed enough that she could use it.

One by one, the elders filed out of the tent.

"What happened here?" asked the leader.

"Lady Rose was attacked," answered Xeen.

The elders looked at each other. A few shrugged.

"Kita defeated her attacker, killed the shaper, and drove Angus away," clarified Snowy. "She was badly injured in doing so."

"Does Lady Rose not speak for herself?" asked an elder.

Kita pushed herself to her feet and picked up Dusk and Dawn.

"Let me run you through and nearly sever your arm and see if you want to answer questions."

She floated off the ground to look down at the elderly group.

"Well, elders, are you going to forsake me or not? Be quick. Unlike you, I don't have time to waste on idle talk."

"Lady Rose, we have made our decision. Canceling the contracts with King Cunningham was incorrect. You have led the people of Arcone astray," the leader said so all could hear.

"So be it," Kita snarled. "Get out of my camp. Your Rose is lost forever."

The roses on Kita's face vanished. A wave of surprise and shock went through the amassed Arconian crowd. The elders raised their hoods and turned their backs on Kita.

"There is one group that can override the elders," said Zidin.

Kita rolled her eyes. "Who?"

"Me. As a great elder, I do more than advise the rose."

Zidin's booming voice rose above the din.

"People of Arcone, I am Zidin of Clan MhicAoidh. I am the last of the Great Elders and the bearer of the great sword, Great White." He held the massive sword high in the air. "Lady Rose has bested me in personal combat and has proven that she can lead the people of Arcone to greatness once again. Great White will stand by her side."

"Aye," said Xeen. "Cunningham is a sea slug that murdered the Rose's mother and captured and tortured Lady Rose. These are insults against Arcone and cannot stand. We will go home before we fight for him again. The great elder speaks the truth. I've seen Lady Rose in action. I stand with the great elder. Who's with me?"

A loud cheer came from the Arconian crowd.

"Death to the jellyfish Cunningham," someone shouted.

Xeen turned to the elders, who had lifted their hoods and fastened their cloaks.

Zidin faced the group.

"You knew of this and more, and still, you side with Cunningham."

"Tradition must be followed," said the elder's leader.

"And what Tradition is that?" said Zidin.

The elder didn't answer.

"As the Great Elder, my job is to ensure Lady Rose follows Tradition. And the insults against her stand up to Tradition. Whatever riptide you used to come to your decision is wrong and doesn't follow Tradition. Go back to camp. I will deal with you later."

The elders turned and left.

"Does this mean you're going to stay?" Kita asked Xeen.

"Aye. We've only heard tales of the great elders from Maud, the Rose matriarch. But we've heard stories of what they have done. If Great Elder Zidin says it is Tradition, then it is so. The only person who can overrule him is Maud."

"The Legion stands ready to follow your lead," said Cowboy.

"Here, here," said the officers.

Frostbane roared and came over and put a paw around Kita. The bear grunted and gruffed.

"He says the bears and war cats follow you," translated Snowy.

"Tell him his armor is magnificent and worthy of him."

Snowy did and replied, "If not for you, they'd still be captives. The armor shows friendship between Kita and animals."

I don't want a repeat of the war cat attack on the ravager camp. How many war cats would've lived if they'd had armor?

"They're good friends."

Earl Cauzul led Jeffrey and a group of nobles.

"We, of course, support the Legion and its commander," said the earl.

Yeah, for how long?

"Thank you, Merc. We will put the king on his throne."

"You know, this does make you the princess," said Cauzul playfully.

Kita laughed.

"Still not going to get me into a ball gown."

"We wouldn't dream of it."

"He would," Kita motioned to Jeffrey.

"You should be in the dungeon," snarled Jeffrey.

"Oh, you and I will have so much fun working together."

"I am king, and this is my region. You can stay in your holes."

"You have no idea what the Legion is capable of or what we have."

Kita put her hand out, and it turned red.

"Feel like playing with fire?"

"Winged freak."

"Then we're all freaks," said Cowboy, changing into his demon form.

Snowy snapped her claws out, and electricity crawled up them.

"Let's go," said Zidin. "We'll leave the king to his horses. Just remember whose army it is."

Jeffrey glared at the big Arconian.

Xeen led the Arconians away, and the animals loitered or returned to the forest. Cauzul took Jeffrey away, teaching the young king what was expected of him. Cowboy and the staff returned to the inn, leaving Snowy and Kita.

Kita took Snowy's hand.

"You want to go look at the stars?"

"From up there?"

"Sure."

"But one thing. I never got to pledge myself to you."

Kita looked at her, confused.

"If it matters, you're covered by the Legion."

"I know, but no one pledged themselves to the most important person on the list."

"Huh?"

Snowy giggled, wrapped her arms around Kita's neck, and looked into her eyes. "I, Snowy, pledge my love, body, and heart to Katrina Logine, forever."

"Oh…" was all Kita could say as Snowy kissed her.

K ITA CAUGHT UP TO Zidin later that evening.

"What's on your mind?" he asked.

"How do you know I have something on my mind?"

"You get this look, like you're either going to steal something or kill someone."

Kita laughed.

"I'm not here for that. I wanted to say *thank you* for standing up for me."

"You were in the right. I'm not sure what the elders' problem is. I may never get an answer, but I can make sure Tradition is followed."

"Speaking of Tradition, I'm going to cancel your life debt and restore all the honor I took."

"I thank you, but I haven't earned it."

"You're my friend and there when I needed you most. I can never repay that."

Zidin nodded.

"I'll still follow you around and do my duty. Though you won't listen anyhow."

Kita laughed.

"I do when it suits me."

"You'll do anything if it suits you."

"True. But you do help me get out of trouble."

Zidin laughed.

"You have a knack for finding it."

"And you'll always be there to get me out."

KITA PUSHED THE DOOR of the SWORD AND DAGGER open.

"Mom! Dad!" she yelled above the other patrons.

Glen looked up from cleaning a stein.

"Kita! What are you doing here?"

"I need your help."

"To do what?"

"I'm going to steal the city."

DURING THE COMMAND MEETING, Forrester covered every detail of the attack on Leedings. His mantra was, "We have no reserves, every warrior counts."

Kita knew the phrase would haunt her dreams.

To her, she had no good options. Her forces outnumbered the garrison, but the garrison was strong enough to hold the city. Without a navy, the city could be resupplied indefinitely. She was working on something better than General Forrester's closing remark, "Either way, we're going to have to go in and drag the rat out by the tail."

When Forrester asked for questions, Kita raised a hand.

"What about the meeting before the battle? The one where they tell us if they surrender or not?"

"That's a formality. King Logine will accept their answer."

"Who delivers the answer for the other side?"

"The commander of their forces and the city mayor."

"Can I go?"

"If you want. These meetings don't last long and are usually not productive."

"I think I'll go just to see."

"Have it your way. Is there anything else?" Forrester asked the group of officers.

There were none, and the tent emptied as leaders took orders to their units.

Kita exited the tent with Cowboy and Zidin.

A guildsman approached Kita and handed her a scroll. She read and then burned it.

"What was that?" said Cowboy.

"Something for tomorrow."

"And what are you planning?"

"A heist."

"In the middle of the siege?"

"At the beginning of it."

"And what are you stealing?"

"The city, but no one else is to know in case it doesn't work."

K ITA GLIDED DOWN THE hill next to Jeffrey and the honor guard. Forrester had chosen a high ridge for their position. On the forward slope, Arconians, legionnaires, the animals, and Yorqian soldiers stood ready.

I hope it's a big enough force to make Leedings think twice about holding out.

The opposing side had erected a canopy for the meeting. Their commander was a tall man with dark hair and hazel eyes. He looked like his best fighting days were behind him. The mayor of Leedings was a short, balding, well-dressed fellow with beads of sweat forming in the cool morning air.

"I am King Logine, rightful King of Yorq," said Jeffrey to open the meeting. "With me is Commander Logine of the Legion of Yorq."

The tall man came to attention. "I am Colonel Hudson, garrison commander for the city of Leedings. This is Mayor Turly."

"Gentlemen," said Jeffrey, "Our offer is simple—surrender and open the city. If you do, we'll spare your garrison and any damage to the city."

Hudson shook his head.

"It's not my intention to give up. The earl is the only one who can surrender us."

"Where is your earl? And why is he not here?" said Kita.

Hudson stiffened.

"He has taken refuge elsewhere."

Kita smiled wickedly.

"Left you twisting in the wind, eh? What about you, Mayor, are you interested in having the great city of Leedings sacked?"

The Mayor mopped his forehead and stammered, "Th-the city stands ready to repel any attack."

"I'll give you a better option. Strike your colors to those of the rightful King of Yorq and join us in returning your region to its rightful owners—the people of Yorq."

"That would be seen as worse than surrendering. We would be traitors to the Crown," said Hudson.

Kita's eyes narrowed.

"The other option is I burn the city to the ground."

"What!" all three men said in unison.

"You know as well as I do, you can hold out forever. Taking the city by force would be costly. The only reason we're after the city is to stop the flow of supplies to New London. I don't need the city to be standing to do that."

"You can't possibly do that. There are no weapons that destroy an entire city," said Hudson.

"You doubt me, Colonel?"

Kita pointed toward the city and wiggled her wings.

Two dozen fireballs erupted inside the city, billowing giant plumes of smoke. As the smoke from the first fireballs drifted on the wind, another dozen burst, leaping into the sky. Soon, most of the city lay obscured in a smoky haze.

The three men looked on in shock.

"How did...that's not possible..." Hudson lamented under his breath.

"Well, gentlemen? I can deliver another salvo if you wish," Kita cooed.

"No, no. The city surrenders, it's yours," cried Turly.

"Colonel?"

"I have no choice. I will not let my men be slaughtered, nor will I lead them into treason. You have my sword."

"Thank you, Colonel." Jeffrey nodded respectfully. "Move your men to the base of the hill and lay down your arms. They will be taken prisoner and treated fairly. Mayor, have the city guard captain waiting for me as well as yourself and the council, understood?"

"Yes, Sire," said Turly.

"Thank you, gentlemen. I will see you both shortly," Jeffrey said with a curt nod.

He grabbed Kita by the arm and pulled her out of the tent. "What the blazing suns happened, Kita?" demanded Jeffrey as they made their way up the hill.

Kita shrugged.

"Dammit, what did you do?"

"What?"

"You stupid, silly girl! Tell me what you've done. I command you."

Kita raised an eyebrow.

They passed through their lines and met Forrester. Enjoying the confusion and stunned looks on the faces of the others, Kita burst out laughing.

"Once you recover, you should tell them," said Zidin.

"Yes, kitten, what is so funny?" Snowy bit out between clenched teeth.

As tears streamed down Kita's face, she gasped for breath. "I'm sorry, but the look on your faces is priceless."

"How can you be laughing when the city's burning?" Forrester demanded. "We need it in one piece."

Kita laughed even harder.

Forrester stood with his arms folded, red with rage.

She recovered enough to breathe.

Kita tried to explain but giggled. "You said yesterday we'd have to go in and drag the rat out by the tail, but anyone who's ever dealt with rats knows you get bitten that way. It's faster and easier if you smoke them out."

"The city is burning!" Forrester yelled.

"It's not burning, it's smoking."

"Dammit, girl! Make some sense!"

"I didn't burn the city, I stole it. Like this."

Kita pulled out a smoke bomb and dropped it. A fireball leaped into the air, followed by thick clouds of smoke. When the smoke cleared, Kita was gone.

"Where did she go?" Forrester demanded. "Did that make any sense to anyone? Never mind. We need to get people to the city to start putting those fires out."

"That won't be necessary, General," said Cowboy.

"Why not?"

"What Kita did a poor job of explaining was our enemy fell for a ruse. There are no fires, just a flash and a lot of smoke. You might say she just pulled the biggest heist in history. I don't think anyone has ever stolen a city before."

"How come she didn't tell me? How come you know?"

"She told Zidin and me. Kita wasn't sure it would work, and she thought you'd be surprised if it did. I guess she got it half-right. I do agree with her—your reaction was priceless."

Cowboy's eyes crinkled with a smile.

Forrester relaxed some.

"Well, I *am* happy. It'll save us plenty of troops and time. Where is she?"

"I don't know, General. If you ask nicely, she might come out. I think you hurt her feelings."

"What do you mean, *I hurt her feelings*? She's the one laughing like a loon."

"And she delivered you a victory without losing a man, Do you think she'd be laughing if the city were burning?"

Forrester huffed.

"She can come out when she feels like it. We need to see about rounding up the prisoners and getting people moving into the city."

Humph.

Kita took flight toward Leedings.

F ROM ATOP THE ROOFTOPS, Kita watched her forces move into the city. She stayed invisible, not wanting to deal with anyone, but did make momentary appearances to handle disputes between her army and the locals. As the sun went down, she drifted into the SWORD AND DAGGER.

Glen greeted her enthusiastically.

"How's my girl? It looks like your plan worked."

"Yeah." Kita sighed heavily. "Thanks for the help. It looked great. It definitely fooled them."

"What's wrong, love?" said Barb.

Kita huffed.

"I thought I did a good thing by doing this. Instead, all I got was yelled at."

"Who's yelling at you? I thought you were in charge?" said Glen.

"I am—kind of—depends on what we're talking about. I'm in charge of everything, but not the details. I guess they got mad because I messed up their details."

"Professionals can be like that—especially good ones. They like things just so. They'll get over it or end up in the river."

Kita laughed at the idea of Forrester floating down the river in a bag.

Sigh. I want to be where I'm wanted and appreciated. And I can't think of a better place than here.

T HE DOOR TO THE inn opened, and Snowy, Cowboy, and Zidin entered.

Kita groaned.

"Ha! I told you she'd be here," Snowy said to Cowboy.

"I didn't doubt she would be. I doubted your ability to find the place."

"Oh stars, what do you want?" Kita's words were slurred and mushy.

"Has she been drinking?" said Cowboy.

Glen nodded.

"Since she got here. I remember her being a lightweight, but she's been knocking it back pretty steady."

Snowy sighed.

"Come on, kitten. Let's get you back to headquarters."

"Why, so you can yell at me some more?" Kita said, looking down into her ale.

"No one is going to yell at you."

Snowy took Kita by the arm, but Kita twisted away, knocking over the stools.

"I'm not going. I tried to be helpful, and all I got was yelled at," Kita screamed in her drunken haze.

"You were yelled at because nobody knew what was happening, and you wouldn't stop laughing," said Snowy, her tail lashing behind her.

"They knew." Kita pointed in Cowboy and Zidin's general direction.

"I couldn't help it. You all thought I set the city on fire. You think I'd burn the city to the ground?"

"I would hope not. Some of us didn't think it was funny."

"Why not?" Kita asked, giggling.

"It's not funny," Snowy yelled, "because I'm still trying to forget the cities I *have* burnt to the ground!"

"See? You do want to yell at me!" Kita screamed. "I'm not going, I want to stay here."

Kita fled upstairs, and a door slammed hard enough to rattle the pictures on the wall.

"Oh, you are not pulling this shit on me again," snarled Snowy as she charged after Kita.

Snowy banged on the door. "Let me in!"

"No! Go away!"

Snowy phased through the hatch, appearing behind Kita. She extended a claw and gave Kita a powerful electric shock.

Kita twitched in the current before collapsing.

Snowy picked up Kita and brought her back downstairs.

"Is she going to be alright?" said Glen.

Snowy nodded.

"She'll be fine. I only gave her enough volts to knock her out."

She handed Kita to Zidin.

"Come on, let's go. I'm tired. I hoped to get to bed early tonight," Snowy said grumpily.

K ITA WOKE UP DISORIENTED.

The big bed had a warm comforter and soft pillows. A dent was next to her to prove Snowy had slept, but it felt cold.

Sitting up, she marveled at the elegant décor. It reminded her of some of the older earls' castles. A vanity sat in the corner along with a large wardrobe. From the floral decorations and the soft colors, the room belonged to a woman.

She scooted out of bed. When the cool air hit her skin, she realized she was naked. She opened the wardrobe. The clothing's conservative style suggested the owner was old. A door led to the bathroom and a shower, and Kita squeaked excitedly.

The shower felt wonderful, but her wings made fitting into the stall challenging. She discovered if she put a wing outside the stall, she could make it work. Finding a towel, she dried herself, then sat at the vanity. Searching through the drawers, she found a metal comb.

Heat it. You never know who has what parasites.

Kita did as instructed, then ran the comb through her hair as she decided what to do with it. She tried several ideas, but she wasn't happy with any of them.

"Let me, kitten."

Kita jumped, but feeling Snowy's hands running through her hair put her at ease.

"I'm sorry for being a brat last night," Kita said in a small voice.

"It's ok, but let's not repeat the lock-oneself-into-a-room bit. It doesn't solve anything and only makes the situation worse. Same with drinking. General Forrester was ready to forgive and forget, once the smoke cleared. Instead, you came back unconscious and drunk, and you were laughed at."

Kita sighed and relaxed as a comfortable silence rose between them as Snowy worked on Kita's hair.

"When do you think we should tell them?" said Snowy.

It took Kita a moment to come out of her trance.

"I thought after this is over. There's no hurry. I have you. You have me. Everything else isn't important."

"That's what I thought. It would be a distraction, otherwise. There, what do you think?" Snowy stepped back, and Kita looked in the mirror.

Two braids ran low on the side of her head. The tails of each braid had been wound together to hold the rest of the hair into a ponytail.

"Oh, I love it. Thanks, love."

Kita reached back to hug Snowy. In the process, her towel fell off. Snowy seized the opportunity to run her hands up and down Kita's body. She stopped to fondle Kita's breasts.

Kita sighed and let out a happy purr.

"We could do that if you want to."

Snowy shook her head.

"We have a staff meeting. I came to get you."

"It won't start without us."

"True, but they will wonder where we are after four hours."

Kita huffed and collected her sneak suit.

"Think of it this way, kitten. You'll be all the more ready when we do get a chance. It's a nice bed. I want to do more than sleep in it."

K ITA DID HER BEST to keep her restlessness under control as the meeting dragged into its third hour. Having studied the architecture and the large high windows of the giant cathedral-style room several times, she had moved on to counting the stones in the wall.

"Why not use the Arconians? They could be good enforcers," said Jeffrey.

Kita finished counting her line of stones.

"Kita, pay attention." Jeffrey slammed his fist on the table.

Kita swore as she lost her place.

Forrester shook his head.

"We don't want to look like an invading army."

"Use Glen's men," said Kita. "They've plenty of experience being enforcers. They can show the city constables how it's supposed to be done."

"Are you crazy?" Jeffrey yelled as he jumped to his feet. "We can't let a crime lord run the constable's office. Why don't we just give him every valuable in the city?"

Kita crossed her arms and sat back, glaring.

"Why not? He already does more to protect the city than the constables do."

"That's only because he forces people to pay him."

"He doesn't force anyone to pay him. People pay him because it protects them from the petty thieves and the constables."

"Now you're saying the constables are crooked?" Jeffrey demanded.

"Yes. They're the worst kind of criminal. They don't need what they take. They just take because they can. Along the way, they abuse their power and take advantage of those they're supposed to protect. Glen's men are a hundred times more trustworthy."

"What about the rest of Glen's activities—smuggling, stealing, fencing, gambling, assassinations?" Jeffrey hissed. "You've spent too much time with him and are corrupted."

Kita jumped to her feet.

"Don't you dare tell me what my business is. Glen cares about the people he protects. He makes sure they have affordable food and are safe. Every copper he makes as Shadow Master goes back to those he cares for. For those who cross him, they are not innocent. They deserve what they get."

"What about the innocent they harm to help his innocent?"

"Those people aren't innocent. They're fat merchants and stuck-up nobles."

"Don't forget which one you are!"

"I've been trying to forget it for years," Kita huffed.

"Yet you had no problem coming back to your noble parents. Did life get too tough on the street for you?"

"Stop it!" Snowy yelled from a few seats down.

"This doesn't concern you," Jeffrey snarled.

"I'm your sister! It does, too," Snowy snarled back.

"When did this happen?" Jeffrey yelled, returning his attention to Kita.

"A couple of nights ago," Kita said, looking down.

"Were you going to tell anyone?"

"We were going to wait until this was over."

"Were you going to give me any time to prepare?"

"Prepare for what?" Kita said, exasperated.

"I'm the King for sun's sake. I need time to get the politics in order. I already have a hard enough time explaining you to the conservatives. I keep them at bay, telling them you'll be unseen. Adding her will compound things."

"Compound what things?" Snowy demanded.

"Look at you—look at her. You're not normal. If we were still a lower noble family, no one would care. But we're not. You should have kept your relationship quiet until I was established and could make sure the political connections are there."

"No! Don't do this!" Kita shrieked as tears streamed down her face. "You sound even worse than the duke. It's my life, not yours!"

Kita put her head on her arms.

Snowy moved to Kita while glaring at Jeffrey.

Violently, Kita shoved her chair back from the table.

"Dammit all to the bloody moons."

She glided up to an open window and climbed outside. She flew to the highest outlook on the keep. Dismissing the guard with a gesture, she dangled her feet off the edge of the wall, then pulled her legs up, wrapped her arms around them, and cried for herself.

Z IDIN KNELT NEXT TO Kita.

"How are you doing, fallen angel?"

Kita hugged him.

"I've missed you," she said, smiling with tears running down her cheeks.

"I missed you, too. I understand congratulations are in order?"

"I guess. No one was supposed to know. I wanted to keep it special for afterward. I guess that's ruined."

Kita sighed.

"Are you mad at Snowy for ruining it?"

"Why would I be mad at Snowy? I'm mad at that jackanapes brother of mine. Make that ex-brother. You're all the brother I need."

"Don't spear Jeffrey from the school yet. You might need him someday."

"For what?"

"I'm sure he could get you good seats to the tourneys," Zidin grinned.

Kita laughed.

"I think someone else wishes to talk to you."

Zidin stepped aside to reveal a nervous-looking Snowy.

"Snowy, what's wrong?" Kita jumped from her perch and took the weeping girl in her arms.

"I'm sorry. I didn't mean for it to come out like that. I just couldn't let him do that to you. I promise I'll make it up to you. Just don't get mad and leave me."

Kita held Snowy at arm's length.

"Why would I leave you? I'm not mad at you. I should be thanking you. You're the most important thing I have, and I wouldn't trade that for anything. I love you, and I'll never let you go."

"Promise?" Snowy asked around tears.

Kita nodded and kissed her. She closed her wings around them and soothed Snowy.

Voices caused Kita to open her wings.

Cowboy, Sarge, Zidin, and Xeen waited.

"Why is everyone here?" Kita said as she held Snowy.

"We came to offer our support. None of us thinks it was right for your brother to say what he did," said Cowboy.

"There is no reason to hide who you are," said Xeen. "The entire Arconian Nation is proud of you and is excited to welcome an outstanding warrior like Snowy. We will have to get you both fitted for kilts." He clapped his hands together with a big smile.

Both girls laughed.

"Doesn't plaid clash with spots?" said Snowy.

"Maybe they can get you a kilt in black and gray. It won't clash as much," said Kita.

"Too bad I can't be like you and hide them."

"Hide these?" Kita said, rubbing her hands down Snowy's sides. "Don't say such a thing. You're beautiful, and you'll look amazing in a kilt. If Xeen can pull it off, anyone can."

"I hope I'm not intruding on anything?" said Forrester.

"Of course not, Forrester. You," Snowy paused when she saw the rest of the general staff with him, "and everyone else, are welcome."

"Thank you, Commander. I just wish to say that the rest of the staff and I would like to express our support."

"Thank you," said Snowy. "It means a lot. We are grateful to have everyone's support and understanding."

A lieutenant came through the door with a large box and presented it to Forrester. He motioned for the lieutenant to put it on the ledge. After the lieutenant left, Forrester poked through the box.

"This was the best he could find in this gravel pit?" he muttered. Some of the other generals crowded around him.

Snowy and Kita traded glances.

Forrester appeared from the crowd and handed the girls glasses of wine.

"You will be the first Legion wedding in history, as I know. Cowboy, you would be the authority on that."

"The closest I can think of is Commander Isa when he married his twelve-year-old bride—"

Twelve-years-old! That poor girl. How can the Legion let that happen? It won't happen under my command.

"— and later made her his junior. Most commanders are married to the Legion," said Cowboy with a chuckle.

"Aren't we all?" said Forrester. "Now, I know you said you were going to wait, but we on the staff thought the occasion should be saluted. When we met, I had doubts, but I'm happy to say Commander Kita proved me wrong. Through your words and deeds, you have earned our respect and loyalty. We couldn't have a finer commander. Here's to you both. May you find happiness in each other and lead us to ultimate victory!"

Kita raised her glass, drank, and kissed Snowy.

Loyalty is the currency of the leader. To spend it, you must earn it. Glen taught me that. What did I do to earn such loyalty? All I did was be myself.

≡X≡S

C OWBOY WALKED AROUND THE bar after getting hot water for coffee. He joined Snowy, sitting at a back table, looking bored. Slinging his saddlebags on the back of a neighboring chair, he kicked another aside and set down his tin cup.

"What are you doing up?" Cowboy asked as he sat.

"Kita's asleep, and I have nothing to do. I hate that she sleeps an entire day away."

"You should be used to it by now. I'd think you'd be with her."

"I was until I got bored. I've been trying to get her to give me manuals on how to be a commander. She keeps ignoring me."

Cowboy smirked.

"There are no manuals for being a commander. La Forge never published one."

"Why? How am I supposed to learn? Kita expects me to follow her around and magically know everything."

"The formal reason is it's too complex to explain The Mass's politics, economics, and military in a book. Juniors follow commanders and learn by observation, instruction, and practice. The real reason is so La Forge can make his friends commanders, and there are no rules for them to follow, so they can do what they want."

"Kita doesn't know anything about teaching," scoffed Snowy.

"I think she's done a good job. Unorthodox, to say the least. It's got Jeffrey tied in knots."

"I don't understand why she has to make things more difficult. Jeffrey's running the city fine. He favors the nobility, but there's nothing wrong with that. Kita only wants to help the poor. The city is happy, but is that Jeffrey or Kita?"

"Depends on who you ask—the majority or the privileged? Kita may be a noble by birth, but she's with the masses by choice."

"I wish she lived in the tower, not this dilapidated shack. She's the commander, for god's sake. There's nothing wrong with a little luxury."

Cowboy lowered his coffee cup.

"Maybe you should talk to your partner about her ethos. I think Kita would die before she abused her position. Better not tell her that about Jeffrey."

"I have the right to my opinions."

Cowboy chuckled.

"And you sure do have a lot of them. Everything Kita does has a reason. She seems to be expanding on what the Shadow Guild taught her about governing."

"They don't govern. They help people, but they're not the king."

"I can tell you spent your life in a lab. You should know there are more seats of power than the person who says they rule over everything. She was an underboss, second to Glen. Kita knows how to handle governing. I'm sure she was set to take Glen's spot someday."

"Ugh. I'm not working in a kitchen or waiting tables. I'm sure as hell not spending my life in a place like this."

Cowboy lifted his hat.

"Are you really in love with Kita or just into what she can give you?"

"How dare you!" exclaimed Snowy.

"You did me dirty. I want to know if you're doing the same to her."

"Why do you care?"

Cowboy leaned back.

"I like to think she's my friend. She's brilliant, interesting, and I know I can trust her. More than I can say for you."

"Oh, shut up. You're the one who punched me. You should be begging my forgiveness. You're an unloyal ass who could care less that he had a wife."

"I am, and I did. You deserved it, and I won't. I cared about you plenty. I'm the only senior researcher who'd put up with you. I never understood why you were a lion in the lab and a mouse everywhere else. You're repeating the same mistakes here."

"You're just trying to get rid of me so you can have Kita. She's mine."

Cowboy's eyes twinkled.

"God, and I thought you were hell. I know you and how you can be. It'd be in Kita's best self-interest—not being with me but getting rid of you."

"I'm perfect for Kita. As soon as she's done playing Legion commander, we're going back to the lab in Razor's Mountains."

"And what will she do? What will you do?"

"Live in the mountains with the war cats like I did before I met her. The war cats know how to treat me right."

"Have you talked to her about this? Kita isn't the type who'll sit around and do nothing. And that doesn't sound like you anyway."

"I lived in Razor's Mountains longer than I was with you. Leaving you was the best thing I ever did. You and your stupid war. There was no need for me to be a part of it."

"Yeah, that was a stupid mistake on my part," Cowboy grinned. "Still, watching your fat ass run the obstacle course was worth it."

"I am not fat!" snarled Snowy as she slapped the table.

"You were then."

"You are such an ass."

"What? Mistakes were made by me and everyone. We all underestimated La Forge. I wouldn't have capitulated to him if I knew he was going to turn the world into a stereotypical racist fantasy land."

"I have no idea what La Forge did. I've only been to Yorq."

"Maybe you should get out more. Might help your attitude."

"My attitude is fine."

Cowboy snickered.

"I've got stacks and stacks of complaint cards that say otherwise."

"It's not my fault your students and junior researchers were stupid and worthless and couldn't be taught."

"None of them were any of that. And you couldn't teach. All you did was yell, berate, and make them do it repeatedly. If they got something wrong, you'd be mean and nasty. I had a lot wanting to quit or move labs. I kept you around as long as I could because you got results. You never wondered why you got the solo assignments?"

"It was because you knew I didn't need help, and they'd only slow me down."

"Your ego is as big as always. I tried to assign people to work with you, but they all called in sick and did so until I moved them to someone else. It finally became so bad I tried to trade you to another lab, but your reputation went far and wide. I guess I paid for my selfishness, requesting you work in my lab so we could be together."

"I was perfect. It was the rest of you that was the problem. And there's nothing wrong with how I teach. I did the same thing my parents did and turned out flawless."

"I'm always amazed you can make everything everyone else's fault and always be the victim."

"I do not. I've done nothing. Kita is the one making it up as she goes along. You should be happy that I'm reining in her random impulses."

"I thought you liked her?"

"I do. I love her. That doesn't mean she doesn't need adult supervision. She's only twenty-four and has a lot to learn."

"Maybe you should leave reining her in to Zidin and me. We're her advisors, and that's our job."

"You suck at it. She has no idea what she's doing. Kita tells me she's making it up as she goes."

Cowboy sipped his coffee.

"I'll have to talk to her about that. We need to have a plan for the city and the war. I'm sure she does and is being opportunistic when changes come about. You and Jeffrey need to understand that she is from the Shadow Guild. She adapts, overcomes, and looks for unorthodox solutions. Which is fine, but she does need direction and a goal."

"About time you saw things my way."

Cowboy scoffed.

"I wouldn't go that far. Do you love her? From what you said, you prefer Jeffrey to Kita. I can assure you, Jeffrey is worse."

"Of course I love her. Jeffrey is more mature and knows what he's doing."

"One of the tenets of being in a partnership is to accept your partner as they are. Kita isn't going to bend to your will. I think she'll do everything in her power to make you happy, but she won't change."

"She's a child. She'll change once I express what I want her to be."

"Then get used to disappointment. I don't like where this is going. I thought you'd changed and would be good for her—give Kita something besides war and governing to focus on, and be another voice of reason. But you're the same old girl with a new paint job. I miss the mouse you—made it easier to bring you to heel."

"You took advantage of me!"

Cowboy raised an eyebrow.

"No. I tried to get through your thick skull that you needed to change directions. You always acted like I'd beat you afterward. I never understood why you let me do all the thinking."

"Because you're a pompous ass that wouldn't let me think."

"The only time I got mad at you for thinking was when you made me that birthday dinner. I appreciate the sentiment, but you should have asked what I liked."

"Your mother told me!"

"Yeah, but she doesn't use vat meat. She said she offered to send a carton of steak, but you turned her down, saying you'd use a meal chit. I do apologize for being rude and throwing it away. I'm sure it tasted fine. I was just mad at the wasted money when we could have gotten the real thing."

"Too little, too late."

Cowboy shrugged.

"It may be a late apology, but it's still an apology. Something I've never heard from you."

"I have nothing to apologize for. You made my life miserable."

"You're playing the victim again."

"That's because everyone treats me like shit."

"That ain't true. You're mad no one treats you like royalty."

"I am. I'm a princess and a junior commander. I've earned the right to be treated like the queen I am."

Cowboy tapped his gloved finger on the table.

"You know, you haven't achieved either of those. You have them because of Kita. You're riding on her shoulders like you rode mine."

"I've earned it! Kita's given me nothing."

Cowboy shook his head and finished his coffee.

"Keep lying to yourself."

He stood up and opened a saddlebag, pulling out a notebook.

"Besides all your faults, I still love you and would be happy if you came and lived with me. We could get rid of the cat body, and I could design a better human one. Honestly, I don't think you'd be good for Kita. Someone with more experience is needed to handle you. And I know Kita. Another shiny bobble will come along, and she'll either lose interest in you or try to have you both. But, like I said, you start being you and drag Kita down, I'll drag your ass back to Dallas. You'll be away from her and be with me. And it's not like I don't have creature comforts. I still have Red Legion base."

"Kita is mine. Don't you dare take her from me."

"That's up to you. I'm sure I can find Kita another girl who'll treat her right."

"If you get in my way, I'll gut you."

"You're a hunter, not a killer. Leave that to Kita. Now, I have some correspondence to write. Why don't you go check on Kita?"

Snowy stood and glared.

"You should be trying to protect me, not her."

"I am. Right now, she needs protection from you. I'll do it for you when you need it."

Snowy extended a claw and pointed it at Cowboy. "Stay away from her. She's mine."

"I'd love to know her opinion on that."

"It is what I say it is."

Cowboy laughed as he picked up his belongings.

"That'll never happen."

He walked across the dining area to another table. He set his saddlebags on a chair and went to get more coffee.

"Just remember, those who copy the powerful will never be powerful."

"You are such an ass." Snowy draped her tail on her arm and stomped upstairs.

THANKS TO
THE FOLLOWING
PATRONS

Thanks to the following Patrons!

—Li've—
Anna Haig

—Kita's Partners—
ParadoxicMouse

—Kita's Lovers—
Monica and Shirlee RichardsonMIller
Michaela Smithies

—Angels—
Adam Dunsmuir
Joshua Le Tourneau
Kat
Noble Seven
Andy Ratka
Lunarsong

Vetlet
Stefan

—Kita's Crew—
5m7kabedfr76
Nora Rockwell

—Kita's Friends—
K.V. Wilson

ABOUT
THE
AUTHOR

L. FERGUS IS A disabled US Army veteran and self-publishing author. After ten years of struggling with their diagnosis, L. began writing as therapy. What started as a bedtime story and a way to cope with symptoms has grown into a twenty-three-book multi-series featuring L.'s antiheroine Kita, the Fallen Angel. Many of Kita's afflictions are L.'s afflictions, and together they work through their emotions (or lack of), pain, anger, and moods. L. and Kita love My Little Pony: Friendship is Magic and adore Princess Luna as they see her struggle as similar to theirs. L. lives in Florida with his cat, Jupiter, and two dogs, Moxi and Valor.

You can follow L. Fergus on
Facebook FallenAngelKita
Twitter @FallenAngelKita
website FallenAngelKita.com

To get the latest news, stories, artwork, and chat with L. consider becoming a Patron at Patreon.com/FallenAngelKita